Presented to Purchase College
by
Gary Waller, PhD Cambridge

State University of New York
Distinguished Professor

Professor
of Literature & Cultural
Studies, and Theatre &
Performance, 1995-2019
Provost 1995-2004

A WATCH

IN THE NIGHT

A WATCH
IN THE NIGHT

A. N. WILSON

W. W. NORTON & COMPANY
New York   *London*

Library of Congress Cataloging-in-Publication Data
Wilson, A. N. 1950-
 A watch in the night / A. N. Wilson. — 1st American ed.
  p.   cm.
  ISBN 0-393-04042-9
  I.   Title.
PR6073.I439W34   1996
823'.914—dc20   96-28636 CIP

W.W. Norton & Company, Inc., 500 Fifth Avenue, New York, NY 10110
W.W. Norton & Company Ltd., 10 Coptic Street, London WC1A 1PU

1 2 3 4 5 6 7 8 9 0

For a thousand years in thy sight are but as yesterday: seeing that is past as a watch in the night . . . For when thou art angry all our days are gone: we bring our years to an end, as it were a tale that is told.

Psalm 90

'Only, I wasn't sure whether you were staying for supper.'

'If that's not inconvenient, I'd love to. You probably want to watch the Shakespeare.'

'I'm in two minds,' I said. 'But supper will be no trouble at all.'

As so often when talking to my cousin Felicity, my last link with childhood, and all that past, I heard myself echoing her mother. Having lived for five years in Aunt Deirdre's bungalow, this was perhaps not surprising. In some moods, I wondered whether I had not turned into my aunt, absorbed her own unobtrusive attitude to existence. Like hers, my days were punctuated by gardening, and walks into Binham, the nearest village.

The bungalow consisted of one large room, with three small rooms off it. One of these rooms served as Felicity's bedroom and was kept for whenever she felt like motoring over in her Polo from Cambridge, where she resided in a modern block of flats called Highsett, near the station. The other bedroom in my small house was a spare, but no one ever visited, and I kept it piled high with junk. I was no longer sure whether I could cope with a guest. I had somehow lost the knack of people, and the courtesies required when in their company, pretending to listen to what they say, and so forth.

The sitting-room was where I existed. It was more or less unchanged since Aunt Deirdre left it. All the furniture came from the rectory – the chinoiserie press, which used to stand on the landing at Timplingham; the long-case clock which belonged to Aunt Deirdre's father, as did the nice little Pembroke table and the large Japanese bowl (mended with rivets) which stood upon it; I used it as the place to keep current bills. The knobbly Edwardian hall bench in the Tudorbethan style came from my granny's house – that of Uncle Roy's mother in Fulham. The water-colours on the walls were by 'poor dear Lavinia' Lampitt, who married the composer Campbell Dilkes. They were a present from old Mrs Lampitt – 'bless her' – of Timplingham Place.

A room contains a life. This contained not my life but the salvaged remains of other lives. My only additions to the furnishings when I had moved in had been two large framed photographs, one of my parents on their wedding day, and another of Mummy taken on one of our Norfolk holidays, her mouth open and smiling, her hair swept back from a young brow. Apart from these two pictures, everything in the room came from Uncle Roy and Aunt Deirdre. Oh, except for the bean bag which was a present from Leman. With my sexagenarian back it was never quite possible to get comfortable on the bean bag.

My cousin Felicity was over seventy now and she looked more and more like Aunt Deirdre. Her thick silver hair was cut in a bob. The fleshiness of her face, and its pinkness, made it seem much younger than it was. Aunt Deirdre had seemed like a Sea Scout, whereas the sexlessness of the features translated themselves in Felicity's case to those of a lay abbess. The intellectual loftiness which marked Felicity's earlier character had given place to a simple and pleasure-loving disposition. She never spoke of philosophy, except to contradict my more foolish explorations into that subject. She had retired from her college fellowship with relief. She liked many of the things which I detested; for example, foreign travel. She had been down the Nile, and to Mexico, and to Japan and to Vietnam and to Romania – all on tours organized for the middle classes, and advertised in the back of the Review section of *The Times*. She liked going to restaurants with friends; and she enjoyed television. When alone, I never watched the thing, which was kept in the corner of the room for her visits only.

From the kitchen, however, where I was putting the cottage pie in the upper oven, and checking to see that the rice pudding was cooking nicely in the lower, I could hear that Fliss had turned on the telly. She knew that the actress playing Queen Margaret was an old acquaintance of mine, but she probably did not know how well we had been acquainted, Dodie Rich and I.

'Didn't she marry your friend?' Fliss asked as I handed her a glass of British sherry (perfectly good, I'm told by those who drink the stuff).

'Yes, and her son's my godson. It's been a blissful marriage. I never remember Julian's birthday. He's at Westminster now.'

The screen came to life with Shakespeare, and silence descended on the two bungalow-conversationalists as, before their ageing eyes, Dodie Rich impersonated Margaret of Anjou. She did so with such majestic confidence that no viewer could for one moment have worried about the historical unlikelihood of a medieval queen of England being black.

There we sat, two old shipwrecks of time, staring into the cathode ray tube. I could not concentrate on the play, and my mind wandered in the way it does to the old days, and the strange fancies which used to fill it in those years of quiet recovery.

The act of love is used in magic rituals to summon up spirits. Have you been watching the pair of us, Dodie and me, during our last afternoon together? Before we take our shuddering farewell, before she goes on to her ordered life of marriage and fame, and before, after one long night of booze, one pilgrimage into the past, one final revel with Kit, the bachelor, I make my retreat from the stage and begin the life which is now mine. As I write, in the new century, I look back over nearly eighteen years of contented solitude and quietness. We have probably spoken more of your words to one another than our own during the last year, in rehearsals and performances. And we both have the habit of quoting you out of context in our ordinary conversation. 'Let's put on manly readiness,' we say, 'And meet i' the hall together', rather than, 'I am now about to visit the lavatory.' It's a tedious trick, perhaps, but one which is hard to shake off; one of the many affectations which I learned as a schoolboy from Treadmill. Dodie picked it up, with much else, from her father. When she ladders her tights, her instinct is to exclaim, 'See what a rent the envious Casca made.'

Now, as she becomes still, and her flattering scream dies down, she adds, with an affectionate giggle, 'Who would have thought the old man to have had so much blood in him?'

Twice her age, I do not mind being described as old. Throughout our surprising association, there has been an element not just of personal flattery but of professional self-interest. As a failed actor, there is no doubt that I was attracted to Dodie's fame. Equally, I had been the means which enabled her to make the switch from being a television star to playing serious Shakespearean roles. She is an intelligent, properly trained actress, and she did not wish to be cast for ever in a television sci-fi series. She is only twenty-seven but already, for five million viewers each week, she 'is' Roxana in *Planet Venus*. A better paid and less ignominious role than mine, you might think (thirty years as Jason Grainger on 'The Mulberrys'), but, still, the sort of 'success' which serious actors dread; for, like a parody of existence, to be stuck in such roles is to wonder whether free will itself is an illusion. You haunt her, as you have haunted all actors with the slightest ambition, with the desire to incarnate your dreams. (What triumphs she has had since she and I parted – as the Scottish Queen, as proud Titania, above all as Cleopatra!) But it was my little Sonnets play on Radio Three at the beginning of that year which had launched her as a Shakespearean presence in

4

the English theatre.

It was a minor piece, *Dear Time's Waste*. The hope that it would be broadcast during prime time had evaporated at an early stage of negotiations with the BBC. I was grateful in the event to be broadcast at eleven o'clock at night on St George's Day. Your birthday.

Funnily enough, when Dodie Rich's name was suggested to me by the director, I had been wholly opposed to it.

'She's a good actress,' he had argued. 'You should be grateful. She's famous. Millions of people watch *Planet Venus*. If anything could make your play attract some notice, that is it.'

'Simon – *darling*' – when angered, I become a 'luvvie', an old queen – 'this is meant to be a serious play about Shakespeare's sonnets. Well, it's so much more than that. It's about the creative process itself. I mean, here you have Shakespeare in the middle of the most sordid emotional mess. He's obsessed by a young man – not sexually obsessed . . . '

'That's *your* story . . . '

'He's not. Look, Simon, let's get this clear from the outset. It will spoil the whole point if you try to give this play a gay angle. He's miserably obsessed, non-sexually, with this beautiful, cold-fish young man. Having such a young friend reminds him of how much of his own life has gone; what a mess he has made of things, all that. And at the same time, Shakespeare, the narrator, is very much involved, sexually, with the Dark Lady. And the two of them, Willie, the young man . . . There's no need to snigger, Simon. Shakespeare does actually pun on this young man being called Willie.'

'Even though he has no sexual interest in him whatsoever?'

'Simon, you've read my play, you've read the Sonnets. For God's sake! Willie and Emilia, that's the Dark Lady, betray Shakespeare, their dear old friend. The two of them have an affair. But out of this sordid mess, this emotional hell, you get Shakespeare transforming the whole situation into art. That's why I quote so much from the plays, Simon. Here's this cold young man, well

5

above Shakespeare's social situation, and he likes getting pissed with Shakespeare and going to the pub with Shakespeare; but when the time comes, he is going to drop Shakespeare – and so you get the relationship between Falstaff and Prince Hal. "I know thee not, old man." That poignant scene comes straight out of the pain we find raw in the Sonnets. Even the name is a joke: Fall-Staff/Shake-Speare. Then there's the Dark Lady. The Dark Lady is this randy, deceitful, demanding predatory *bitch*! If she'd been to bed with anyone else, and she went to bed with lots of other men, nothing would have come of it except a dose of the clap. But this ghastly woman, Simon, happens to have gone to bed with William Shakespeare, this modest, unaffected, slightly colourless actor-manager – and out of that experience he wrote *Antony and Cleopatra*, the golden crown of his work . . . '

'You've said all that before, Julian. I still think that Dodie Rich is made for the part.'

'There just seems something so obvious, and, as it happens, so false to history, and so worthy, and so BBC-in-the-1980s, about casting a black actress as the Dark Lady.'

'Nobody's black or white on the radio, Julian. We are all as colourless as you think Shakespeare was.'

Dodie proved me wrong. She brought musicality and inventiveness and rage to the part. The small supporting cast, the Young Man, his overbearing aristocratic mother, the Rival Poet, and the assorted actors and players, were all perfectly competent in the radio production. It was my own performance as the author of the Sonnets which disappointed me. I never got the right modulation into my voice. I *heard* it, that gentle rise and fall, that irony, inside my head, when I typed out the play, but I quite failed to convey it on air.

My ability to act had deserted me. Too long on 'The Mulberrys'! In impersonating you, I was probably *asking for it*, summoning your spirit from the vasty deep. If so, you failed to appear on the night. I'd wanted to catch a certain actorliness in your manner of delivery. At the same time, I had imagined you as being one of

6

those actors, like Guinness, who is chameleon – that's what I meant by colourless. You would take on, and become, the role you were playing, rather than being one of those strutting self-parodists like Hubert Power who has been the same in nearly all his roles for the last twenty years – bombastic, loud, mannered, *au fond* quite stupid. My rendering of you, though, which was meant to be subtle, came over as merely toneless.

And now, for the first and last time, I am in Dodie's flat. We have been having this 'thing' all year, but our lovemaking has been occasional. A borrowed flat. The Nelson Arms at Sherdingley Staithe. That nice old hotel at Southwold.

Dodie has become a regular guest at Staithe, but I have never visited her flat in Fulham. Nor has she ever known the significance, for me, of its address. She was living in the top floor of what had been Mrs Webb's house. My granny used to live two doors down. It was at the end of this garden, during the war, that I sat and clung to Mummy – until we were evacuated to Norfolk, and I was sent away to boarding-school, and she and my father were killed in that raid on Southampton. Number 21, Alderville Road, London SW6.

When Dodie first told me that she lived here, I was visited, as I am so often these days, by the thought that there's – if not a divinity that shapes our ends, then an extraordinary symmetry over which we have no control. It was here that the child was so often brought to play, and to sleep. And it is here now, half a century later, that the man lies naked on the floor.

'Who would have thought the old man . . . '

We are both naked when Dodie says these words. I lie on the kelim rug in front of her electric fire. Her long face, with its very intense, lively eyes, and its broad smile, takes in my final gratitude and puzzlement. We are not, and never have been, in love, so there remains something a little sad about these couplings of ours. But I could never get over my simple thankfulness that one of the most beautiful young women in London should have wished to do this wonderful, if slightly sad, thing, with a balding, skinny, not very good actor. There would have been so many other ways of being kind, but perhaps Dodie did not know them. I think she wanted to do it, and yet the enterprise was doomed; we had too much in common, not too little, a shared inner inheritance which had nothing to do with the theatre.

It comforts me, then, to think of you there, since it enables me to forget the other spirits who might hover and watch us as we commit this comparatively trivial sin.

Dodie and I are in the small sitting-room. It is a cosy place for winter. Beside the fire is a low armchair, upholstered in orange. My feet are touching it. Near my head is a coffee-table littered with magazines and a well-filled ashtray.

Dodie features on the covers of many magazines at this period. It is no surprise to see her face staring from the mag on the top of the pile. It is merely surprising that the photographer has conveyed none of her animation. The impassive, perhaps impassible, features might have been those of Roxana, the intergalactic space traveller who had made Dodie famous, but they were hardly those of your Dark Lady. Across her right cheek in headlines of different bright colours is printed a truncated index of further items contained in *Metropolitan*. Printed in yellow: *NOBLESSE BULIMIA an investigation into the eating-disorders of the well born*. In bright pink, immediately beneath, **Derby and Sloane: GORLEY SWALLOW GOES TO THE RACES** (the mag was the June issue; annoyingly, it was a good piece), and in blue, just to the right of Dodie's neck and just beneath her domino ear-rings: *MAN OF MANY ARTS*. MR FIXIT. WACQUI LEFEBVRE INTERVIEWS RAPHAEL HUNTER. This, too, is an article which I can remember, even though it is months since I read it. 'Whether you need funding for an opera or advice in setting up a literary prize, you won't go far in the arts world without Sir Raphael Hunter crossing your path . . . '

Beyond the coffee-table, the sofa, covered with a vivid yellow and green cotton bedspread. Above the sofa, the mirror in which

I cannot see myself (I am too low down on the floor) but in which I can see the nimbus of Dodie's hair touching her shoulders. It is black at the brow, but gold as light plays through its outer, delicate tendrils. Dodie's hair is a fluff not a fuzz, it is light in texture. Her face, the colour of *café au lait*, is high-browed; and in her nakedness it is the bones of her sculpted beauty of which one is aware, the nodules of her spine, the even coat-hanger of her collar bones, the strength and straightness of her neck. She could easily be an Ethiopian princess or, as she was destined to become for cinema-goers the world over, the Queen of Egypt.

This is the moment when I wonder if *you* might be watching, as this most elegant of Cleopatras bestrides the puniest of Antonys. It is the curious trick of perspective which enables me to look in the glass and to see the reflection of the woman with whom I am still joined while remaining invisible to myself. It gives rise to the weird fancy, not that I am exactly non-existent, but that, having made myself your devotee, I have become your dream, able to materialize only when, Prospero-like, you raise your wand.

It is perhaps superfluous to attempt an explanation for this strange idea lodging itself in my imagination. We have, after all, had an intensive year – you, my Dark Lady and I. Dodie has had her triumph as Titania in Victoria's production of the *Dream* – a production which has made her everywhere spoken of as the new star in the Shakespearean firmament. My Sonnets play, which had started as *Dear Time's Waste*, has been performing itself inside my skull for much longer than twelve months, and has by now passed through many transformations. Your sonnets are, notoriously, a subject by which men and women become obsessed. I am still in this state of mind, a Shakespearomaniac who cannot stop reading and rereading the poems and the plays.

It is only fair to admit that I have been mad.

I do not believe that my Shakespearomania is mad. My views about you are the eminently sane, middle-of-the-road ones. I have never, in my approaches to Shakespearean problems, ridden any hobby-horses. My mania has never taken the form of wishing to pretend that you were someone else, such as Bacon or Marlowe or Queen Elizabeth or (a theory favoured by Father Linus Quarles, SJ) a cartel formed by the more literary-minded members of the Society of Jesus. Nor have I been attracted by the discovery of ciphers or secret messages about astrology in the Sonnets, nor by those I would call the lobbyists who wait to catch you, sir, as you run from the stage door of the Globe and claim you for their party: Shakespeare the right-wing patriot; Shakespeare the Catholic; Shakespeare the dissident; Shakespeare the Gay Rights campaigner. Rather, I have lived and breathed what I took to be *echt* Shakespeare for more than a year.

As I did so, it became different in kind from other forms of literary enjoyment. It goes without saying that I have always read you, but since I began to read you to the exclusion of almost everything else (except journalism) I had become conscious of a phenomenon: not that I was viewing all existence through a Shakespearean glass, but that I was, little by little, ceasing to exist as a person in my own imagination. I no longer knew or cared, quite, who I was.

This has grown, this sense, in the time it has taken me to write these chronicles, these *Lampitt Papers*. I am shaking loose from the tyranny of my own history, my own genetic and emotional inheritance. After the night which will be described in the following pages, and my parting from Dodie, I shall travel lighter towards old age.

Where do we get our ideas of human personality? They are not innate. They are all imbibed from the surrounding culture. Human beings might, I suspect, have as little self-consciousness as other mammals if they had not been taught to regard themselves as 'souls'. The beginning of wisdom in the New Age is to Find Yourself. The beginning of wisdom in the Christian Age now past was to lose yourself, but of course many Christians, from Augustine to Wordsworth, have shown no interest at all in the Gospel injunction to deny self, viewing, rather, the entire scheme of creation and redemption, from the first moment that the

10

Almighty exclaimed *FIAT LUX!*, as a drama involving themselves and their own relationship with the unseen First Cause. I have never undergone a course of spiritual instruction, nor sought a guru to teach me the *via negativa* or the path of enlightenment. After a diet of Shakespeare, Shakespeare, Shakespeare, I find myself, however, losing the notion of my own identity. I feel the need to be passive and docile in its true sense. You taught me. Lying there, beneath Dodie, and not being able to see my reflection in the glass, I have this whimsical idea that you might perhaps even be controlling events; and I never feel it so strongly as when I see Dodie's noble head in the mirror above the sofa.

(Of course I don't *believe* that you are there; but this journey has taught me the value of holding on to useful mental furniture, such as church, even when – or especially when – you don't believe. Blessed are those who have seen, but who have not believed.)

Sensing perhaps mere post-coital *tristesse*, Dodie takes my face in her long pink palms. Moving from her position on top, she lies beside me and enfolds my little white body in her brown swimmer's shoulders. (Dodie is a thirty-lengths-a-day girl.) My cheek nestles beside her breast. How quickly the act of generation turns the would-be father, rutting and thrusting, into the vulnerable child in a mother's arms. The big hard assertive fellow becomes foetal and vulnerable.

Alderville Road, where I had lain and had my nappies changed! And where, in those beautiful days before the war, I had my paradise. Mummy, pushing me in my pram to Hurlingham Park. The little rose garden there, where Mummy sat with Granny and Mrs Webb, smoking their cigarettes on the benches while I drove round the paths in my pedal car. Alderville Road, where the Metro Goldwyn lion roared, the credits rolled, and the drama began – the me-show. Mummy gave me the impression that everything I did and said was of consuming interest and importance; an impression which Mrs Webb was polite enough, in her abrasive fashion, to confirm. Is that why Mummy's death was so difficult to accept – no more audiences for the me-show?

11

There literally were me-shows in Alderville Road. Here I had erected my puppet theatre and, before the captive audience of Mrs Webb, Mummy and Granny, I had insisted that they watched whatever drivel I performed, clapped at my songs, laughed at my spazzy jokes. Acting on stage as a grown-up I have often been reminded of that captive audience of three, sitting there during my 'shows' – Granny shamelessly closing her eyes; Mummy, wide-eyed and apparently genuinely impressed by everything I did and said; Mrs Webb, who liked her money's worth, providing instant, usually generous, commentary on my performances. 'Oh Tommy Handley made that joke when we were listening in last week. My! He's got a memory, this boy.' She chuckled at the joke and esteemed my ability to repeat it. Already an actor, I wanted to be given credit for words which were not my own, I craved more and more attention and adulation.

'Baby,' says Dodie. She could not have spoken more accurately, as she kisses my head, conscious of my sadness, but not, of course, aware of you watching and directing this final love scene.

Years before I ever went into hospital, I would have periods of fear, totally irrational, that I was being watched at intimate moments – when defecating, for example, or when copulating, or when sleeping. Such moments are full of anxiety, rendering the act itself impossible. Sleepless on a pillow, impotent in a woman's arms, full-bowelled but paralysed on the loo seat, I would be frozen with terror: the body had taken me over, and was ungovernable by the will. To know that Shakespeare is watching over me, however, provides comfort, not fear. Better the kind and tolerant eyes of Shakespeare than the merciless stern and unmoving eyes of the First Mover.

Lord Alfred Douglas says in his book about the Sonnets that you were puritanical in your attitudes to sex and that you were almost certainly chaste. It is an example of the way that your readers project all manner of their own preoccupations into your works (particularly into the Sonnets) without having any evidence for their faith. Overshadowed for ever by the great

12

scandal of 1895, Douglas had been constrained to prove to himself that you were not Oscar Wilde, even though your name and sonnets had been invoked during the trials. I see you as a much more genial figure than Douglas's Shakespeare, which is presumably why I want you there when Dodie and I lie together for the last time.

Advocates of what they would call morality might inveigh against the superficiality of 'casual sex', thereby failing to see that when comparative strangers make love (Dodie and I had met only once when we first did so) there is often more tenderness, certainly more pathos, than in the routine couplings of the married who take coition for granted and probably go into it, sometimes, with rather less excitement than they would plan a dinner party or a summer holiday. Victoria in one of her earlier essays – it is the one about Chaucer's *Troilus and Criseyde* – speaks of the two lovers as they lie there, their vulnerability, the ease with which their happiness can be destroyed – making them in that moment an archetype of human experience, and of the fragility of happiness itself.

The Timplingham Titties. Another of those emblems which become archetypical. In the roof-beams of the parish church at Timplingham were carved the figures of Carmelite friars in their choir-robes. Like the winged angels who are to be found in other churches in East Anglia, these figures stared down from each boss above the aisle, all the way up the south side of the church, almost all the way up the north. Above the pulpit, however, one figure stood out. Instead of the fifteenth-century cleric, with his pudding-basin hair and his gathered rochet, a full-bosomed young woman bared her chest. Sargie called them the Timplingham Titties.

They were certainly so distinctive a feature of the church that even my fastidious uncle, the rector, could not forbear to point them out to visitors. For many years they caused me imaginative

13

or emotional difficulties. We like to believe that Christianity wages war against the carnal side of life, and that is partly because it's true, partly because we ourselves wage that war. We want to credit God with the idea that sex is wicked because we find it so frightening. It's very convenient to have a religion which tells us that orgasms are sinful – because our pursuit of orgasms is something which causes us so much pain and embarrassment and confusion.

How to cope with this bare-breasted woman staring down on my uncle's crinkly head as he stood in the pulpit and expounded the Gospels in his moderate, well-educated Anglican way? That took, and takes, a lot of learning. You, the genial Shakespeare – what if you are more like God than the Unbending First Cause? And what if the all-forgiving, all-knowing Earth-soul were more fully incarnate in you than in the Galilean exorcist?

I'd never supposed for a moment that the Timplingham Titties were going to be exposed once more; nor that church should form a part of my relationship with Dodie. No. I could not leave Staithe, the house I lived in, the place I loved. That was my creed when the summer began. It all had to do with believing myself to be an indispensable cog in the machine. Although unmarried to Victoria, I felt towards her the unwilling attachment of the married. Part secretary, part housekeeper, part guide-dog to Victoria, whom I had come (in part) to loathe, I should have found no moral possibility of escaping the thrall, the comforting womb of Staithe. (I think I now understand why Rice Robey called Mrs Paxton 'The Great Attachment' – both why he was in subjection to her, and why so compulsively in need of other emotional pursuits.) I 'couldn't leave' Victoria. To sleep with other women, even though I had never, technically, succeeded in being Victoria's lover, was a betrayal. That was the inner mental furniture, the state of my mind, at the beginning of the summer.

We once planned to marry, Victoria Amt and I. That had been

14

the idea. We had even tried to have a sexual relationship. These were the years which followed my madness, and which followed what was madder than my madness, that brief marriage to Sonya. Victoria Amt's kindness to me was my salvation. Without it, I should have been mad, or suicidal, or destitute. The calms of Staithe, the established routines of that house, the possibility of a tranquil frame in which to work: all these Victoria provided.

Dodie knows more than most people about my strange relationship with Victoria. She knows, by the time we lie there for the last time together in Alderville Road, that this relationship has changed, that I am 'free' from Victoria, and that it is something else, or a cluster of other things, which prevents me from committing myself to Dodie and, more importantly, which prevents her from committing herself to me.

Of course, at the moment of our last lovemaking, Dodie knows more than I know myself. I have not really absorbed the fact of Victoria's new life. I am still reacting as if I were responsible for her, and presumably this is because I so desperately need to stay in the comforting womb of Staithe. After my breakdown, and my slow recovery in hospital, and my recklessly absurd marriage – which lasted less than a year – I had gone to Venice and met Victoria. She had suggested Staithe as a healing place. She lived in the house only for a part of each year, and she was glad to take on a caretaker-lodger. Only later did I discover that Victoria attracts dependants in the way that some women compulsively buy shoes. It suited her magisterial character to fill the cottages and the spare bedrooms with a floating population of hangers-on. I was in no position, financially or emotionally, to turn down the chance of becoming one of the Fairies of Staithe (as, inevitably, they, we, are known in our profession).

By the time I am lying on the hearth-rug in Fulham with Dodie, Victoria is in no position to mind about my having a sexual partner other than herself. She has her new attachment after all. (As a matter of fact, it is only slowly dawning on me that Victoria would never have minded if I took lovers, as I have done from

15

time to time since going to live with her.) It is something quite different which has come between us, Dodie and me. It is our shared sense of – how can one put this? Our shared sense of Anglican seriousness? Catholic guilt is easy to write about, and presumably quite exciting to feel. If you die without making an act of perfect contrition, you will be whisked off to hell and punished everlastingly. Very exciting if you believe, or even if you 'believe', this. If you're Anglican, though, this exciting world-view seems like kids' stuff.

Dodie and I can't pretend to anything so clear-cut or garish. We don't think there's a torture chamber devised by a Cosmic Sadist filled with homosexuals, divorcees and emotional inadequates. But we both have church in the system, while not being very sure what we believe. (She is more *croyante* than I, praying each morning, and receiving Communion. I can't quite do that. Even now, so many years after that afternoon, I seek the churches in which there is no service in progress, preferring to wander in wistful silences than to mouth words which aren't quite sayable.) And Dodie takes a high view of marriage. My two divorces rule me out as a life partner – and it is a life partner, and perhaps children, which she wants. That is why, although we have enjoyed the last year, we both know that this removal of clothes, this lying together on floors, has got to stop. Dodie, much more than I, has absorbed the wisdom of the Timplingham Titties. She considers it almost inconceivable that the Almighty should be as censorious of our sexual nature as the Pope; and that if He takes any interest in it at all, it must be an amused interest. (I'm Anglican enough not to be too sure that I even believe in the Almighty, but I still carry round the infantile sense that He doesn't approve of *this*.) It isn't the sex – which we both enjoy – which causes Dodie to be troubled. It is her sense that life – even if there is nothing beyond the grave and there is no account to be made of it to the recording angel – can't be frittered away, can't be played with. When she meets the right man (and it is quite obvious for a number of reasons that I am not the right man) she

16

wants to stand before an altar and make vows for life. At the same time, her genial attitude to the act itself suggested that this was how we should spend the afternoon – not a stiff little meal, or a series of notes, but a last ride together. Then she would come with me to the party I was attending, would leave on her own. Thereafter we should meet only as friends.

She says, 'I love these moments. I'm going to miss them.'

'Me, too.'

'It's such a great act of trust, even when . . . '

Even when it is impossible for us to imagine a future together. Rather, it is impossible for her to imagine a future with me. Rather, it is impossible for any woman, anyone, to imagine a future with me. It is becoming increasingly difficult for me to imagine a future with me.

'We're still friends, aren't we?' As I ask the question, I regret the cliché. We never were, exactly, friends, and we are certainly not going to be 'friends' in the future – if by friends is meant people whom one sees regularly or whose company one seeks out. For a complex set of coincidental reasons, I am destined to be godparent to Dodie's first child. But friends?

'Oh my dear.' She is wiser than I am, and she holds me, expressing in this gesture less of sensuality now and more of solicitude. I feel myself, as I did during my year or more of 'treatment', being regarded as a hopeless 'case'.

A chilly instinct tells me that this might be the last time, not merely with Dodie, but *ever*.

(Who knows? That instinct has proved right so far; and I write these words so long after that evening.)

I want, therefore, to concentrate on the this-ness of the moment, on the exact quality of Dodie's skin, on the pores of the shoulders and the softness of her breast against which my cheek is lying. I am trying to concentrate on these immediate and physical things, but my mind has raced off again on this insane thought that *you* are there, watching.

I am having what I call my Bishop Berkeley thoughts. To think

17

about Bishop Berkeley while lying with a naked intergalactic goddess is a chronic example of bad timing. I know that. Like getting an erection in church.

But, Berkeley. His theory of perception. His idea that the *esse* of the universe was *percipi*. Felicity (my philosopher cousin) stops her ears when I try to repeat my 'ideas', as I did to her only this morning before writing this paragraph. Felicity says I get it all completely haywire. If I do, so what? I'm not trying to pass an exam in Berkeley's theories of perception; just using my understanding, or misunderstanding, of what he wrote as a basis for my own vision.

Since, oh, before I started to think, and probably since that dark, liquid, comfortable time before I was born, experience has seemed – if not something one could control, at least something which one could adjust, a bit like a TV transmitter. Colour, sound, channel, could be changed or modified. The world was not that which is the case; the world was what one happened to be noticing or thinking about at the time. At this point, Doctor Johnson kicks the stone; but common sense doesn't help. Berkeley's question would be: how do we know that the stone exists *when Johnson is not there to kick it?*

Answer – Berkeley's answer – God sees it. It does not interest me whether this was an original idea, nor even whether I've got it quite right: the idea of the universe not as a thing, not as an entity which is or is not the case, but as God's dream. I find the idea satisfying, a way of avoiding going round and round in circles in one's head, when trying to work out, without some external arbiter of truth, whether one can test the verifiability of any logical, mathematical, or linguistic system. (Quite possible, I find, to enjoy swimming about inside this Berkeleyan idea without *believing* in God.)

Pure solipsism, the contented sense that our 'lives' have no reader, no audience, would be an enviable accomplishment. (Is it what Zen Buddhists hope to achieve?) But it is rare, and, to a Westerner, unnatural. The family photograph-album; the boring family memories, spoken aloud formulaically when we meet our further-flung relations at funerals or Christmas dinners; the involuntary processes of interior memory: all propose the analogy of story or performance as a trope by which to read experience. The reality of self (I write as an actor, rather than a poet or a mathematician) passes as speechlessly and meaninglessly as a tree unless it is observed.

A few real bores might behave as if every experience which they undergo is of perpetual interest to friends. These are the ones who will go to the trouble to narrate their day, put into words the visits of gasmen or doctors or their own humdrum pilgrimages to hairdresser, dentist, supermarket. Most of us are deterred by a fear, if we articulate such diurnal dullnesses, that we shall be boring. So, for convenience, we construct an inward Berkeleyan fiction that our drift through time actually has a shape, a story. It is as if our lives were a comprehensible sequence of events, directed by Something Outside Ourselves. Hence, on a small scale, the concept of Guardian Angels, writing our deeds in their book. Or, in the case of the 'famous', the fantasy that a truth could be told about their lives by the chronicle form, the biography.

For those with a mind to absorb grand schematic ideas, there is Providence, the Fates, destiny.

If I'd ever been able to overcome my scepticism about Christianity, I should have been troubled by the egotism which believes that the Author of the Universe interests Herself, Itself, or Himself in all our passing whims and actions. There were Christian boys at school who seriously supposed that God, like our headmaster the Binker, paced about listening near their beds, concerned about whether they masturbated. The fiction that one's life is observed perpetually by the First Cause seems imaginatively less plausible than the idea that it is an occasionally observed, haunted thing, teased by night-visitants; a picture which flickers in and out of focus; a 'story' which remains untold, quiescent until drawn out in sporadic episodes. This belief has its finest expression in Homer, where the gods and goddesses are as

19

capricious as the fairies in your *Dream.*

I don't know when I decided to fictionalize, and at the same time to accept you, Shakespeare, as my Guardian, my personal Divinity. Probably it was when I was mad. But there can be useful forms of madness or mental game. Keats was not mad and he conceived of Shakespeare as 'a Good Genius presiding over me'. I find it more congenial to accept this fictitious genius 'observing' my life than to imagine the metaphor of the First Cause, who would have it in His Power to avert famine and plague but chooses to remain impassive.

But thou, Shakespeare, unto whom all hearts are open, all desires known, and from whom no secrets are hid, keep up your playful, randy watch, your voyeuristic guardianship, as I lie on a rug with big-limbed Dodie Rich.

She makes a circle on my forehead with her finger and slowly walks her fingers over my nose, across my lips and down past chin and neck to traverse my chest.

'What are you thinking about?' is her question.

I have drifted into thinking about *Dear Time's Waste* yet again: my absolute failure to capture your essence when I wrote that play of mine! Just as I do not suppose that Uncle Roy, when he worshipped the Blessed Sacrament, really identified the Bread of the Altar with the Historical Jesus, nor do I have many (any?) thoughts about you, the glover's son from Stratford who became a successful actor-manager, while I am reading the plays. It is the godlike mind and imagination which created Hamlet, Lear and the *Dream* (my favourite) which I revere and with which I commune.

I reply to Dodie: 'I've been thinking how lucky I am, how happy you have made me.'

'You lie. You are thinking about old Shakespeare. I can always tell when a Roman thought has struck you.'

'Everyone makes up their own Shakespeare, just as everyone makes up their own Jesus.'

'And was I supposed to be your Dark Lady? Or are you trying to tell me that all year you have actually been in love with Kit?'

Not Kit Marlowe, but Victoria's nephew, Kit Mayfield.

I say, 'Ow! That hurt. There'll be no more fun from that quarter if you yank it. What do you think you are doing – pulling the plug out of a bath?'

As Dodie says softly, 'I'm pulling the plug out of something, darling,' my mind absorbs itself in the mild little family joke which was shared between me and my parents and Granny. The Day War Broke Out was, for me – a stomping child of four – the Day God Pulled the Plug out of the sea. We had been walking, Mummy, Daddy and I, across the flat sands at Mallington Beach (ten miles along the coast from Staithe) and at that age I could not understand where the sea had gone. It seemed a reasonable hypothesis that God had pulled the plug. Together with everyone in the country, we looked back on that day as one on which all our lives changed.

Mummy and Daddy were destined to be killed three years later in an air-raid, leaving my life irreparably scarred.

'Are you, though?' With her plug-pulling exercise, Dodie insists upon an answer. 'Are you in love with Kit? Is that why you had to get involved with the Sonnets? Because you had some stupid English fear of gayness?'

A flicker of Old Bore rises from a leather armchair in the corner of my mind to wonder whether the old Gaiety Theatre, full, no doubt, of what would now be called Gays, would have a fear of Gayness, or merely of the ghastly word; but, choosing to mix with so many people younger than myself, I'd be having these tedious thoughts all the time unless I put a check on them.

So I say: 'Of course I'm in love with Kit. Aren't you? Isn't everyone?'

Back at Staithe, I play these painful games with Leman, pretending that Kit is an object of desire, not only to myself, but to all men of my acquaintance.

'To tell you the truth . . . ' and Dodie pauses. I find that I care what her answer will be.

21

She toys with her reply, rolls it round in her mouth like a sweet, before releasing, ' . . . I could never be in love with Kit. I can see he's kind of cute, but I don't go for that public-schoolboy, giggly, gentle thing.' Kissing my forehead, she adds, 'I like older men. And he's a cold-hearted little boy, isn't he?'

'Oh, don't say that!'

I speak with real passion.

'You do, you do love him!'

I say, 'I just hate the thought of him hurting anyone.'

'By anyone you mean little What's-her-name.'

Dodie always speaks of them both as 'little' – the cold-hearted 'little' boy and 'little' What's-her-name. Kit is a tall young man, easily six foot. Leman, if not quite as tall as Dodie, probably stands five foot eight in her Doc Martens.

Dodie has met Leman constantly throughout the summer at Staithe and is perfectly well aware of what she is called. There is no need for the affectation, little What's-her-name. Dodie knows nothing of the 'full story'. Yet, isn't it odd? – she has a dazzlingly successful acting career; she is comfortably off, and will be rich; she is famous; her face is on the cover of every magazine; she is saluted in restaurants like royalty. But Leman, in her old shoes and her oil-stained overalls, can provoke in the intergalactic space goddess such spite!

That morning, at Staithe, I found Leman in the kitchen garden. It is a brick-enclosed area which summons up mental images from children's stories – Mr McGregor running around the edge of the cucumber frame, waving his rake; Diccon cupping an injured bird in his palms and finding the secret garden. Leman, and all those silly, embarrassing feelings which I have for her, lead back, no doubt, to a secret garden of childhood, inhabited before Mummy's death, never recaptured or re-entered.

Leman wore corduroy trousers and a grey games-jersey dating from comparatively recent schooldays; but it would be wrong to think she was boyish. There is a roundness, and a sensuality, and a softness of limbs and skin which no boy ever had. Nor is her modulated musical voice remotely boyish. Over trousers and a jersey, she wore the blue overalls which she puts on for tinkering with machinery.

'Fetch me that spanner, Angelo,' she said.

'Do you mean this spanner?'

Her son spoke in no less deliberate tones.

'It will do.' She applied the instrument to a bolt on the underside of a rotary digger which was evidently in need of repair. Leman is as much at home in the world of machines as in that of nature. She can service cars, mend mowers and electrical devices, dig, hoe, fertilize.

'Would you like another spanner, Mum?'

'No, thank you, darling. You can go back to helping me tidy the bonfire.'

Leman was squatting just outside her shed, a creosoted larch-lap construction which she made her own very soon after arriving at Staithe. Before she came, the warped door of the shed closed only with difficulty, and its interior was scarcely penetrable – a couple of rusted mowers, garden tools in a variety of decay, clutter of all kinds filled and wasted its space. Leman had arrived; oiled the hinges, mended the lock, cleaned away the grime and cobwebs from the panes, and managed to get the windows open within a matter of days. Now, inside, the mingled smells of earth and wood were pervaded with creosote. Order had come to the shed. Tins of oil, empty jam-jars, boxes of plant food and plant pots stood neatly stacked on the shelves.

Beside the shed, the compost heap; and beside the heap, Leman and Angelo piling refuse to be burned. The child staggered about adding his own handfuls of dead weeds and twigs, an intensely serious expression on his face suggesting fear of her disapproval should he drop earth or weeds on the path. I am sure she never spoke an unkind, nor even a severe, word to her son. He like the rest of us (and Dodie's jealousy is a compliment of its kind) felt in her presence as though he should be on good behaviour. In the best sense, Leman is awe-inspiring.

'So!' A word she uses so much and which, when she loops it on the end of sentences instead of a full stop, has such a power to enrage Victoria – 'You're off to London – so!'

'There's this party.'

'There always is.' She said this with a pealing laugh, the ex-prisoner who had been released from bondage, the child let out of school.

Some time after school (and she wisely gave university a miss) Leman felt it necessary to get a job, and she had landed the unlikely position of assistant to Gorley Swallow on *Metropolitan*. She hated this – a fact I found unsurprising. Strange to say, however, she had lasted in this job several years, 'subbing' the material as it came in, and perhaps even helping to frame the excruciating puns (of the 'Derby and Sloane' variety). There were also, of course, the numerous 'drinks parties' in the early part of each evening.

There is a circuit – not a clique, nor an inner ring, nor a secret society, but a circuit – of Londoners who can be relied upon to turn up for 'red or white', or, at the more ambitious parties, champagne or orange juice, absolutely regardless of whether they have any interest in the supposed occasion of the gathering. Private views of paintings which no one in the room wishes to buy, 'launches' of books which no one in the room will ever read, provide common excuses for such assemblies. Leman often found herself attending them in olden time.

'Where's your party?'

'Dylans.'

'That place is truly ghastly.'

'It used to be a pub called the Black Bottle in my day – hardly a resort of the *jeunesse d'orée*. Now they've turned it into this club. It seems an appropriate place to celebrate a biography of Day Muckley.'

'Who's Day Muckley?'

Leman never felt the slightest shame about ignorance of this kind. Given the fact that Day Muckley's novels had now been televised and made into films, and his name had even become synonymous with a certain kind of North Country bluff, honest charm among those who never read his books – 'We're not in a Day Muckley novel now,' some Yorkshire MP said not long since on the radio – I might have been astonished by Leman's ignorance. But she seldom listened in (to use Mrs Webb's phrase), nor did she much go in for reading, except for seed catalogues and maintenance manuals of machines.

'He was just an old drunk I used to know ages ago.'

'Everyone you knew was a drunk, so!' She laughed.

The extent to which Leman always hated the magazine, always hated London, never felt at home other than when doing what her father had always done, mucking about in cars, gardens, boats, reached crisis point in her mid-twenties. She could not live with her father – a retired, rich businessman whom she disliked. She could, though, reasonably hope to find some position in which she was allowed to do the things she was good at, and which she had learnt to do with him. The problem, for her, had been to find anyone to recognize that her talent did not lie in the direction of magazine layout so much as in odd-jobs, gardening, keeping a small 'estate' or large smallholding in smooth working order.

The arrival of Angelo, whose paternity was unrevealed to anyone, precipitated her desire to get out of London. Discontent with the vacuous world of magazines hardened, with the arrival of the child, into true despondency.

'We can't open a refuge for unmarried mothers and fallen women,' said Victoria when the idea was at first suggested by Gorley Swallow. (*All* women, without any exceptions in my experience, feel threatened by Leman, and Victoria, with her sensitive antennae, felt threatened even before she had met her. Her milky eyes rolled unsympathetically, and her lips, far older than her years, twitched.)

More than anyone else in the universe, of course, Victoria Amt is permitted violent swings of opinion. Her hostility to the notion of having 'a girl from glossy magazines' living in Gardener's Cottage at Staithe changed very quickly when Leman and Angelo moved in.

'Lemon? What sort of a name is that? Why not Orange or Tomato?'

'It's Leman, not Lemon. She just happens to be known by it.'

I heard again Gorley Swallow saying, 'Isn't it a medieval word meaning lover?'

'That seems no reason to adopt it as one's name.'

'I don't think she did adopt it, Victoria.'

'It seems at the very least affected of her parents to have chosen it.'

'By contrast. It was imposed on them also; Leman is her surname.'

'Then why not use the name she was given in baptism?'

'I doubt whether she was baptized.'

'Oh?' Given Victoria's ancestry, it is perhaps not surprising that she is obsessed by the question of Jewishness. Jewish herself on her father's side, she cocked a blind head for telepathic hints from Gorley Swallow about this vital question.

'The Lemans have been Quakers for generations. Cumberland Quakers, which is rather unusual. She felt unable to live up to Arabella. A name, she felt, which required flounces.'

It took less than a week for Victoria's scepticism to dissolve.

Soon, it was 'That child is a genius. Mr Goddard told us that car couldn't be mended until he got a spare part from Cromer. Leman has cleaned – what was it she cleaned, Gorley?'

'The plugs, Victoria. And fitted a new steering-box.'

'I do not know what a steering-box is; but I can recognize genius.'

She unquestionably, Victoria, had gifts of intuition about the resemblances of the material world; but could she guess quite what a powerful effect Leman produced on those gifted with sight?

Dodie's beauty produces an instant response of a very obvious kind. She is simply amazingly sexy. Leman has more power to disturb, even though, with her working boy's clothes and her short bob of hair, she does not seem to be making so much effort with her appearance.

One eye of Leman's is a very slightly different colour from the other, a fact which, if you stare into them, is hypnotic. A casual observer of Leman's eyes would probably say that they were hazel. (But there, you run into difficulties; it is hard to imagine a casual observer of Leman. Her face is the sort which stops hearts.) In fact, her eyes are the deepest midnight blue, flecked with a pale spider's web of gold. It is this which gives them, in some lights, a very blue appearance and in others, a hazel. Close up, their colour recalls the Middle Ages, the sky in some illuminated manuscript, the encrusted blue and gold of a church ceiling or a royal shield.

I had fallen in love with Leman before I met her. William, who was an habitué of the evening parties just mentioned, used to speak of her; and then I heard of her from Gorley Swallow. I did not love her simply for her failure to endure working for him on *Metropolitan*, though that negative quality alone was beguiling. Before she became flesh, Leman was already an idea in the head, a visitant to the planet, but not one who was quite at home in the world of human activity, in terms of social rules. Even when I had come to know her and had been stabbed through the heart by her beauty, I thought of her as a stranger, a mermaid who had swum in from the sea by mistake, or a creature of faerie who had mysteriously stayed behind at Staithe when the other visitants had vanished from sight.

Her natural practicality, her ability to mend fuses, tinker with lawn-mowers, replaster walls, seemed to such a clumsy person as myself only to increase the sense that she was a stranger on the earth. She was not a spiritual being, merely an alien, like one of the Homeric deities who were able for their own capricious purposes to transform themselves into beautiful serving-maids in order to converse with mortals, before returning to Olympus. She was the least urban, the least modern young person. She belonged to the world of nature. Plants grew for her. Animals – particularly her West Highland terrier, Trump – had a natural affinity with her. And there was Angelo. Sex, clearly, had been part of the picture – perhaps always was. I was so pathetically enamoured of Leman, though, that I could not allow my imagination to accept her as a sexual being. I had even gone through phases of wondering, quite seriously, whether Angelo was the result of parthenogenesis.

Throughout the last year, the two women have become, among other things, the two beings in the Sonnets. Dodie is naturally the Dark Lady. Leman for me, much more than Kit, is 'my better angel' – though there has never been any reason to suppose that the two, as in that disturbing poem, had conjoined, nor that my angel had 'turn'd fiend' by loving the dark woman.

Dodie, indeed, has never made any secret of being irritated by my soppy feelings for Leman (which could not be disguised, even though their extent, like their seriousness, is unplumbable, even to myself).

Could it be the difference between falling in love with a face and lusting after a body? You don't have to be homosexual to understand Plato's *Symposium*. It all starts with faces – the crush, the longing for something not easily defined. Leman's face destroys sleep. I think about it, dream about it and seem to see in it the possibilities of another life in which I have become finer, purer, stronger. I would love to have been hugged and held by Leman.

I sometimes still fantasize about being allowed to go on a camping holiday with her and falling asleep with her under a blanket and the Milky Way. It is still true, nearly twenty years later, as I write these words. Angelo is a young man. His half-brother and half-sisters – Jeremy, Theo, Henrietta – descend in order scattered by a year or two. What pointless havoc would have been caused if I'd declared myself to Leman and if – unlikely, I know – she'd been interested. In times past, my sense of her as a goddess to worship would not have prevented some blundering, selfish attempt; but now we are 'friends' – it's a friendship, though, with this sense that by saying nothing, I've saved everything. By doing nothing, I haven't overstepped into embarrassment.

That first year, however, it was painful to watch the blossoming relationship between Leman and Kit. When I say that I am worried by Kit's capacity to hurt, I am indeed referring, as Dodie discerns, to little What's-her-name.

'She's tough. She'll look after herself. She's done exactly what she wants in her life, and that's what she'll go on doing,' Dodie says.

The generosity which women can assume when discussing the merits of other human beings quite deserts them when the person under discussion is a member of their own sex who is widely or universally admired. Much to the chagrin of the others, Leman is universally admired – in the village, on the farm, and with visitors to the Festival.

'You're simply jealous of them both – Kit and little What's-her-name. You'd like to fuck either of them and you can't stand the idea of their fucking one another.'

Having delivered this judgement, Dodie stands up to fetch cigarettes and a lighter. The crudity with which she had expressed herself seems like a simple lie; but if she had said it more subtly, would I recognize a picture of what had taken place in Staithe during the summer?

That bright May day, six months before!

It was going to be a glorious day. Skinny, toothpaste-breathed, pyjama-clad, I paused on the half-landing of the broad oak stair;

through the tall window I saw sunlight glint on a full tide. The sea came ever closer to the house, year by year. According to one survey, it will overwhelm the house and the garden within a few decades. Staithe will vanish beneath the waves. We can say, literally, after us – Kit, Leman, the children – the flood.

At low tide, when the beach became a limitless stretch of sand and the waterline was out of sight, it was hard to believe in the threatened deluge; easier to imagine it at high tide when the waves reached the dunes and, in spring, covered the salt-marshes themselves.

So do our minutes hasten to their end . . .

It was a preternaturally warm morning for May, but only the hardy would have considered it bathing weather. My parents, both quite tough, favoured this stretch of coast for holidays before the war, but they often had to concede some justice in Mrs Webb's contention that, 'You take a risk with the North Sea even in the height of summer. Look at my husband's brother Graham and Mablethorpe.' If we were ever told what befell Mrs Webb's brother-in-law at that northern resort, the record of it has vanished from the annals. How well I recollect, though, at Holkham or Brancaster, or on the blowy stretch of sands at Mallington, that numb of pure cold when I emerged from the ocean, warmed only by Mummy, wrapping my small limbs in the towel which smelt of her.

From my vantage-point I discerned two figures emerging from the water. High tide at Staithe produces an optical illusion. Though the house is more than half a mile from the shore, the perspective cast by differing land levels makes it appear much closer. Only the size of the figures bobbing about in the water gave a true sense of distance. They appeared as darkened stick-creatures in that blinding morning brightness, rising out of the glacial silver water and emerging on to the sand. I found the scene so beautiful that I balanced the tray on the broad polished stair and continued to watch as the figures, presumably naked, came out of the sea hand in hand, dried themselves hastily and broke into a run.

They came in our direction, the direction of the house. For a while, as they ran over the sands, they became invisible. Then, much closer, their heads showed over the springy grass of the dunes. They came into the drive, but they were not heading for the house. Rather than cross the garden in our direction, they loosed hands, ran along the narrow path at the side of the kitchen garden wall and were lost to view behind shrubs and trees. Leman, presumably, was heading for Gardener's Cottage, which she shared with Angelo; Kit, for the rooms above the disused coach-house which was where he lived when not in his flat in Shepherd's Bush.

Their youthfulness made me wistful. The sea, the sunlight on the park and shrubs and budding trees and burgeoning hedges, all seemed as young as they.

Though the landscape was so distinctively that of North Norfolk, the picture became for me, in that bright morning, like one of those huge imagined scenes in the work of the late Poussin, where the happiness of two figures, small beneath trees and a huge sky, is threatened by some impending disaster of which they are unaware.

I prayed to Shakespeare, who knew all the tricks played by love, to look with mercy on this scene. It seemed like an expulsion from Eden; but, in his benign hands, it could be transformed into a comedy in which every spare character is neatly paired off with another by the end of the fifth act. O Shakespeare, you knew the tormented evil in the heart of Iago, the petulant confusions of Lysander and Demetrius, the jealousies of Leontes and the lust of Cleopatra. Look with mercy upon us. In sooth I know not why I am so sad.

In the foreground of this epiphany, I saw the field which bordered the garden; I saw the thick cliff of rhododendron, an explosion of white and purple; I saw the rose garden, its grass

31

grey-silver with dawn. For a moment, I could believe that Leman and Kit were just such 'creatures of air' as the notorious supernatural visitants who appeared to Victoria's grandfather over eighty years before.

Downstairs in the hall, the long-case clock chimed six.

What was I doing, at fifty-something, so much further into the wood than halfway, having such feelings as churned through my pyjamas, as I stared at that day of days? Men of my age were meant to be the chairmen of committees, or headmasters, or company directors, or magistrates, or – like Timpson, head boy of Seaforth Grange in my day – a bishop. That great world, which it is the destiny of Englishmen to control! Those classrooms at Seaforth Grange – how they urged us to take the world seriously! On the walls hung pictures – General Wolfe on the Heights of Abraham, General Gordon meeting his end at Khartoum – suggesting that whether in life or in death, the Britisher's duty was to do. In this sense I had never 'done' anything; hard to see, after Suez, what one would 'do', even if built with the moral fibre of the old pioneers of Empire.

Without Aristotelian functions to perform, we retreat into dreaming our Platonist dreams. I was tormented by the suspicion, the thought, the certainty, that because the young people had taken a dip together, they must have spent the night together. No moral reason existed, as far as I was aware, why they should not have done so; neither of them had other attachments. The blunt serrated knife, though, was ripping through my vitals as I thought about it: all the old symptoms. If feelings about Leman could only be kept on the level of that harmless *crush* on her – which everyone knew I had . . . Couldn't do anything about it, of course; could not even talk about it, nor tell anyone – except you.

> It wearies me, you say it wearies you;
> But how I caught it, found it or came by it,
> What stuff 'tis made of, whereof it is born,
> I am to learn . . .

In my head, there were no extravagant lengths to which I should not go for Leman's sake. Since my love was undeclared, and she could not possibly have guessed it, the tasks which she had so far set me were modest – to give her a lift, when her own van was in need of a spare part, to some garage in Cromer; and the jealous, but delicious, torment of watching the easy way in which she spoke to the garage mechanics, told them in precise detail what was wrong with the van, and what 'part' was required; and the lascivious but friendly smiles of the young men as they too basked in those lapis-lazuli and golden eyes. Once we went to the nursery at Holkham because she was running short of organic peat. Rather than performing such easy and mundane roles, I should have been just as willing, had Leman commanded it, to crawl naked to Walsingham, carrying the Cross. Equally, if she had told me to kill myself or to kill another person, I should have obeyed her.

Kill Claudio . . .

You knew the extraordinary degree of power which is exercised, usually involuntarily, by the beloved over the lover.

And I could imagine the troubled expression which would pass over Leman's sensible face if I told her the truth; and then, as she recounted to some third party my 'really embarrassing' declaration – that's what she'd call it – I could see how her sensual uneven lips would divide and how her white teeth would smile. To protect her from committing this cruelty (which would kill me) I have kept my secret safe. You alone, Shakespeare, are told about it. The others are enabled to smile at my 'crush'.

Turning from the window, I picked up the tray, mentally checking that it contained Victoria's manifold vitamin and Ginseng pills. The large butler's tray with handsome curved handles had come from the rectory at Timplingham. So did the large blue and white porcelain Worcester breakfast cups and saucers, which my uncle had inherited from *old* Mrs Lampitt,

Victoria's maternal great-grandmother; so, you could say that the china had come home. Not that Staithe was ever 'home' to the Lampitts.

Victoria inherited the place from her mother. At that stage, fifteen years ago, Victoria, whose father had died as an American citizen (having started life as a Czechoslovakian Jew), was teaching in the University of California. Staithe was an odd inheritance, not quite something to boast about. It had an unhappy reputation, both in Victoria's large and extended family and also, in so far as anyone still remembered it, in the life of the nation. The life of Campbell Dilkes, the composer who had largely rebuilt the flint-knapped seventeenth-century manor-house with its twisty brick chimneys in grandiose Tudorbethan style, and who inhabited the place for the first four decades of the century, was one of those careers which had to be 'lived down'. Even Uncle Roy, who took an indiscriminate interest in any branch of the Lampitt family, had never taken me to Staithe during my childhood, though it is only a quarter of an hour from Mallington, an hour from Timplingham.

Lavinia Lampitt had married Campbell Dilkes in 1893, the year of my uncle's birth. At that stage, from the modesty of his parents' semi-detached in Alderville Road (next door but one to Mrs Webb) Uncle Roy was hardly in a position to hobnob with Dilkeses or Lampitts, but in the proprietorial and deferential tone which he always adopted when that dynasty was under discussion, he would refer to 'poor dear Lavinia' – a locution picked up from 'old' Mrs Lampitt of Timplingham.

Campbell Dilkes was beyond the pale. He had committed some sort of unpardonable sin. Perhaps this fact, and the absence of any loyal friends, explained the decay of the house and – such as it was – of the estate.

When Victoria and her sister inherited the place, all this started to change. The hundred acres were leased to a local dairy farmer. The three cottages and the rooms above the coach-house

34

were renovated to a basic degree, plumbing and electricity being installed. These places, uninhabited since the war, became at least a potential source of income from 'holiday lets'. The large house began to have some sort of life again. Victoria's sister Juliet and her children came for extended trips during the school holidays. In the year of coming into her inheritance, Victoria left her job in America and became a Professor of Elizabethan Drama at the University of East Anglia, only an hour's drive away from Staithe. She began to treat Staithe as her almost permanent residence. And yet the central figure in all this – the man who rebuilt the house and created the garden – remained someone whose life was not quite mentionable.

The Munnings portrait of the old man hung on the landing, as I passed by with the tray. Once, when she still had her sight, Victoria had looked up at him coquettishly and said, 'You wicked old fraud!' Of course, I knew about the music, and the house, and the theatre. But the rest of what I knew about Campbell Dilkes was gathered piecemeal – largely as a result of Kit's researches; and I certainly had only the haziest idea of how the débâcle came about. All sorts of absurd euphemisms had been used in the family – and, by extension, on the lips of Uncle Roy; 'That was the year old Campbell Dilkes came a cropper' was one, I recollect.

Campbell Dilkes, through the medium of Sir Alfred Munnings's brushwork, looked down from the panelled walls: at first glance, a country gentleman, in his Norfolk jacket, his breeches and his socks. In his lifetime, the locals had called him 'Squire' without any obvious irony. Staithe is behind his head in the canvas, its twisted chimneys rising to English elm and grey clouds. His puce face, with its thick white moustaches, seems, at casual glance, to be that of any old Colonel Blimp who might have shot pheasant in the winter or sat on the magistrates' bench. No doubt, Campbell Dilkes was such a man, but, in the wistful look of those piercing blue eyes, there is another creature, a dreamer of dreams, a glimpser of visions.

Before I ever set eyes on the picture, his daughter, Victoria's mother, said to me, 'Of course, we offered the National Portrait Gallery the Munnings, but . . . ' Her voice had trailed away. I had no idea then why the National Valhalla should have scorned this reasonably accomplished oil painting of a minor but interesting musician. Munnings caught the fact that there was something tremendously sad about the face of Campbell Dilkes, and I always thought so, even before Kit told me his story.

Entering Victoria's bedroom, I announced, 'Leman and Kit have been having a dip.' I placed the tray on the round table by the east window through which light poured. I could never have slept in a room through which so much sunshine intruded but it made no difference to Victoria.

'Rather them than me. Now you have remembered . . . '

'Ginseng, Cod Liver, Multivite and Iron Capsules.' I spoke rapidly, testily, to curtail her question. I so seldom forgot her pills. Why did she make this request each morning? Would she have done so if she knew what a disproportionate rage and pain it caused? Christ, how it spoilt the sunlight, this pointless rage.

I turned to look out of the window: that at least was something which Victoria was unable to do. That was one thing which I was better at than she was – seeing. I waited for the intense, scalding irritation to subside. Through the window I could see the knot garden near the theatre which, together with his friend Masefield, Campbell Dilkes had built in the first year of the new century. Here, too, dancing around the topiary, the fairies had appeared to the composer in 1908.

'Leman and Kit have been having more than a dip.'

Victoria's announcement was authoritative, as if she had visual evidence for the assertion, which was delivered in her mild, deadpan American accent. She took a bite of Rich Tea and continued, with her mouth full.

'I am extremely worried about those two.'

There was nothing which caused me more pain, nor was there anything I liked better, than talking about Leman.

'What is there to be worried about?'

'Kit is quite obviously having some sort of an affair in London. This, equally obviously, is making Leman extremely unhappy.'

'I was thinking how very happy they looked, just now, as they came running back from the beach.'

In fact, it had been impossible to make out the facial expressions of the young pair, but I felt the need to keep my end up. Victoria could be pardoned for considering appearances deceptive. She ignored my remark.

'It is disastrous. Leman is simply perfect here. If only Kit would leave her *alone*! She has been so happy since she came to us. It has been like the fulfilment of a vocation. Her child is happy. Leman, for the first time in her life, has found things to do which make *her* happy. Now this! If we lived in a just world, of course, Kit and Leman would be compatible. I can think of no better mistress for Staithe than Leman, and no worse master than Kit. Yet one day it will all be his. If I died today, he would inherit it. His mother is dead. His father – wherever he may be – is a dead loss. I feel responsible for the boy. I was starting to feel dependent on Leman. Look at the gardens since she came; a wilderness has been tamed. It has been like the coming of God, with the rough places made smooth. And the way she looks after the chickens, and the rapport she has with Mr Loder and his herd.'

'In none of this does there appear to be a problem.'

'The problem is Kit's history of emotional disasters. Have you no memory? Georgia?' – a girl at Kit's college who had attempted suicide – 'The ludicrous Botney?' – his moral tutor, a man with a bow-tie who had a nervous breakdown and was still receiving treatment at Fulbourn Hospital – 'Hiney?' – the Scandinavian au pair in the London household where Kit first lodged when he began his grown-up life in London.

'Hiney was just trying it on. She admitted eventually that anyone could be the father of that . . . '

'That really isn't the issue.'

'She went back to Trondheim, didn't she?'

'You are wilfully missing the point. If the same thing happens to Leman, we shall lose not only a delightful companion but a gardener, a prodigiously talented odd-job person, a chauffeur and an estate manager. It was Gorley Swallow's stroke of genius to get her.'

Even Victoria had the habit, which everyone had, of referring to this individual by both his names. One never said just 'Gorley' or just 'Swallow', but always 'Gorley Swallow'. Trying to avoid such references at so early an hour, I said, 'Of course Leman is a marvellous asset; but since there is no evidence of her breaking her heart over Kit, we surely do not need to become too worried just yet.'

Victoria's exploratory fingers crept around the rim of her cup and fished for a soggy blob of Rich Tea, dunked too long.

She said, 'Gorley Swallow said that she never got the hang of *Metropolitan*. He said that, contrary to what is supposed, it requires a particular kind of intelligence to work on a magazine of that sort.'

'Would that be the kind of intelligence which other people call unintelligence?'

'It is cheap to belittle forms in which we have no experience and no wish to excel. Gorley Swallow says that as an experiment they even offered Leman a shopping column for one month. She submitted a humourless feature on the best old-fashioned ironmongers and hardware stores in central London.'

'It sounds much more interesting than most articles about shopping which I have read. Or, rather, which I haven't read.'

'Your boring crush makes you blind, blind. Who else in this place knows how to service a tractor? Mr Loder said he'd written off the old John Deere until Leman got her oily paws on it. And the electrical system in this house. She rewired the place, remember? This is the woman Kit has to mess with, when any one of the girls in the village would have done just as well.'

Bolt upright in black silk pyjamas, pencil thin, Victoria had a neatness of appearance unusual in one of her disability. Her iron grey hair, very thick, was cut extremely short. Her milky eyes rolled in all directions as she spoke, providing the only touch of anarchy in her otherwise composed features.

When she had woken up blind, five years before, in that Californian apartment (she was in the middle of a short lecture tour), and when the implications of the calamity had begun to dawn (Victoria without sight), her friends and admirers had all assumed that her career in the theatre was over. (The condition, for which nothing in her previous history had prepared her, was immediately pronounced incurable.) They supposed that she would retire to Norwich and that sympathetic reading-slaves would keep her abreast of modern scholarly journals, enabling her to do a little work of her own.

In fact, it was university life which she reduced, deciding in effect to abandon academic research altogether.

'A man may see how this world goes with no eyes, but I would defy him to master the catalogue of the university library.'

In any case, for some years, and certainly for as long as I had known her, Victoria had found the academic world alien. Hers was the last generation in Eng. Lit. circles to attempt humanist criticism and scholarship in Shakespearean studies. She wrote her doctoral thesis during the liberal-humanist Wilson Era: Dover Wilson, F. P. Wilson and Wilson Knight represented the range and agenda of 'the subject'. In that lost age, structuralism, deconstructionism, post-marxism, post-modernism, all lay in the future. The new critics in their various guises, not quite philosophers, not quite scholars – the Barthesians, the Derridans, the Paul-de-Maniacs – hovered in the wings. As someone who had never been educated at a university, but who was steeped in Shakespeare, I reacted to their utterances, when heard at third hand, as might a mystic who had heard about the disputes at a theological synod of the Church. Their disputations were arid, but what they were discussing had become for me the living fire.

By the time Victoria returned from the American job, inherited Staithe, took up her chair at East Anglia, the New Critics were triumphant in the English faculties of the United States and France, poised to take over in England too. Readers who were actually interested in Shakespeare's plays, their sources, their analogues, their textual history, their content, their great themes, what they were actually about, how they were written, would continue to enjoy Victoria's books of essays. (It was no surprise to me to discover that Dodie had read some of Victoria's essays in the course of 'doing' *Othello* and *Measure for Measure* at A level.)

The pushy undergraduate, though, wishing to earn street cred, would have very little time for reflecting on the character of Cleopatra, still less on what Shakespeare owed to his reading of North's Plutarch. Such stuff belonged with A. C. Bradley in the U-bend of critical history's plumbing arrangements. The 'texts' were no longer books to be submitted to, nor attended to, they were toys to be played with; one was almost tempted to add, toys for self-pleasuring.

This development in the academic world, wholly inimical to Victoria, added energy to her theatrical preoccupations.

It was said (by several bigwigs on both sides of the Atlantic) that, when she went into academic life, the theatre lost one of its great Shakespearean directors. From undergraduate days she was an active member of the Marlowe Society, and she never saw the study of Shakespeare as a purely academic exercise. The stage and not the page is where he lives. It is a sentence from her essay on the Globe, but it was deeply believed and lived.

Inheriting Staithe, with its Edwardian amphitheatre, was a gift from the Fates which Victoria did not spurn. Even when the house had a leaking roof and no functional heating system, Victoria had persuaded her sister to spend money having the amphitheatre restored, the brickwork repointed, and the canopy built over the stage and over the 'box' area of the best seats.

The Marlowe Society came over and gave a performance of *Comus* there before the building work was complete. And so, on the very site where Campbell Dilkes had seen the fairies, Sabrina fair had sung of the 'mincing Dryads'. In the same summer, Victoria put on a production of *Love's Labour's Lost* which amazed everyone by being a local sell-out.

Ten years later, there was the Staithe Festival, attended not only by locals but by visitors from Norwich, Cambridge, London and further afield. Television stars such as Dodie and knights of the theatre such as Sir Hubert Power were pleased to be associated with it. Sherdingley Staithe, the little town a mile or so from the house, was now taken over annually for Festival week. Rooms in the one hotel of any substance – the Green Man – and all the boarding houses were booked up by the Festival Office. There was even talk of reviving the theatre at the end of the pier (which had become a bingo hall) for productions larger in scale than the garden theatre at Staithe could allow.

The amphitheatre seated only about two hundred. The productions there had become so popular that it would have been possible to sell these seats five times over; but the charm of the amphitheatre was its smallness. For a week each year, Staithe was now a haven of Shakespeare-mania. Not only were there the plays, put on each afternoon and evening in the amphitheatre; there were the talks, the seminars, the theatre workshops and the discussion groups, all enormously popular. All these things emanated from Victoria's magnetism, her alarming enthusiasm, her organizational skills.

Her capacity to command was undiminished by losing her sight. To direct, to shape life according to her dictates, was her natural mode. Were it not for her rolling, milky eyes, it was hard to believe that she really was blind. I have watched her directing many times. We were all amazed by her uncanny sense of the whereabouts of actors on the stage.

'You need to come down, darling, five yards, I should say. No, no – whoa! That's too far! Back a few paces. That's more like it.'

These instructions, which would have been commonplace on the lips of any other director, seemed uncanny when spoken by someone who supposedly could not see what was taking place, and who had lost her sight only a short time before. Perhaps her grandfather really had communed with the spirits and learned to see what could not be seen by mortals? Some such magic lurked in the blood? Or in the place?

It was inevitable, given her magisterial and natural capacity to command, that Victoria should have taken over my Sonnets play; even so, on that beautiful morning when I had watched Kit and Leman emerge together from the sea, I was not aware that the play was about to be snatched from me so brutally.

Still upright in pyjamas, Victoria said, 'I've asked Gorley Swallow to join us, when the others come over for the read-through.'

'Is that wise? We don't want everything we have said repeated in some gossip column.'

'Gorley Swallow would never betray a friend . . . '

'I thought that it was on the betrayal of friends that he had built his professional life.'

' . . . and a little publicity never hurt any production. This, after all, was your thinking when you decided to cast a television star as the Lady in your radio version of the play.'

'It wasn't actually my – '

'Dodie is coming over this morning, as you know. She is in the area anyway. Now, before she comes, I want your views, your candid thoughts about her.'

Victoria could no longer stare me out of countenance in the way that she did when I first met her, but she had an uncanny capacity to concentrate psychic energy in the direction of one particular individual, so that it felt as if one were being stared at. It was by no means impossible that Victoria had guessed, or been told by spies, the nature of my relations with Dodie. Victoria and

I would never have discussed such subjects; we lacked the vocabulary; we should have been no more equipped, linguistically, to indulge in emotional 'sharing' than to have a dialogue about computer programming or Rugby League. The fact that a subject is not mentioned, however, does not mean that it is absent from the atmosphere.

Sex, when Victoria and I had tried it, years before, in Italy, had been a disaster; after a couple of 'goes' we decided to call it a day. I say 'we decided', but the fact (not so strange if you consider it) is that Victoria and I never discussed this matter, never alluded to it in all our time living beneath the same roof at Staithe. The sexual failure no doubt produced its own painful bond, however, a secret of which both of us were perhaps ashamed; or a tormented frustration, a feeling that if only I had hovered around for long enough, I, or we, should have managed to get this side of things right.

The great sexless marriages of the nineteenth century were sometimes closer knit than those where the inevitable children and the humdrum routines of family life deflected attention to other individuals within the household. In a sexless union, attention between the two partners can be total. Many marriages begin with sex, pass through a phase of shared family life and end up, after twenty or thirty years, as (all but or actually) sexless unions in which irritation and mutual dislike are as strong a cement in the structure as love. The Carlyles managed to 'fast-forward' to this state of things after a single botched honeymoon night; to stride from youthful passion to old-aged hatred in the space of a few frustrated nocturnal hours at Craigenputtock; and to maintain, in addition, all the obsessive love which lies buried in such a painful unfulfilled relationship.

Victoria and I had never married; we had never even ex-perienced the sexual-cum-intellectual friendship of the sort she had once enjoyed with Raphael Hunter. There were, however, Carlyleish elements in our strange relationship. If she had not gone blind, perhaps, I should have left Staithe. When I had been in the place five years, though, and she returned from that lecture tour of the United States with no sight, no amanuensis, no nurse, no companion, it was inevitable that I should hover around and do what I could in the way of helping with letters, cooking and carrying trays about the house. I had performed a similar function in the past in the life of Sargent Lampitt; I knew how it was done. It suited me to live at Staithe. My bedroom here was large – it was a perfect retreat. I also had the use of a small sitting-room and a somewhat fuzzy black and white television set on which I could watch *The Criminals*, a weekly American comedy show to which I had grown addicted. I had given up my London flat. There could be no doubt, however, who was in control; and the very week I gave up my flat, I felt the prison door slam behind me.

We never discussed any of this. There were no written ground-rules, which in a paradoxical way tied me down all the more. In no marital sense did I owe Victoria loyalty; but I had developed guilt sensations if I was not on hand to act as her servant. On the nights which I did occasionally spend away from Staithe I felt it necessary (she always said it was needless) to arrange with Leman to come in and make Victoria's supper, provide her with her whisky and, in case of need, sleep in the house overnight.

'I think we should be candid with one another about all this. I happen to think that is very important. Otherwise the meeting will get nowhere.'

'I hadn't realized that it was to be a meeting. You said last week that we might have to have a read-through, especially since Dodie is in the neighbourhood today.'

'Do we have any idea why?' Victoria's question flew out impulsively.

'Any particular reason why she should not have been?' I countered.

Victoria was suddenly flustered. A natural liberal, and in many ways more American than English, Victoria is far touchier on the subject of race than I am. Why not simply say that blacks are all but unknown in North Norfolk – that it is very surprising to think of one there – that in London one saw nothing distinctive or odd about Dodie being black, but that as soon as one imagined her in Norfolk, one realized what a gap existed in England between town and country? All these thoughts occurred, and they all lay behind Victoria's impulse to ask what could possibly have brought Dodie Rich to our neck of the woods. Victoria's natural good taste was disgusted at herself, however, for this reaction, and she began squirming.

'I mean – a famous television star, one would suppose that she would take her holidays . . . '

'Somewhere with coconuts and palm trees and silver sand?'

'Of course not.' Words failed her, since the suggestion that this was a surprising place for a holiday revealed once again the set of Victoria's mind. There was undoubtedly the suggestion here that some more exotic location than Staithe might be found for a young woman who would probably feel more at home in the Seychelles or the Caribbean. Not only was Victoria a modern, liberal American with an understandably exaggerated horror of 'racism'; she was also a woman with skeletons in the family cupboards, ghosts which she wished to exorcize. Her liberalism, particularly on the racial question, was obsessive, which was why she so often found herself getting tangled up in embarrassment when real black people were involved.

'It's very important that we should all try to be frank,' she repeated, 'at the meeting. As you know, I want to start rehearsals for the *Dream* at once. The question remains whether your play, or some version of it, is put on for one night of the Festival.'

'What do you mean – some version of it?'

'I told you Hubie is coming over too this morning?'

This was news.

'Is he to be in the *Dream*? I always think Theseus such a boring part; and you can't be thinking of Hubie as Bottom. Though – now you come to mention it . . . '

'We must not prejudge anything. We must wait for the meeting.'

I sat there in her bedroom watching her, hating her and fearing her.

I had been given to understand that she did want to have a production of *Dear Time's Waste* at the Festival. Now, I felt like a student whose dissertation might or might not be acceptable to the examiners.

Victoria added, 'Gorley Swallow sensed that there was something a little vulgar about Dodie's radio performance, but not necessarily so vulgar that it could not be refined, given the right director. Candidly, I cannot yet tell whether this was the fault of your director on the radio or whether your play, which is very nearly there, very nearly saying something interesting about Shakespeare, is not in fact falling all the time into the Victorian vulgarity of supplying a story which the Sonnets themselves so tantalizingly and so successfully always refuse to tell.'

I knew these words to be true, which is why they made me so speechlessly angry.

I retreated into the garden and watched the cars arrive – Hubert Power in a Rover 2000, Dodie in a taxi. At the end of the gravel path, in khaki shorts, Leman was bent over the onion troughs, sieving earth. Her terracotta legs, muscular and sculpted, were such as Poussin might have painted had Enid Blyton lived in the seventeenth century and that French Master been asked to do illustrations of George in the 'Famous Five' stories. Always drawn to the tomboys in Tasso, Poussin would have liked George, I fancy. He'd certainly have loved Leman.

While I had the thought, Gorley Swallow could be seen taking his gentle, shuffling steps across the yard from Dairy Cottage to the larger house.

'They are all assembling,' I said, having wandered down the path intent on wasting Leman's time. I was contemplating cutting the meeting altogether, and determined, whatever befell, that I should be late for it.

'All except Kit,' I added. 'Where is he?'

Leman looked up and wiped her brow with the clean back of an otherwise earth-blackened hand. She looked extremely amused.

'He's so naughty, so! Is he really meant to go to Victoria's rehearsal?'

'She says it isn't a rehearsal, it's a meeting. I had thought it was a read-through.'

'Kit's off, pursuing his secret life.'

'Victoria will be displeased. She wants him to appear in my play as the young man.'

I knew, having asked her before and been astonished by the reply, that Leman had never read a single one of Shakespeare's Sonnets. When I had pressed her about this and accused her of affectation, she had asked, first with blushes, and then with giggles, whether 'I wandered lonely as a cloud' was one of them.

'Kit felt the need to go cottaging I think.'

'Not with Raphael Hunter?'

'I expect so.'

It was our standing joke that Kit's 'secret life' – it was becoming obvious that he had something up his sleeve – consisted in surreptitious expeditions to satisfy homosexual lusts. Neither Leman nor I believed this was the case, which is why we made the joke.

'He's told me his secret by the way,' she said. 'I mean, what he is really up to, the real secret.'

'Which is?'

'You'll have to get him to explain it himself. Why he can't tell Victoria I can't imagine, but he thinks she'd go spare, so!'

'What is all this? What secrets, Leman?'

But she laughed and went on with her sieving.

The brightness of the day made the drawing-room at Staithe Stygian in its impenetrable shadow. The smell of last night's wood fire lingered in the air, mingling with cigarettes – Dodie's

Marlboro Lights and Hubie's Gauloises.

The two women, Dodie and Victoria, were silent and stood at statuesque right angles to the two men whom I found in the room, Hubie Power and Gorley Swallow. None was seated. Thoughts of the Chorus in a tragedy – memories of *Samson Agonistes*, the school production staged by Treadmill – came to mind at the sight of these four upright shadows.

It was no surprise that Gorley Swallow was speaking when I entered the room. Even the great actor, Sir Hubert Power, was silent.

'Sheeks,' said Gorley Swallow, 'Sheeks.'

I recognized that he was discussing the author of the Sonnets. Whether the others, their ears less well attuned to Gorley Swallow's distinctive and confiding manner of speech, caught the name 'Shakespeare' I could not be sure. His habit of lowering his voice, speaking at times in a near-whisper, guaranteed maximum attention from those who noticed that his lips were moving. Victoria, knowing such things by instinct or magic, craned forward to catch his phrases. It was a remarkable fact that, while Gorley Swallow had spent almost his entire professional career in what might be regarded as the most frivolous end of journalism – glossy magazines and gossip columns – his idea of himself was serious; he always spoke of himself as an intellectual and – more baffling, since he had no publications to his name apart from the magazine articles – as a 'serious' writer. One could not but admire the strength with which Gorley Swallow believed in himself. His deeply held view that, despite all appearances, he was someone to be taken seriously, was easily absorbed by women, less readily adopted by the men of his acquaintance, who were, perhaps, more censorious of his preparedness to devote so much conversational space to the subject which interested him most: himself.

'Of course, I wrote some sonnets once,' he was murmuring. 'They were terribly sad.'

Tall, stooping, a little younger than myself, and therefore perhaps fifty, Gorley Swallow stared into the dark room with that expression of wistfulness which women found so beguiling. Grotesquely huge feet were clad in shoes which would have been more appropriate for the promenade of some southern seaside resort: dark blue moccasins. Thick blue corduroy trousers. A hairy grey tweed jacket. A grey jumper and an open-necked white shirt. His bespectacled face was, as usual, concentrated, with his lips pursed and his small porcine eyes glinting behind large specs. He had a full head of hair, much more abundant than mine, but the effect of personal oddness was greatly increased by the fact that he never seemed to brush it. The dishevelled dark mop stood on end in a style reminiscent of the Phiz illustrations. One remembered Pecksniff. The effect was rendered even odder by the central tuft which, in contrast to the surrounding oily dark, was pure white. The face, though, was not the face of Pecksniff; it was that of Sir Andrew Aguecheek.

'Like Sheeks-mumble,' pursued Gorley Swallow's just audible, mincing tones, 'my sonnets were chiefly about loss, love, time. Terribly sad themes, you see.'

'They are also the theme of *Dear Time's Waste*.'

Since we had not assembled – surely? – to discuss Gorley Swallow's sonnets, it seemed fair at this point to call the meeting to order; but I had spoken out of turn.

'What's that?' asked Gorley Swallow.

'My play,' I said.

'About me?' For a moment Gorley Swallow's face lost its sadness. 'You have written a play about me?'

One of the annoying things about Gorley Swallow was that I never quite knew when he was teasing me.

'Does Kit know the time?' asked Victoria.

This question was presumably (on most metaphysical levels) unanswerable. Reaching no one, the inquiry hung in the wood-smoky shadows and floated over the lumpen furniture, some 'good', some contemporaneous with its original owner, Campbell Dilkes.

Feeling myself and my play on trial, I sadistically waited a minute or two before revealing, 'He won't be coming.'

'He told you this?' – from Victoria.

'How very tiresome' – from Hubert Power.

'He did not tell me, but I gather he has sloped off.'

'To London, we may take it,' said Victoria crossly.

Since I shared her assumption, I murmured some assent.

Hubie Power was an old friend of Victoria's, but it was years since I had met him – not since I had been married to Anne. We had once found ourselves being dragged backstage to Hubie's dressing-room. He had just given the finest performance of his life, as Uncle Vanya. This was the night I witnessed Isabella Marno with her legs wrapped around Raphael Hunter, and began to realize many of the sad things which Shakespeare (doubtless, Gorley Swallow too) wrote about in sonnets.

Hubie had never in my estimation 'done' anything much since that *Uncle Vanya*. That is, while playing all the major roles – his television Othello was widely praised, and his Prospero, Cymbeline and Lear had all been hailed in recent time as masterpieces – he seemed to me to have developed habits of hammy self-parody which it was hard not to find ridiculous. One went to see Sir Hubert Power imitating himself, not to see an actor transforming himself into one of Shakespeare's characters. That was my view, always (I noted) one which was howled down if I tried it out on non-theatrical company. Power was certainly a very popular actor and it was only among the profession that the particularly meretricious, even absurd qualities which he brought to his craft were apparent. His manner of delivery – imitated not only by us actors but even by vaudeville comedians and 'impressionists' on TV comedy shows – was something which he now carried into private conversation. At the news that Kit had gone absent without leave, Sir Hubert looked very disappointed. His thin lips tautened as he put a cigarette between them and held the lighter between trembly, slightly orange fingers.

'This is sad! Sad indeed!' he declaimed. One felt that some Victorian melodrama were being enacted. The exaggerated manner in which he pronounced dentals made the two 'd's of *indeed* come into the room like gunshot.

Like many people battling with booze, he had decided to keep himself impeccably neat. His hair was sleek and combed in a style which would have seemed very smart in the year of Noël Coward's first performance in *The Vortex*. Its chestnut brown was remarkable in a man who must have been past seventy; indeed, it was even richer and glossier than when I had last seen it at close quarters thirty years earlier. Yellowing bloodshot eyes looked sadly, but also furiously, out of the lightly pomaded face. Why was he so angry, and so sad – did he not have a knighthood, and success, and the praise of all the theatre-going world?

He wore a spruce little check sports coat, cavalry twill trousers, yellow socks and highly polished brown shoes, a rig which suggested a country solicitor, life and soul of the local golf club – but, once again, a golf club frozen in history. Was he in fact 'in costume'? Had the curtain just risen on one of those sets which never appear these days in the West End theatre but which survive perhaps in rep: an old-fashioned drawing-room comedy? Scene: the drawing-room. From the open french windows comes the twittering, electronic and far too loud, of garden bird-song . . .

'But I found Kit so charming when you introduced us, darling,' said Sir Hubert. 'I'd found the prospect of working with him really exciting.'

The implications of this strange remark did not dawn on me at first. *Dear Time's Waste* was to be performed for one night at the Festival. That had been agreed, hadn't it? And since I had made the part of Shakespeare my own on the radio, it followed, didn't it, that I should play Shakespeare in the production at Staithe? Didn't it?

'Well, Kit should have let us know he wasn't coming,' said Victoria, 'but we had better start without him.'

Having filled his lungs with tobacco smoke, Sir Hubert looked as if he were trying to contain something greater than a cough; his bluish complexion, which Victoria could not see, might easily have heralded a seizure. I remembered, for some reason, the only bitch review of Hubie's *King Lear*. Everyone else praised it extravagantly, except the critic in the *Observer*, who compared the poignant moment of tragicomedy when Lear tears off his clothes – 'Off, off, you lendings!' – with that traditional part of stage business in a Christmas panto, the Dame's striptease.

'I think', said I, 'that Kit has probably gone up to London for one of his mysterious lunches.'

'It cuts so terribly into one's day, luncheon,' said Gorley Swallow. 'That is why I generally prefer dinners. A really good luncheon, however . . . ' His voice trailed sadly away, implying that it was several years since he had eaten anything between the hours of breakfast and sundown – as though life had been a perpetual Ramadan. That teasing little smile played across his face again and I felt cross with myself, once again, for having been 'had'.

'Perhaps Kit couldn't get out of it,' went on Gorley Swallow charitably.

'He could have told me he wasn't going to be here,' said Victoria.

No doubt Kit had his own reasons for having gone off, his own reasons for not wishing to discuss my play. There was something unquestionably embarrassing about this 'meeting'. Did she really intend to humiliate me by discussing *Dear Time's Waste* with, of all people, Hubie Power and Gorley Swallow? And was it part of the ritual to make Dodie a witness of my humiliation? When they all began to dissect my poor play, however, I found myself strangely detached, and it was difficult to prevent an idiot smile from playing across my face.

'Well,' declared Sir Hubert Power, 'the first thing to go must be the title.'

'I quite agree,' said Gorley Swallow. 'A disastrous title. I've always found that titles are the hardest thing to write.'

'And why not' – Hubie pursed his lips; he held the palm of his hand flat, like a conjuror revealing, now an empty palm, now an abundance of silk squares springing by magic from his fingers – 'why not, quite simply, *Dark Lady?*'

'Suits me,' Dodie simpered.

It was surprising that she gave me so little support.

I felt that Hubie's vulgarian suggestion did not require an answer. One assumed that Victoria, the Shakespearean scholar, would soon put him right. I was astonished when I heard her quiet voice murmur, 'I agree.'

I ventured to speak.

'The title *Dark Lady* hardly conveys what the Sonnets are about, still less what this play is about. It would be like calling a play based on Dante's *Inferno* . . . '

Words failed me and I wished I had not begun the analogy game. It was too much like the competition at the back of the *Spectator*. Just the sort of thing Gorley Swallow would love, of course. Already, he was supplying, in a not very good American accent, '*Journey to Hell and Back. Beatrice, I Kinda Miss You.*'

'*Dark Wood*' was Victoria's contribution; for some reason, the others found it funny.

'For a start, only a handful of Shakespeare's Sonnets have anything to do with the dark woman, or with her involvement with the young man.'

'It seems such a pity that Kit isn't here,' said Hubie petulantly. 'You see, darling, if you are still thinking that he and I might . . . '

It was of some interest to know what Hubie and Kit might be supposed to be doing together; and it was also of some interest to know where Kit had gone to, what he was up to, whether Victoria's speculation was true and whether he was indeed having an affair in London. Victoria, however, interrupted.

'The difficulty', she said, speaking to a crowd of undergraduates inside her head rather than to us, 'is found in the Sonnets themselves; in the way they work as a literary form.'

'I always find', said Gorley Swallow in his mournful little voice, 'that when I'm reading them, I think they are about me and my friends.'

'It's a very intelligent point,' said Victoria reverently. It was hardly believable to me that so intelligent a woman was prepared to defer to him.

'It's the same trick in *Hamlet*,' she said. 'Everyone identifies with Hamlet, everyone imagines themselves saying the soliloquies.'

'That's where I happen to disagree,' I said. True, there had been many occasions during my youth when I should cheerfully have murdered my uncle, but the resemblances between Claudius's character and that of Uncle Roy were not conspicuous. 'I do not identify with Shakespeare the sonneteer. I think the Sonnets are a series of poems about a very specific set of circumstances. They are about a feckless young man whose mother wants him to marry. Shakespeare is enlisted by this *grande dame* to persuade him to do so, and Shakespeare himself becomes infatuated . . . '

This obsessive burst from me provoked Victoria into seminar mode.

'But, Julian! You must see that this is a late Victorian or Edwardian love story which you are imposing on an Elizabethan sonnet-sequence. You've been reading too deeply in James Petworth Lampitt's *Shakespeare's True Story*. In that work, you will recall, my great-uncle . . . '

I blushed to see Victoria lining herself up with those whom Sargie and Uncle Roy would call, in their specialized use of the term, the buggers, or the absolute buggers, denigrators of Jimbo's bellettrist approach to the art of literature.

Gorley Swallow and Hubert Power laughed; so did Dodie though she plainly did not know what we were talking about.

'All that Bosie Douglas, seeing into Shakespeare's soul sort of crap,' laughed Hubert Power.

'You see' – and really Victoria's satire was wasted on so small an audience – 'my great-uncle convinced himself in 1926 that he knew exactly the story which lay behind the Sonnets. He established that the Mr W. H. of the dedication was the young man of the poems – that itself is by no means a matter of certainty. Then he took it as read that Mr W. H. was William Herbert, later Earl of Pembroke, and that the Dark Lady was Mary Fitton. Shakespeare in this version of events becomes a rather snobbish, sexually ambivalent, metropolitan *homme de lettres* who enjoys staying at country houses and who, at the behest of an aristocratic lady, vouchsafes to take the young man of the house under his wing. It's very much the sort of thing which happened to Jimbo Lampitt himself. Bless him. You remember the absurd excitement in the family when he went on that walking tour in Belgium with Lord Esher? But back to the Sonnets. Jimbo Lampitt, I mean, William Shakespeare . . . '

Gorley Swallow yelped with laughter.

Like everyone else in the family, Jimbo had ostracized Victoria's grandfather during the 1930s, but there had once been a friendship between Campbell Dilkes and Jimbo. Such disloyalty ill became her.

'The *homme de lettres* develops an obsession with the young man. Together, they explore the low life of London, the brothels and the taverns. They confront the man who appears to obsess the poet as much as the man he loves – namely the Rival Poet. Cue for the entry of Hugh Walpole. I think the passage in Raphael Hunter's biography of Lampitt when he draws a parallel between Lampitt's life and the Sonnets is definitive.'

I recognized all this bilge as being inspired by Hunter's book.

'Hunter's book is every bit as subjective as anything Jimbo wrote,' I said. 'As a matter of fact there's hardly any evidence of a friendship between Jimbo and Lord Esher. You seem to forget that I have spent quite some time thinking about the Raphael Hunter phenomenon.'

'Haven't we all?' said Hubert Power.

It was an interjection which surprised me, but Dodie then made a remark which compensated for her willingness to side with the others about the title of my play.

'Raphael Hunter?' she asked artlessly. I am sure she spoke for her generation. Hunter's star had been on the wane for some years. People in their twenties had barely heard of him.

'He wrote that remarkable book about the American financier. Virgil D. Everett Junior,' said Gorley Swallow.

'Oh, yeah, right,' said Dodie annoyingly. 'The one who made money out of the Vietnam War? It was all serialized in the Sunday papers. That was really yucky, some of that stuff – about making boys screw prostitutes, and watching? Do you remember?'

'His first biography', I said, 'was of one of Victoria's many distinguished relations – one James Petworth Lampitt.'

'Of course,' said Dodie. 'Didn't he do that telly series about Victorians based on Lampitt's books? It was great. I remember my dad watching it when I was about fourteen; making me watch it for my GCSE project on the Crimean War.'

'Hunter', I continued, 'purported to tell the story of James Petworth Lampitt. But I have never met anyone who actually knew Jimbo who thought that it was an accurate portrait of the man. Biography is a branch of fiction. There is, for example, not one scrap of evidence that Jimbo was ever in love with a young man. Who knows, perhaps Hunter was drawing some morbid self-portrait.'

Hubert Power, the umpteenth fag alight, positively shone at this piece of malice. There was the unpleasing chance that he might actually prance across the carpet and embrace me. He made a sound like 'Hoo, hoo, hoo' as smoke billowed from mouth and nostrils.

Then occurred an example of that uncanny phenomenon: Victoria's blind eyes resting on Hubie and his visibly feeling her unspoken call to order. She was the stern teacher who appeared to see misbehaviour in the classroom even when she had her back to the children and was writing on the blackboard.

Hubie sharply returned to the subject of the Sonnets. In spite of his momentary delight in my analysis of Hunter's oeuvre, he knew, as far as the Staithe Festival was concerned, on which side his bread was buttered. He must appease Victoria's academic vanity by parroting what she had just said. He appeared to find no difficulty in slapping me down, undermining a fellow-actor who had made the mistake of trying to write a serious play.

'The Sonnets are a series of snapshots,' he said crossly. 'They are moods, many of them moods which we all recognize immediately because we've been there before. They don't really have a story.'

'In that case, you are missing the point of *Dear Time's Waste*,' I began.

Like children ganging up, they all chorused, '*Dark Lady*.' It had some of the playground rhythm and jauntiness of a skipping rhyme.

'OK,' I said. 'Literary historians of Jimbo Lampitt's era – I don't happen to think they are as ridiculous as you do; but let us grant, they had a tendency to think they could explain the Sonnets in terms of things external to the poems themselves – historical events, actual figures in history. That's not our way of reading a poem these days. We see works of literature – indeed, we see whole language systems – as being self-contained, and to a large degree self-referential, so we're not too worried about the possibility that these poems might refer to actual people, real experiences. Common sense, though, tells us that they do, that they must. Take Shakespeare and the Rival Poet.'

'Which has nothing to do with your kind remarks just now about your rival biographer Raphael Hunter.' Hubie's feeble pleasantry brought general applause.

'Now, whether he was Marlowe' – I was determined to ignore that last remark – 'you remember:

Was it the proud full sail of his great verse . . . ?

That sounds like Marlowe's "mighty line", doesn't it? On the other hand, it could be a pun. Sail/sale. A salesman might have been known as a chapman, someone who makes a cheap, chap, or sale. So we might be talking about Chapman here. The point is, whether it refers to Chapman or to Marlowe, the line perfectly obviously refers to someone, to a real person.

> No, neither he, nor his compeers by night
> Giving him aid . . .

that's the School of Night, you see. And, as we know, the Sonnets are absolutely crammed with contemporary references which we can identify to our satisfaction if that's the way we like to read them.'

'I sometimes prefer the footnotes to the poems themselves, I'm afraid,' said Gorley Swallow. 'You can imagine how Kit would have written it all up in the *Evening Standard*. "The Stratford scribbler, upon whose friendship with Mr William Herbert I commented last week, has always nursed a sense of grievance against his fellow-poets, I can reveal. Flamboyant bachelor scholar of King's School Canterbury, Christopher Marlowe, whose *Tamberlaine* has been going through such painful teething troubles in rehearsals has – "'

'We must get on.' Victoria spoke sharply. 'There's a festival in Staithe this summer. It is the tenth we have organized and Julian has asked me if I would consider putting on his Sonnets play in addition to the *Dream* which we already have scheduled. Perhaps for just one performance only. Now that involves an horrendous amount of organization. And work. And expense. If the play were perfect, of course, this would justify the expenditure. But as Julian would be the first to admit, the play is not perfect.'

'It seems an odd word to use of a play,' I blustered. Now, quite suddenly, I felt furious. 'Apart from *The Importance of Being Earnest*, can you name to me a perfect play?'

'Racine's *Phèdre*?' asked Gorley Swallow.

'Victoria's point, surely,' said Hubert Power, 'is that none of us wants yet another Shakespeare-in-Love piece. I mean, it really needs – isn't this what we are saying? – the play needs cutting down and making into a script which is much simpler. We are looking for a strong story-line of course . . . '

'*Macbeth* even. Perfect in its way,' mumbled the quiet voice of Gorley Swallow.

'A moment ago,' I replied to Power, 'everyone seemed to be agreed upon the opposite.'

'Would you say *Waiting for Godot*?'

'Shouldn't we be allowing Shakespeare to speak for himself?' was Hubie's *coup de théâtre*.

'Look,' I said, now conscious fully for the first time that their collective density was going to destroy the play by a sheer inability to see what I had been trying to do in *Dear Time's Waste*, 'let's take Gorley Swallow's point about gossip columns. There is that side of literary criticism. Modern biographies rest upon such an approach. People do actually want to know if Shakespeare knew a Dark Woman. It's a perfectly fair point of view – whether she's Emilia Lanier, which is her name in my play – she's got to be called something and Emilia Lanier seemed as good a candidate as any – or whether she's Mary Fitton, or whether she was someone else we have never even heard of. Fine. But my play starts from the opposite end of things. Fairly obviously, Shakespeare is obsessed by a Dark Lady – she's bossy, she's overbearing, she comes into *Love's Labour's Lost*, she comes into *Antony and Cleopatra*, and of course, she appears in the Sonnets:

The worser spirit, a woman coloured ill.'

As if I were not speaking, had not spoken, had never written a play on the subject, Victoria turned to Hubie and said, 'I think what we all have in mind is really something between a simple reading of the Sonnets by you, Hubie, and a few very brief enactments – little more than tableaux from the supporting cast. Dodie, you'll be here anyway, doing Titania, and as we said before, if you felt able . . . '

'That would be great! 'Course!'

'The young man – all he really needs is languid good looks, but there are things which Julian's – er – script brings out – even if we are only going to use the script as a basis for what we do, and play about with it a little.'

'Please,' I said, 'do not feel constrained by anything I have written.'

'I knew he would take that line. Didn't I say, Victoria, that if you handle him right, old Julian is never any fuss?' said Gorley Swallow.

'So,' Victoria gulped girlishly, 'all that is required is to go down on bended knee, Hubie, and wonder, ask, beg, whether you might consider coming over to Staithe this summer for one evening in order to play William Shakespeare for us?'

Ours is a very strange profession. If Sarah Bernhardt as an old woman with a wooden leg could play an (apparently not disastrous) Hamlet and Bella Marno aged fifty could have been one of the most successful Peter Pans ever known on the West End stage before settling down in her retirement as Lady Caroline Grainger on 'The Mulberrys', there was presumably no reason why Hubert Power, a good quarter-century older than Shakespeare was when he died, should not have played the thirty-something-year-old Shakespeare in – yes, damn it, in *Dark Lady*, which was – again, damn it – a much snappier title than *Dear Time's Waste*.

'Oh,' said Gorley Swallow, 'and what about the *Alkestis* of Euripides?'

Dodie sensed my humiliation that morning; surely one of her motives for offering consolation. Already, at that stage, there was something unsatisfactory to both of us about this resorting to sex. Undressing in my room at Staithe, while Victoria and Gorley Swallow had driven into Sherdingley to walk Hubie Power to the end of the pier, I felt I was betraying something or someone. It was a vision, and not Victoria, whom I was betraying. When yearning like a boy for Leman, I was pure. Whether it was early religious programming or an innate sense of alienation, who can say? There is nothing like sex to awaken my feeling that I am not at home in the body, but a tenant there. Dodie was different. She seemed happy enough, a greedy child with a lolly at a fairground.

Ah! but those tears are pearl which thy love sheds!

Not long afterwards, she repeated her desire to drive over to Walsingham.

I knew that she was Church of England, as I was, and that this was something which she took more seriously than one would ever have guessed. Since we had never got to know one another very well, however, we had fallen into the habit of stereotyping one another. Still too aware that she was someone famous on television, I envisaged an 'exotic' life for her when we were not together, imagining that she chose to spend her time with other famous people, or with the rich. Her protestations that this was not (wholly) the case and that for most of the time she led a very 'normal' life were written down in my mind as inverted modesty, an attempt to ensure that I felt no resentment at her commercial success. For her part, she retaliated by repeated assertions, despite all denials on my part, that, merely because I lodged at Staithe, I was 'posh', out of her class. Perhaps she half believed this, as I half believed in the jet-set life for her.

My own reminiscences to her of childhood – the modest house in Fulham, the rectory at Timplingham – had perhaps made as little impression on her as her much more diffident allusions to her own home life had made on me. She came from Birmingham, but her parents now lived in White City, not far from the BBC. (I immediately thought, when I heard this, that it was appropriate and imagined that her father, occasionally alluded to as a man of serious tastes – witness his fondness for Hunter's historical documentaries on television – had something to do with the 'media'. Her mother was a nurse.) She told me that her parents read the Bible together every morning, but I am afraid I merely guessed this was normal behaviour for Jamaicans.

61

Walsingham, though, was almost the last place on earth with which I should have associated her. It is a village some fifteen miles east of Staithe, tree-surrounded, brick- and flint-built, nestling in the vale of Stiffkey. It is dominated by the ruins of a medieval abbey, despoiled in the time of Henry VIII, who, until his quarrel with Rome, had been a keen devotee of the shrine.

Towards the close of the eleventh century, the Virgin Mary was said to have appeared here to Richeldis, the lady of the manor. A sacred well had sprung up on the site of the apparition, and Richeldis caused to be built a replica of the Holy House of Loretto (itself allegedly the home of the Holy Family of Nazareth, which had flown to Italy by miraculous means). From the time of the Reformation, when the monastery was sacked and the shrine despoiled, until the twentieth century, Walsingham had lain quiet, as had almost all the monastic ruins and holy wells and shrines of medieval England. Miracles and apparitions of Mary had gone the way of the fairies, as in the old poem:

Witness those rings and roundelays
Of theirs which yet remain,
Were footed in Queen Mary's days
On many a grassy plain;
But since of late Elizabeth
And later James came in,
They never danced on any heath,
As when the time had been.

By which we note the fairies
Were of the old profession,
Their songs were Ave Maries,
Their dances were procession.
But now, alas, they all are dead,
Or gone beyond the seas,
Or further from religion fled,
Or else they take their ease.

62

It was appropriate that Campbell Dilkes, the witness of fairy dances, should also have been a devotee of *Ave Maries* and 'the old profession'. A keen Anglo-Catholic, he had been delighted when the vicar of Walsingham during the 1930s had revived the old devotion of Our Lady of Walsingham and built a modern Holy House on the site of what he believed to be the very well where Richeldis saw her vision. Dilkes had composed settings of the *Salve Regina* which had been used at the Anglo-Catholic congresses of those days, and he was himself a lay Guardian of the Shrine, loving to process through the streets of Walsingham with his fellow Guardians, following the statue of the Madonna and wearing a blue velvet mantle, not unlike the robes of the Garter.

Even if it had not been for the other excesses which unhappily resulted in his being sent to prison, Campbell Dilkes could not have hoped, by those pious observances, to have endeared himself to his wife's family, the Lampitts, a resolutely secular tribe. My uncle Roy was chiefly tolerated by them because he was so affectionately and eagerly prepared to shoulder the problem of Jimbo's brother Sargie. Jimbo's dismissal of Uncle Roy as 'Sargie's tame parson' had caused offence when it was first repeated to my uncle and aunt, and if Aunt Deirdre wanted to restrain some particular outburst of Lampitt sycophancy in my uncle, she would never hesitate to repeat it.

'You must have been coming to Walsingham all the time when you were a kid,' said Dodie, as we bowled along in Leman's van – the only available lift. Though Leman was at the wheel, and Dodie in the front seat, she contrived to address all remarks over her shoulder to me alone, rather as if the van were being propelled automatically and the driving-seat were empty.

'Actually not. I don't remember ever coming here in those days.'

'I thought with your uncle being a priest . . . '

Uncle Roy certainly was aware of the attempts by the Walsingham brigade to introduce full-blown Latin Christianity to the Norfolk countryside. Coming from the Catholic wing of the Church himself, he might have been expected to sympathize, but he viewed the whole thing with absolute dismay. Father Delmar, a whimsical retired priest who had settled just outside Timplingham for his retirement, was always popping over to Walsingham. In my aunt's phrase, the man 'couldn't keep away from the place'. She always spoke shudderingly, as if the Baroque, not to say Firbankian, delights of the Marian shrine were an addiction on the same level of turpitude as alcohol or erotic deviation. Uncle Roy did not think this, but even before my antennae had learnt to pick up the signals he gave out, one sensed that the Walsingham shrine offended not so much the canons of doctrine as those of good taste – possibly, even, of class. Quite how deeply all these things were connected was something which dawns on me only in retrospect. I answered Dodie Rich's question carefully, lest my reply seemed too harshly to put her down.

'Uncle Roy was certainly high, but Walsingham was not his sort of thing.'

Having emerged from the lower end of the middle class himself, Uncle Roy was jealous of the smallest social and aesthetic distinctions and shibboleths. There was no logical reason why the Sarum Rite should be more gentlemanlike than the Baroque, but such, unquestionably, was the case. 'St Mary the Virgin' was all right as the dedication of a church, but too much interest in her was, well, *peasanty*. As for the habit of referring to her as 'Our Lady' – Uncle Roy always put the words in heavy inverted commas, finding Delmar's artless use of the term quietly amusing. I came to feel, by the time I'd grown up and lost all ability to believe in the orthodoxies, that no one who was quite 'the thing' would talk about Our Lady. She 'went' with lace curtains and plastic flowers. Such thoughts rose to the surface as Leman's van bowled along, but I was glad I had not voiced them.

Dodie said, 'We used to go on the pilgrimages as kids quite a lot. It's fantastic. My dad loves it.'

'You've mentioned your father several times this morning, Dodie, and I don't remember you saying more than ten words about him before today.'

She turned back and said with a smile so sexy that it felt embarrassing to see it, and to respond to it, in company, 'We don't know one another very well – yet – do we?'

Angelo started an independent conversation which rescued us from this line of talk, and Leman, concentrating hard on the road, turned to me and asked, 'Are you going to call on your aunt?'

Aunt Deirdre now lived about four miles outside Walsingham in an extraordinary bungalow somehow expressive of her character. It was hard, as you approached it, to imagine quite why anyone had chosen to build a house on that exact spot, since it stood in three-quarters of an acre of garden, almost every bit of which would have made a more suitable site for the house. It was the garden of course which had attracted her to this strange little dwelling, which consisted of one large room, with three small bedrooms leading off it, a tiny kitchen (Baby Belling, miniature fridge) and an even tinier bathroom. The house was the longest possible trek from the village of Binham, its nearest inhabited point. It had no views, but it was exposed on all sides to the wind. Built in about 1962 by a farmer who had almost immediately recognized his mistake, it had actually remained empty for several years before my aunt got it so cheap and moved in. Its complete absence of any aesthetic merit or social pretension was, perhaps, an eloquent comment on her childhood in a big Victorian parsonage near Lowestoft, her forty years or so of married life in the Georgian elegance of Timplingham; but if so, there was no verbal disloyalty to my uncle's memory.

Leman, unsurprisingly, since she shared many of my aunt's attitudes and tastes, had made friends with her, and often came with me when I drove over to see her. They swapped cuttings, tips; there was talk of mulching, pruning, raking and hoeing.

'Now I have this silly back,' my aunt would say, 'it's been a wonderful help to have you and Leman lifting those bags of compost.'

Astonishingly, as I write these words – so many years after the year which I describe – this bleak bungalow has become my home. I am perfectly happy here. How surprised almost everyone in my life would be – Aunt Deirdre and Uncle Roy especially – to know how often I find myself, now in my seventh decade, pausing in the shrine at Walsingham, and meditating on that day with Leman, Dodie and Angelo. *Incipit vita nuova.* That could be said of every day no doubt, but there was a change after that morning. I have certainly travelled lighter, and more cheerfully towards death, as a result of it. I wonder if it is possible to convey why, or how.

Walsingham is a place of obvious, outstanding beauty. Since that May day, it has become part of my life. Some of its fascination is that it is tree-surrounded. In all seasons, but particularly in the spring when the boughs are coming into leaf, you feel that peculiar protection which comes when brick meets green, when roofs are towered over by branches. Some of its charm is architectural, although, apart from the ruined arch of the old abbey and a handsome eighteenth-century manor-house in the abbey grounds (occupied by some relations of Pat Lampitt, incidentally), there is no serious architecture. The low-lying houses in the village streets, dating from the late Middle Ages and the sixteenth century, have an unquestionable charm.

The modern Anglican shrine, so much beloved of Campbell Dilkes in the last decade of his life, makes no attempt to blend in. Outside it resembles a suburban church of the period which would have been more at home in Woking or Carshalton. Inside, its peculiar doll's-house scale – dozens of chapels all too small to accommodate more than one and a half people – and its atrociously ugly statues would certainly not have been to Uncle Roy's taste. This building, though, has a certain 'power' which I should not choose to analyse or to explain.

*

As the van turned the corner into the village street, Leman let forth a high-pitched 'Oh, no!'

'Pull over,' said Dodie. 'Let's get out and watch.'

Familiar with the place since childhood, she would have been immediately aware of what was going on. Leman, as uninterested in religion as she was in books, would probably have been unable to distinguish – in terms of emotional pull – between this and any other traffic obstruction. She would have been as unexcited by it as by a large truck blocking the street – perhaps rather less excited, for the truck would have provided her mind with something on which to feed.

We had scrunched to a halt in the main village square, and could see the procession coming towards us. A band of Sea Scouts was playing a hymn, which, for all my early familiarity with Anglicanism (perhaps because of it, for this was surely pretty *recherché* stuff?), was unknown to me. Four other boys, also in Sea Scouts' uniform, carried aloft a statue of a black Madonna, dressed in a stiff little golden cope and draped from the head with a spray of white Brussels lace. Some dozen men in blue velvet cloaks followed them, singing lustily. Behind them was a crowd. From where we stood it was impossible to number. I thought it was a few dozen at first, since the street turned a sharp corner, and I could not guess how many more would emerge. In fact, there were hundreds of people. Some of them carried banners suspended from poles which swayed like the sails of old galleons against the pale blue sky, proclaiming the parishes from which they came. I saw the names of Newcastle, Manchester, Birmingham, London and Plymouth. Involuntarily, I was taken back to an earlier scene of life when I had witnessed just such a procession in France, when staying with Madame de Normandin at Les Mouettes.

Ahead, the swaying, doll-like statue, and the Guardians; behind, a great concourse, which snaked its way down the entire length of the street and beyond it to that fringe of the village

67

where fields began.

In Brittany, during my teens, shortly after discovering sex, I had been taken to a *pardon* in which a statue of the Virgin was similarly paraded. Barbara, the girl in question, and her mother, Thérèse, had accompanied Madame de Normandin and myself. Then, as now, the hymn was unknown to me. I found myself, in Walsingham, revisited by some of the emotions which had welled up in me forty years earlier in Brittany. Was it simply memory which moved me? I felt tears pricking my eyes as the procession went past. I was transported, so that it would not have been possible to distinguish, during that quarter of an hour, between the earlier experience and the later. They had become one. An earlier self came back to join the desiccated, confused man in the mid-fifties. I am one of Nature's Nazis, too easily moved by processions, music, crowds. It was certainly nothing to do with belief, this strange experience, but it felt deep and elemental. For a while, at least, I forgot my company, and the edginess, bordering on open hostility, which the two women were displaying towards one another.

Leman had been adopting that determinedly larky approach to the whole thing which characterizes those who are embarrassed by displays of religious emotion.

'Isn't it great? Look, Angelo! Look at the men in funny little hats.'

'They're birettas,' said Dodie sharply.

It was surprising that she wanted to get this straight; her knowledge of the correct terms for ecclesiastical millinery was suddenly reminiscent of those peculiar people, occasionally encountered during any rectory childhood, who take an obsessive interest in liturgy and its outward trappings. Strange enough in the clergy, this taste usually suggests, when manifested in the laity, imbalance if not derangement of mind.

('Ayve ironed and pressed all Mr Ramsay's albs and amices, though Ay quate understand if he wishes to wash his corporals himself.' A line spoken by one of my uncle's few parishioners, a music teacher called Miss Dare. It was often repeated in the rectory. Even Aunt Deirdre found it funny.)

The reason for Dodie's unusual possession of such knowledge, and for her wanting to come to Walsingham that morning, was about to be made clear.

As we watched the clergy go past in their bewildering array of continental clobber, Leman gigglingly remarked, 'Kit calls them Walsingham Matildas. Did you have to dress up like that when you were a little boy, Julian? So!' She turned to Dodie and explained, 'Julian grew up in a vicarage.'

'Really?' said Dodie with heavy irony. It was difficult, certainly, to believe that Leman had taken no notice of any of our conversation in the van, which had made it clear that Dodie had heard about my childhood.

'What do you think, then, so?'

'Of *what?*' There was something really quite snappy about Dodie's question.

'Of the Walsingham Matildas?'

Certainly, they were a distinctive sight. Chiefly, perhaps, through the power of a sobriquet to impose or strengthen a preconceived notion, they appeared in my eyes more Firbankian than they probably were.

'I think one of them's my dad,' said Dodie proudly, and she waved at one of the priests, no less fantastically arrayed than any one of the others, who waved back cheerfully from the throng.

Shockingly, he seemed rather younger than myself, and certainly better preserved. I do not know why I should have been surprised by the fact that Dodie's dad was a white man, or rather a reddish man, with plump, well-shaven cheeks and, as was revealed when the biretta was raised and waved, a bald pate, and well-trimmed hair at neck and temples.

'Well, well, you are full of surprises,' I said.

'I said I'd meet him afterwards – when the Mass in the Abbey grounds is over.'

And we watched the procession file past, more and more –

there must have been hundreds, perhaps thousands, of people –
and troop through the gates into the grounds of the medieval
ruins for Mass.

So, this was our shared thing, Dodie's and mine – High Church.
We had known about it before the day in Walsingham, but that
was the day which – without our having to talk about it – put the
kybosh on any idea of our seriously continuing to be lovers on any
long-term basis. It made us realize (though we knew it already)
that neither of us wanted to marry the other; and it reminded us
of our shared knowledge that, at the back of our minds, culled
from childhood churchgoing, was the idea that marriage was the
only legitimate way for two human beings to live together as
lovers. Dodie, unlike me, never had guilty thoughts about sex
itself, as far as I could see. But we were to find, over the following
months, that though we were both visited by sexual impulses from
time to time, and were to gratify them, there could be no future.

So (as Leman would say), that was one of the consequences of
our day in Walsingham. If, however, I had thought that it was a
day which would merely reveal something new or strange about
Dodie, I was mistaken. It was the day when another set of
mysteries, nothing to do with myself, began to be unfolded. It was,
no doubt, one of those strange days when things began to
coalesce. My own past and future became clearer to me. But so did
the past of others. Staithe and its mysteries, past and present,
Staithe and its inhabitants – Kit, Victoria, her mother, her
grandfather – were to be brought into focus and, if not explained,
then unveiled. Things which had never been quite spoken about,
matters which had not been discussed openly for fifty years, were
about to have an airing.

'Good Heavens,' said Leman, as we sat outside the Bull, 'so Kit
did not go cottaging in London after all.'

'Richer pickings here?' I volunteered, unable to get out of this
slightly tiresome joke.

We sat with pints of cider in plastic tumblers. Angelo was
eating nuts out of a bag and drinking Coke. The Mass had been

70

continuing in the Abbey grounds for nearly an hour, but some of the pilgrims, clerical as well as lay, appeared to have absented themselves for at least a part of the ceremonies, and to have filled up the patch of ground beneath the old inn sign.

And there was Kit, standing in characteristic pose, tall, horse-faced, laughing, a cigarette alight, his ear cocked towards his interlocutor who, much shorter than himself, seemed, to outward view, to be a Walsingham Matilda.

A surprising development, this, in a young man who, to the best of my knowledge, had no more interest in religion than did Leman. As far as I could tell, hardly any people of their generation *did*. My parents' generation, for the most part, lost belief. I am the in-between generation, certainly not able to believe in the way that our ancestors believed, but unable, quite, to forget what it was like when belief was taken for granted. I and my generation will be like fairies since the reign of Queen Elizabeth: we will be obsolete, soon to be lost from sight, glimpsed only in unlikely moonlit spots. For Kit and Leman and their friends, who have only the haziest grasp of simple Bible stories (Leman the other day made it clear in conversation that she did not know the story of David and Goliath), the thing has gone. They lack the edgy hostility to church which I had when young; but the baton has been dropped in the relay race, and they simply don't know what the Judaeo-Christian tradition is, or was.

'Hi,' said Kit. 'This is Trevor.'

The porky young man – specs, a linen jacket bought at Oxfam, an embarrassing bow-tie, and an even more embarrassing Panama hat – came up to Kit's shoulder. His pink face sweated on the upper lip and if, as I wildly, but only momentarily, assumed, he was Kit's secret, he was certainly a surprising one.

'Kit didn't feel quite up to another Mass,' said Trevor whose plummy voice seemed no more convincing than the hat. 'We went in the shrine, didn't we?'

'Trevor's been showing me the ropes,' said Kit.

'We got him sprinkled, didn't we?' said Trevor, casting an

admiring glance up at Kit. He spoke as if he had just had a cherished *objet d'art* cleaned by experts. 'And we heard Father Aubrey's Mass – slightly better than what they'll be getting in there, I can tell you.'

He shot scornful glances in the direction of the old Abbey and let out a shockingly deep bark of laughter.

Noticing that this was all slightly above our heads, Kit introduced Trevor to Leman, Dodie and myself. Clearly no fan of *Planet Venus*, the young man showed no recognition of Dodie. It seemed vain to ask who Father Aubrey was.

'Trevor and I were at Cambridge together,' said Kit.

Since this must have been true of about two thousand young people, it was not much of an explanation.

'When I heard he was doing this book, I said to him, "You've got to get the details right",' Trevor added.

'Oops,' said Kit. 'It's still a secret, you know. Or meant to be.'

'Me and my big mouth,' said Trevor inaccurately, before pursing his sweaty little lips.

'We thought you were in London,' said Leman.

'We missed you at the meeting,' said Dodie. 'You're meant to be the young man that Shakespeare was in love with.'

Staithe and Walsingham seemed, at that moment, spiritually miles apart. But I could not stop myself talking about the meeting which Kit had missed, the extraordinary cheek, as it seemed at that moment, of Victoria hijacking my play, and giving the most important role in it to Hubert Power, the probability that the old ham would spoil the part. Embarrassed by my bitterness, Dodie and Leman tried to soothe me. In my egotism, I forgot the question, with which the day had begun, of Kit's secret.

Was he having an affair, and breaking Leman's heart? It did not look as if this were the case. She stood there in the sunshine, with a glass of cider in her hand, looking entirely confident in his company. She knew, of course, what the secret was, which was why she was able to make the mildly tired jokes about Kit's other life. She knew what I was only about to discover, that Kit's secret was an innocent one, though one which he had the most understandable of reasons for concealing from Victoria.

It was, quite simply, that he had undertaken to find out for himself the secrets of Staithe, to tell the story of Campbell Dilkes.

I had known Kit Mayfield since he was a teenager, but I had never really known him.

His aunt Victoria's way of caring for him was to express constant anxiety about him. From the first, she had regarded her sister as a 'problem', and her sister's children as an extension of that problem. Kit and his sister were being brought up all wrong, as Victoria, with the certainty of the childless, could see. Kit was spoilt. Kit was at the wrong school (Westminster). Then he was reading the wrong subject (History) at the wrong college (St John's). Now he was doing the wrong line of work, spending half the week on the gossip column of an evening newspaper in London, and for the rest mysteriously lolling about, doing Victoria knew not what, and – as she supposed – creating emotional havoc in the heart of her reliable factotum, gardener and odd-job person, Leman. At the time of his parents' divorce, before I came on the scene, Kit had been a source of anxiety because he was, at different stages, being openly upset by the separation, and then, by contrast, putting too brave a face on things. Then had come the appalling year of his mother's cancer, and Victoria's sense that she was now responsible for the boy.

Throughout all this period, Kit had struck me as a polite, good-humoured, clever human being, who was emerging from adolescence with remarkable aplomb. Certainly, he had much more charm, self-confidence and social grace than I had at comparable ages. True, he was the sort of person with whom others fell in love, and this was not always something he dealt with intelligently or kindly. But, as I often tried to tell Victoria, there were human beings on this planet with worse problems than being extremely good-looking and slightly 'cold fish'.

What I had failed to grasp about Kit was where, if anywhere, the hidden depths and sorrows might be. That he was saddened by his mother's death was obvious. I'd underestimated, though, the extent to which he was worried by the inheritance of Staithe – not so much by the place, the farm, the theatre, the money (should there turn out to be any of that left when Victoria handed the place over to him) as by its unmentionable past.

I have written in the previous pages of Campbell Dilkes, who built, or rebuilt, Staithe in Edwardian days, and whose portrait by Munnings was so familiar to me when I lived in the house. I've alluded to the apparitions of 1908. But I am writing nearly twenty years later, and at the time I am not sure that we even spoke about the fairies until Kit wrote his book. Although I have already told the reader that Campbell Dilkes was an enthusiast for the shrine at Walsingham, I don't remember being told this fact myself until Kit began to tell us that day outside the pub. The whole story had been suppressed. The Lampitts alluded to it, of course; therefore, Uncle Roy included sad references to 'poor dear Lavinia' in his repertoire. True, Uncle Roy commended Campbell Dilkes's musical skills; spoke of the symphonic poems as if they were rather better than the symphonies of Mozart. But this was because Dilkes had married a Lampitt. Uncle Roy's Christianity taught him that the good things of this world have been dispensed through the channels of grace. Similarly, the country in which we happened to live, though seemingly organized, enriched and delighted by many different families, was really only of interest in so far as it benefited from contact with what he called the Blood Royal. The Lampitts were a conduit through which good things came to England. The Attlee Government was to be praised because the Prime Minister had been sensible enough to appoint the Honourable Vernon Lampitt to the Cabinet. The Suez Canal brought benefits to the race because one of the engineers responsible for its construction had some small Lampitt connection. By a comparable token, Dilkes's music was to be claimed for the Blood Royal by virtue of his marriage. How furious

74

Aunt Deirdre would become when the 'theme tune' for 'The Mulberrys' started up on the radio, if my uncle – no fan of the drama – would put his head round the kitchen door and ask, 'Did I hear *The Surrey Rhapsody?*' (The Mulberry 'theme' is indeed drawn from a passage in this rather jolly piece by Dilkes.)

But, for the other matters – including the prison sentence – silence. Better not spoken of. Uncle Roy and Aunt Deirdre had the habit of treating almost every subject as classified information which it would be 'better' not to air with the village.

'We won't talk about the election in the village,' my aunt announced in 1945. 'Just in case people get funny ideas.'

It had been a tense week in the rectory, my uncle ecstatic at the Honourable Vernon's triumph, my aunt furiously shocked by the country's disloyalty – as she saw it – to Churchill. She spoke of Attlee's victory, however, almost as though it were something which could be 'kept' from Jill in the Post Office if not spoken about.

Obviously, from the Lampitt point of view, Dilkes's débâcle was a blot on the scutcheon. It was a shock, when I came to live at Staithe, to discover that the same rules applied. I knew that Campbell Dilkes was a composer. I knew that he had built the theatre, and that there was some occasion when he believed himself to have seen the fairies. I knew that he had died in prison some thirty years after the apparition. Beyond that, he was a mystery; and we did not discuss him.

'You won't tell Victoria, will you?' asked Kit.

'Course not – though she will presumably notice should you ever finish your book, and should it be published.'

'I want to get it all done. You see, I'm very anxious to set the record straight about the old boy. I'm not trying to let him off the hook. I just want to fill in the picture. It is so creepy having in the family cupboard a skeleton which we aren't even allowed to discuss. So I'm gradually going round, meeting people who knew him, picking up information. Trevor has been very helpful with the religious side of things. My great-grandfather even had a special stall in the Shrine church. They've painted his name over it, together with the other occupants'. John Selwyn Gummer is the present holder of the office.'

We all laughed.

'It's a gorgeous title,' said Trevor.

'What is the book to be called?' I asked.

'Need you ask?' said Leman, who was obviously already in on the secret. '*The Fairies of Staithe.*'

'What's the old man supposed to have done which was so wicked?' asked Dodie.

Before Kit needed to think of an evasive answer, she waved, and her father came across the square.

A convivial hour or so was passed before Dodie and Father Rich went back to London together on a charabanc with his parishioners; Leman, Kit and I – in the van – returning to Staithe when we had dropped Trevor at Sheringham where he caught a train. I wished I had spoken more to Dodie's father, but I felt shy with him. His pleasure in the pilgrimage, his dullness, his amiability, all contributed, irrationally but certainly, to our shared knowledge, Dodie's and mine, that we were not going to be life-partners.

Trevor, who had become something in advertising since coming down from St John's, appeared to spend every available moment in one Anglo-Catholic shrine or another. Father Rich seemed quietly impressed that he had served Father Aubrey's Mass, and joined in Trevor's laughter at Leman's friendly suggestion that Father Aubrey might be lonely without us, and that we should ask him to join us for cider and potato crisps.

'I don't think that would be quite Father Aubrey's idea of pleasure,' he said quietly. Though he was in fact quite conversational, this was the only sentence that, at this distance, I can remember him uttering. It was one with which Trevor, amused at the very idea, wholeheartedly agreed.

*

Walsingham was not the end for Dodie and me. We had our year. And the most exciting part of it, from the sexual point of view, was when we played opposite one another in Victoria's production of the *Dream*. I had never had such a success on the stage. I don't mean, by 'success', critical praise, still less money – neither came our way as a result of one week's performance in a tiny Edwardian amphitheatre in North Norfolk. But we both enjoyed that confident, intoxicating feeling that the audience was in our control, enthralled, even on the night when it drizzled and was rather chilly. The intensity of our quarrel as Oberon and Titania, the fury of it – owed vastly, no doubt, to the chemistry between us as human beings offstage. However tired we were during that phase of rehearsals and actual performances, we always had sexual energy. There was an interval of twenty minutes at Staithe when we felt such an overpowering need for it that we disregarded the risks of discovery and simply went in the shrubbery.

Since Shakespeare and the Walsingham Madonna were now our patrons, we had a shared sense that we had become bewitched during the summer. While our congress enlivened our performance as Fairies, the hatred between Oberon and Titania was a ritualized enactment of our inevitable eventual separation.

When the procession had rounded the corner of the street at Walsingham that first day of May, Dodie had exclaimed:

Shall we their fond pageant see?

And she wished, she told me afterwards, that she had not said it, because it allowed me to return with:

Lord, what fools these mortals be!

Actually I did not think that the Walsingham Matildas were

fools, and I certainly did not intend the insult which she nosed out, the insult to Father Rich himself. I said the words automatically, without thinking, and if they had had any application, then this would have been to the parade of my own past, which moved in unceasing line before my ineffectual gaze, reminding me that while others, such as Father Rich, became useful parish priests, and others, like Trevor, went into advertising, and others, like Hubie Power and Dodie herself, became famous, I had achieved absolutely nothing with my life. Nothing.

'We are borrn into this worrld for a purpose', said the Binker in one of his sermons at Seaforth Grange. 'For a purpose.'

Darnley, my dearest friend at that date, and for many years afterwards, was always able to reduce me to hysterics by repeating this highly questionable observation from the lips of our paederastic headmaster. Sometimes, it was enough for Darnley to say, at some supposedly grown-up gathering, years after we had left school, 'A purpose, a purpose!' and I should start to laugh. If I had been taken in, even a little, by the Binker's words, I should surely have wanted to be something useful, as Timpson, say, Head Boy in our day, had become – he was now a bishop – or Garforth Thoms, who went into politics. Or at least I could have done what Daddy did, hold down an ordinary, sensible job, and have a child, fight for his country.

Aunt Deirdre once, during one of my school holidays, asked me to help sort jumble, preparatory to a parish sale. These jumble sales were never particularly well-organized affairs. A few heaps of old clothes, a few books in old orange-cartons, joined the home-made jams and chutneys on the trestle tables. Any remotely usable or saleable item would have been snaffled in the first quarter of an hour of the sale. The 'sorting' beforehand was therefore undertaken with the specific purpose of weeding out any desirable items and holding them back for ourselves. Many of Aunt Deirdre's clothes and most of mine during the austerity years were acquired in this way. The Edgar Wallaces, the Agatha

Christies and Ngaio Marshes which comprised my aunt's sole reading matter were also salvaged from the jumble piles.

'Here's one for you, old thing,' she remarked one day in the hall; and she jauntily threw across the dog-eared book. I looked at its title as it landed on the Victorian encaustic tiles beneath my twelve-year-old knees. *Something to Do.*

Finding ways to occupy a truculent and unhappy nephew must have taken up much of my aunt's attention during the school holidays, though it never occurred to me to consider myself, or my presence in the rectory, as an inconvenience. *Something to Do* had a chapter devoted to the manufacture of field telephones ('Simply pierce two old cocoa tins and attach them with pieces of knotted string: see Fig. A'). This was a difficult one; my aunt was not willing to be parted from old cocoa tins; nor with string sufficiently long to make a decent field telephone. Even if such a device had been within my powers, though, there would always have been the difficulty of finding someone else to hold on to the other end of the telephone and say, 'Roger and Out.' I fell back on the less ambitious sections of *Something to Do*: identifying birds and trees; keeping a Nature Diary; making a pressed flower collection; various exploits with *papier mâché*; and – here at least Aunt Deirdre was quite indulgent – 'Make your own garden'.

I had not realized when I was twelve that what she had thrown across the encaustic tiles in the rectory hall was not so much a children's book as a profound Chekhovian problem which has afflicted all human beings lucky enough to have been born into a culture where they were not obliged to sweat and toil in order to eat. Take away the obligatory ox-ploughing, the labour-intensive threshing, the primitive grinding of meal; take away the turning of clods, the drawing of spuds, the breaking of stones – and you are confronted with this yawning gulf of emptiness which cannot be filled for ever by *papier mâché*, nor by Start Your Own Museum. *Something to Do*, ah, something to do!

'I think this whole year' – says naked Dodie, in Fulham, in December – for this is where we began, and this is where we continue, and the reader must forgive me for interrupting myself – 'you wanted me to be your Dark Lady. You wanted Kit to be the Earl of Southampton. You wanted What's-his-face to be the Rival Poet.'

'What's-his-face can always be trusted to crop up – if you mean Raphael Hunter. Scarcely a poet though. And a Rival? He is just one of those people who have punctuated life . . . '

'But admit. You have been playing games, weaving shapes.'

'Sometimes I have felt him hovering in the wings.'

'Raphael Hunter?'

'*Him*. Himself.'

You, my Patron!

'You're nuts. Deranged.'

'I don't think it's true that he's really there. Or on one level I don't think it's true. But the imagination needs stories which are not completely true in order to learn some of the serious lessons. Perhaps the whole reason I felt drawn to make a dramatic shape out of the Sonnets was that I wanted to write about the situation at Staithe. One could not become as obsessed as I was by the Sonnets and not recognize that they are concerned with universal themes, and because they are universal, they apply to us. Was Kit my Southampton, my young man?'

'You're in love with Kit, Julian. Admit it.'

I am silent. There is a limit to the amount I can plausibly tell Dodie about the revolution which has taken place in the course of the summer, about the changes which have occurred to me. She has been so consoling and she has been so generous. Yet, one could not go on and on and on needing to explain. About Staithe, about Victoria, about Leman and Kit. About Campbell Dilkes. About me, come to that, and about my past. The trouble with attempted explanations is that they foster the illusion that there might *be* explanations.

With what speed and directness, you always place us there – Wham! – in the middle of a story. 'I thought the King had more affected the Duke of Albany than Cornwall.' 'Nay, but this dotage of our general's o'erflows the measure.' How vividly we feel ourselves in the middle of the story. We run after the characters to overhear them. 'Now, fair Hippolyta, our nuptial hour draws on apace . . .'

More swiftly than any novelist, you distil the whole essence of your characters, throw us into their midst. If you had been telling the story at Staithe, you might have had two attendant lords, walk-on roles, to plunge us in.

First Lord: They do say that Miss Amt being blind . . .
Second Lord: And desirous to hand over the good husbandry of Staithe to her nephew Kit . . .
First Lord: Ay marry and there's the mark, in that word husbandry. For while the fair young Leman doth love him, this merry wag doth affect to London to mingle with all manner of folks, which doth in equal measure grieve Miss Amt and Leman, who would have him husband in name and deed.
Second Lord: It were a merry tale to be told did not more inkhorns swarm round Mistress Amt than flies round stale lark pie at Michaelmas. For one old player, one Julian ~~Ramsay~~, who half dies of love for the Lady Leman, hath written a play . . .

name.

First Lord: At which the wits make many a tilt . . .

Dodie puffs on a cigarette. She says, 'When lovers part and say

81

they want to be friends, one of them really means it, and the other, just as often, can't wait to get the hell out. But I really want us to go on being friends.'

'Thank you. So do I.'

'It just doesn't make any sense – this – our being like this.'

With the wave of an arm, she indicates our nakedness.

'I agree.'

'I'm not sure I can quite face coming to a party with you and Kit, though.'

'Oh, do come. It was such a good idea of ours, that we should go immediately into a social world, and say goodbye without emotion, in a crowd.'

'It sounded like a good idea when we discussed it on the telephone. Now, I'm not so sure. You still haven't said where the party is.'

'At Dylans.'

'All parties are at Dylans.'

'Someone's written a biography of Day Muckley, some young American. I knew Muckley a bit. I thought . . . '

'You knew everyone, my dear.'

'No I didn't. Gorley Swallow knows everyone. I've known a handful. When I knew Day Muckley he was very much down on his luck. He was a regular at the Black Bottle, when I worked there as a barman.'

'That was before the movie, before *The Calderdale Saga* on TV?'

'Precisely. Funnily enough, it was Hunter who was responsible for reviving the poor old Best-Seller's reputation. There was this extraordinary episode . . . '

I have started to laugh.

Dodie interrupts. She has several times warned me of my tendency to tell anecdotes.

'I know. He was sick on live TV.'

'Have I told you all my stories?'

'You should write them down, my dear.'

Perhaps to shut me up, perhaps as a final gesture of kindness, she lifts a knee and mounts me. We come to a climax just as Campbell Dilkes's *Surrey Rhapsody* is coming through the speaker of the bathroom tranny. The music is instantly recognizable to anyone in England. Dodie is a listener more than a fan. The sound is only just in earshot.

'Oh, oh, OH!' says Dodie, whose perfect manners over seven or eight months have never allowed me to guess whether these exclamations reflected genuine enjoyment. They certainly had brought life to me at a stage when it wouldn't have seemed unreasonable to have given up on that side of things.

'You old darling,' she says, as we lie there, hugging.

And if this were not enough to remind me of the emotional mess in which I have lived my entire life, the murmur of 'The Mulberrys' brings the familiar feelings of remorse and self-reproach that I have not made a more valuable or exciting selection from *Something to Do*.

Like myself in his mid-fifties, Jason Grainger has settled down. In fact, parallels, sometimes grotesque, between his situation and my own, had been disconcertingly close. Jason had been my bread and butter, my ball and chain; for an artist who means business, these things are the same. For more than thirty years, I have been assuring myself that I am on the point of leaving 'The Mulberrys'.

When tempted to take myself seriously, I have seen Jason Grainger as the murderer of my talent. Without him, I might have shown a spark of something greater; I might have achieved more. No doubt this is a romantic idea of artistic possibility. The important element is not poverty, but risk. 'The Mulberrys' never made me rich, but they made me secure, they made me feel I never had to try. It is probably pure conceit and vanity, but there was something extraordinary about some of my schoolboy performances in productions by Treadmill. Very little I ever did as a grown-up could match them; very little I ever did since leaving school was done or achieved with pure motivation. I don't know if it is me, or England, or a deadly combination of the two, but it seems that everything one does after the age of twenty in England

83

is tainted in some way, by social rancour or its companion vice, snobbery; by money-greed or money-envy; by the necessity of getting on; by the desire to shock or the desire to be respectable. What happened to the innocent vanity of the schoolboy who simply wanted to show off and who must have been one of the best schoolboy Richard IIs since Shakespeare wrote the play?

Some of this innocence has been retained by Hubie Power, which is what enabled him to be so memorable a Vanya when I first saw him on the London stage, and which made him, even at this most incorrigibly vulgar, mannered and camp, an actor in an altogether different league from myself. When I recall that one night at Staithe – Hubie as Shakespeare in *Dark Lady* – I shudder. But the audience loved it. He had something that I lacked, and which in grown-up life I have always lacked. I don't know how you would define this 'something', but I believe I killed it dead in myself years ago.

There's an old gramophone record of some nondescript fiddler playing Campbell Dilkes's symphonic poems, with the London Philharmonic, conducted by Sir Adrian Boult. It is the flattest, dullest noise you ever heard. One year at Staithe – this is the sort of organizing power of which Victoria is capable – Yehudi Menuhin came and stood at the edge of the stage in the amphitheatre. He played for only five or ten minutes, the solo parts from Dilkes's symphonic poems. Very average music, but on that violin, beneath that bow, angels would have wept to hear it.

Shakespeare was not the only artist of whom it could be said that he 'led a life of allegory: his works are the comments on it'. All artists could be so described, the Salieris as well as the Mozarts. Campbell Dilkes was in this sense the archetypal second-rater, the Salieri of Edwardian England, quite popular in his brief day but wholly the prisoner of his own time, class, place and era. Most of the dramatists of the Elizabethan and Jacobean period have 'dated' in a way that Shakespeare so mysteriously has not.

Kit, who only lately took his degree, says that most 'cultural historians' these days regard the very concept of 'genius' as spurious. The works of Shakespeare, seen from this perspective, are simply what would result from the needs (political and economic) of Elizabethan theatre audiences, the comparable requirements of his aristocratic patrons, and his own origins in the petty-bourgeoisie, which rose to greater prominence as a result of the Reformation. There would be some interest in this theory if it seemed even faintly plausible. It does not account for the fact that Menuhin can make the flesh tingle with a piece of music which, played by anyone else, sounds completely dull. As for you, my patron: you could take such forms as the history play and the revenge tragedy – truly absurd when worked up by Kyd or Beaumont and Fletcher – and make of them *Hamlet* and *Henry IV*. The cultural historian who fails to identify an 'it', a mysterious 'factor X', is simply disregarding an observable phenomenon.

When young, we all hope that some such 'genius' will be ours. And here another voice comes soothingly to my aid when the Mulberry debate conducts itself inside my head. Is it the voice of Satan? It says that there is nothing disgraceful about being Salieri, or Campbell Dilkes, or Day Muckley, or Alfred Noyes. An artist who has done a job as well as it could be done, unpretentiously and cheerfully, has no reason to look back on life as a waste. Surely it is mere vanity which makes me hate Jason Grainger? To some it was given to be Hamlet; to others to be a much-loved radio 'institution'.

Anything wrong with that?

Satan asks this question inside my head in the smooth, insinuating tones of Jason Grainger himself. Jason, who was such a shady customer when he first drove his sports car into Barleybrook thirty years ago, is, of course, now positively genial and respectable. His marriage to the Lady of the Manor and their decision to convert Barleybrook Grange into a 'country-house style' hotel has proved a notable commercial success.

And how did the word 'style' creep into that sentence?

Lying beside Dodie, naked, I can hear Jason and Lady Caroline talking to one another in the bathroom.

'Thank you darling. Mm! Really dry; that's how I like it.'

This is Lady Caroline – Isabella Marno, very much come down in the world. The younger members of the cast call her the Dry Run; I have no idea how they hit on this cruel idea and I'm not sure they are right, but the script-writer, to satisfy the schoolboys of both sexes in the cast, invents lines for poor Bella in which dryness is a constant theme. This camaraderie among the cast of 'The Mulberrys', incidentally, and the fact that we all get on reasonably well with our producer, is a great change from my early days in the show with Rodney Jones as producer (poor Rodney). It is something about which I have mixed views.

Jason, in my voice, or I in his, replies: 'My dear! Mm! So agree! It really does pay to select a decent sherry.'

Jason's voice is as antiquated as his drinking habits. Most other voices on the BBC have become more demotic. Even the Queen has stopped saying Crawss and Lawss. Jason's pseudo-posh, as poor Rodney once called it, sounds more pronounced with the years. Sometimes when I hear it on the radio I think it is Uncle Roy speaking to me. This has its own cruel appropriateness. Jason was the son of the village blacksmith and ended up speaking – well, like me. My granny did not speak 'cockney', nor did her friend Mrs Webb. But there was a distinct twang in some of his mother's vowels which made Uncle Roy wince when he heard her, particularly if she were speaking in front of Sargie.

Do other countries in the world contain thousands of individuals who mind about this sort of thing?

'My God,' says Dodie, 'it's you. One minute I hear you talking in my ear and the next you are talking from the bathroom. It's surreal.'

She jumps from the bed and, having turned up the volume, she returns.

As half England knows, Les Mulberry's wedding is (in Jason's words) 'coming up in two weeks' time'. (I mock this phrase but can I be sure that I have never used it myself? Ever?)

'And everything's catered for,' says Lady Caroline Grainger.

'We have the food ordered, the menus fixed, the rooms booked. The musicians have all that they require in the ballroom. Oh, Jason, you're not going to tell me that the musicians have cried off?'

'Worse news than that, I fear, Caroline,' say Jason's orotund tones. 'Pierre has chosen this particularly delicate moment in the fortunes of Barleybrook Grange Hotel to hand in his notice. He has been offered the post of *chef de cuisine* at a prestigious London hotel and he is leaving us in a week. I'm afraid that unless we come up with something, there will be no one to cook the food for Lyn and Les's wedding.'

And a blast of Dilkes's *Surrey Rhapsody* leaves us all on tenterhooks for another day.

'I'm not sure it's a good idea my coming to this party.' Dodie says this so convincingly that I momentarily wonder whether she means it.

'No, no, you must keep to your bargain.'

'But truly, I shan't know anyone.'

'You'll know Kit. He and I are having dinner afterwards. You could join us.'

'I'll come to the party, but then I'll slip away. I won't eat with you.'

Dressing, she says lightheartedly over her shoulder, 'Who knows? If I come to this party with you, I might meet the man I'm going to marry?'

That is the sort of strange magic you bring to pass in your comedies, isn't it? The men and women take their partners for the dance. Though you are there, keeping your playful watch, I do not know that what Dodie says is true and that two years after this evening, she will give birth to my godson Julian.

Party-clothed, Dodie, in a cloth-of-gold coat which would have been the envy of the Walsingham Matildas, and black trousers and large gold pendant ear-rings, looks so beautiful that our cold decision to end our love affair seems totally crazy. Yet, pushing through the circular doors of the club and handing in our outer garments at the desk – her black cloak, my black tweed coat inherited from Uncle Roy – I feel a complete certainty that a new phase has been entered, and that there is no turning back. You are there with us, and I think, I'm older now than you were when you died, when all the great plays had been written, and when you had retired to New Place, and at length had been buried beneath that mysterious epitaph in Stratford Church. Your life gave more than any writer has ever given to the world, and mine has given nothing. The pattern of that life can still be one to follow. After the follies and tempests of middle age, a calm, a decision to put the frenzies of ambition and love behind one.

> *But this rough magic*
> *I here abjure . . .*

And I feel sad and calm, knowing that there stretches ahead the quiet self-contained life, punctuated by reading and reflection, in which I no longer need to strive for possession of another human being.

'Dylans,' I say with contempt. 'What a mess they have made of this place. And to think of it when I first knew it – so empty most of the time, so charmingly down-at-heel.'

'When?'

'When it was a pub called the Black Bottle.'

Wide-eyed, she says, 'Wasn't it always a club?'

For Londoners of Dodie's age, Dylans – slightly old hat and already surpassed in reputation and chic by newer, smaller clubs – is as much a part of the landscape as Nelson's Column. Archaeologists, trained to sift through dust and shards, can make out from the rubble of a field, the remains of a former habitation – where the garde-robe once stood, and where the Great Hall, destroyed by fire in 1393. To the untutored eye, the mounds of springy turf look as if they have been there for ever. For the last fifteen years, Dylans has been regarded by those who do not go there as a haunt of writers and actors. On the rare occasions I have been taken there, it has been stuffed with advertising executives and spivvy literary agents. Its chromium-plated bar is a straight parody of a comparable snazzy dive in Manhattan. Even the food on offer in the over-priced restaurant – clam chowder, hamburgers with chilli sauce, swordfish, caesar salads – seems designed less to nourish the palate than to make American visitors feel at home and Londoners feel in the swim. Such wholesale reordering of the interior has taken place since it was the Saloon Bar of the Black Bottle that I find it difficult to guess where I once stood as a barman, exchanging insults with Cyril. (The whole place became 'too much' for him in the end. When he had his stroke, the brewery decided to sell the site to a conglomerate of agents, publishers and con-men. Dylans was born.) The name had been seized upon because the Bottle (as Treadmill liked to remind me) had been one of the many pubs in the world where Dylan Thomas had made a nuisance of himself. By the time the fixtures and fittings had been installed – the large leather sofas, the low glass coffee-tables – so much of the shabby feel of the old Bottle had been obliterated that the Welsh poet would have found little here to recognize.

Some publicity girl had been responsible for the huge blown-up photograph of Bob Dylan behind the bar. *N'importe quel Dylan.* Both Dylans in all likelihood were unheard-of by the younger clientele.

Furious complaints from Pete Carnforth, the one surviving Black Bottle habitué to use the club, led to an absurd compromise. Beside the picture of the American rock star was placed another, equally large and no more aesthetically pleasing, of the Swansea bard, cigarette in hand, double chins bulging over his frayed collar.

'It's a fucking disgrace. I was a friend of Dylan's. He was the best poet of the twentieth century,' Carnforth averred.

Both these statements were questionable. Pete, though, was in his way as much of a snob as Gorley Swallow, though a snob who limited his area of interest to Soho. To hear him speak these days, you would think he had been on the closest terms with all the great names; and there was hardly any Soho 'character', from Julian Maclaren Ross to Dylan Thomas, from Francis Bacon to Jeff Bernard, whom he did not reckon to have known better than all the other drunks who made the same dismal claims. Dylans, then, it was. Not Dylan's – since there now seemed some doubt as to which Dylan had given his name to the place; and not Dylans' as some pedant had suggested; but simply Dylans. And this was the venue for the party to celebrate a new biography of Day Muckley.

This popular novelist of the pre-war years had made his name writing solid Yorkshire family 'sagas', rambling middlebrow stuff which as a young man I found dull to read, and therefore easy to despise. He was very much down on his luck when I knew him, poor old Muckley. He made such a pathetic figure in his drunkenness – incoherently sparring about religion with Pete Carnforth, splutteringly claiming to have a beautiful mistress – that I never took anything he said very seriously. It is still painful to record the last night when I saw him alive, however, and to see again in the mind's eye the blood which poured from him as he haemorrhaged. His frog eyes were fixed on the sight of me in the arms of his 'mistress'; perhaps the last thing he saw in this world. The woman was Debbie Arnott – not the pillar of the literary establishment who is famous today, but a scatty, Bohemian, lovable person of whom I grew very fond. When my affair with Debbie began it did not feel like an act of betrayal at all. She was an old acquaintance of mine, going back to the days of childhood – she had lived in Timplingham. Watching her 'cope' with Day Muckley's drunkenness I had somehow felt released from ideas of loyalty. Our going to bed together had never been planned. We both felt kindly towards the old boy.

Dodie and I climb the stairs to the party which is being held in an upper room at Dylans, and we are confronted by a mountain of copies of the biography. Day's sad face, his belligerent mouth, his froggy eyes behind pebble-thick specs, recall for me, not our hours of conversation in the bar, but only that moment, the moment of his collapse, his realization that I had cuckolded him.

'Love,' Debbie said that night to him, 'it's not what you think.'

One would assume that she felt even more guilty about the episode than I did; she was, after all, so much closer to Day Muckley. This alone, quite apart from the fact that we were destined to move in very different worlds, would explain the fact that we had drifted apart. We have all moved on since then. The dead change as well as the living. Raphael Hunter, strangely enough, had been the man who did most to rehabilitate Day Muckley's literary reputation, while making himself a tidy sum writing the script of the TV adaptation of *The Calderdale Saga*. Given the mania of London publishers for commissioning biographies, it was inevitable that someone should have noticed that Day Muckley had not yet been 'done'. The young author of the book – probably very well regarded, but quite unknown to me – had no reason to guess that I had ever been acquainted with Muckley, and I am glad to say that I had not been 'approached' for reminiscences. The biographer's account of Muckley's lugubrious end owed much to Debbie's manipulation of the facts. She emerges, indeed, as the heroine of the book, nursing Muckley through his final days and providing him with the companionship which a cruel wife denied him. There was some truth in this picture, even if there was no truth whatsoever in the details of the last chapter. In this version of events, she sat alone in her house waiting for Day Muckley to come back from the pub. She knew he was unwell, and when he collapsed she had gone with him in the ambulance to the Royal Free Hospital.

*

Dodie and I are now entering the room where the party is taking place. About sixty people are squashed together. Almost none of them could possibly have known Day Muckley, and it is open to question whether any of them have any interest in him. They have come because it is a party. Dodie need not have worried that there would be no one whom she knew among the guests.

Standing in the midst of the crowd, mumbling semi-audibly about himself, Gorley Swallow embodies his own paradox. Aware of who everyone 'is', he feels no absorbing interest in anyone there but himself.

' . . . once thought of having instruction for Catholicism myself,' he is murmuring sadly. A reference, one took it, to Day Muckley's religion. 'But there was great simplicity about his faith, I should imagine.'

I say, 'He once compared God with Stalin. I never felt quite the same about him ever again.'

'About God? Or about Stalin?' asks Dodie.

Gorley Swallow asks, 'Is that in the book?'

'No, he said it to me on many occasions. In this very place.'

'It's hard to remember that he lived long enough to have been a member of Dylans. This place used to be a pub once, you know. I forget what it was called. It might have been the Red Lion.'

Gorley Swallow peers at me. Since making the discovery, or having the suspicion, that all his conversation was an elaborate form of tease, I have been hesitant about responding to any of his more conspicuously foolish 'mistakes'.

'Is Victoria here?' I ask.

'I find it very difficult to look after Victoria and keep an eye on my company at parties. In fact I find parties altogether very difficult. Knowing quite what not to say, pitching the level.' From the way he speaks, it seems the quietest saddest little confession ever to have fallen from human lips. He adds, as if this is even sadder, 'We are having some friends to supper a little later.'

Is there a pause, and is he about to ask me to supper? Has he already buttonholed Kit, and are we just to reassemble round the table in Gorley Swallow's house off the Gloucester Road? This is not how I had envisaged spending this evening. I have that sense, by now habitual in the presence of Gorley Swallow, that he is sizing me up, tormenting me, allowing me to wait. He knows that I have now discerned the possibility of his asking me to dinner. He knows that it is the last thing I want. Should he let me off the hook, or should he not?

'It is nice', he says, 'to see Augusta here.' He is peering myopically and disconsolately at the party swarm and deciding that the company is not up to much; Lady Augusta Wimbish, by virtue of lineage, is the only person here worth noting in his trainspotter's log-book.

'It is amazing to me that she is still alive,' I say. 'She must be at least a hundred and fifty-two years old.'

She sits in the far corner of the room, wedged down beside the ashtrays and the peanuts, an etiolated creature whose gaunt timorous features look a trifle more animated since her husband died. At her feet, and on his knees, is the trim ascetic figure of Father Linus Quarles, SJ in a black suit. We do not know if he kneels so as to be on a level with her face or in deference to her ancestry. The priest has, presumably, like Gorley Swallow, trawled through the crowd of minor novelists, 'publicity girls' and poets in open-necked shirts, the literary editors of newspapers and the figures vaguely 'known' from television appearances, and decided that Lady Augusta is the most interesting person in the assembly.

'I was able to quote to Augusta the opening paragraph of a short story I once wrote,' says Gorley Swallow. 'I think I got it word for word.'

A wrinkled old man who appears at my side says, 'Julian. I didn't know you attended thrashes like this; but then, you were an old friend of Day Muckley's.'

Typical of Darnley to remember that, several years before Noah's Ark set sail, I had enjoyed repeating to him Day Muckley's richer *mots*. Did Darnley also remember that I had been Debbie's lover, or was this something which I had kept to myself? When young, one is so open about one's emotional and sexual adventures that one forgets in later times whether aspects of one's 'secret life' are in fact part of the common joky folk-history of gossip.

My age, Darnley looks considerably older than Noah, his face a mass of wrinkle, his hair already so white. It is not difficult to see that life has treated him roughly. (A rocky marriage, one always understood, had ended in his wife's death some years before.) To my shame and sorrow, for Darnley is one of the beings in the universe whom I loved the most, we have drifted apart. At Seaforth Grange as children we had been inseparable companions, and I often remember how the larky, fresh-faced boy had made Granny and Mrs Webb laugh with his jokes. Had them in stitches, they would have said.

He sniffs imperiously. It is difficult to know these days, though he laughs a lot, whether he quite retains his old sense of humour. On the last few times we've met, there has been a worryingly thin division between his actual self and the spoof High Court judge voice which he usually adopts for comic effect. (Is this hint of pomposity the price he has paid for being a newspaper columnist, which is how, a little ignominiously, Darnley now earns a living?)

He says, 'I thought of you the other day.' He fixes me with silver-blue eyes. Here the High Court judge was surely speaking? 'The . . . er, highly regrettable case of Timpson, our old schoolfriend.'

'The bishop? I missed it. I hardly ever read the papers these days.'

True, but a tactless thing to blurt forth to a journalist. However well balanced, journalists, particularly in the higher reaches of the trade, believe that everyone reads the papers as carefully as they do themselves, seeming unaware of the fact that most human beings buy at most one newspaper a day, and concentrate, when they have done so, on the sports pages and the crossword puzzles, leaving the 'columnists' and the leaders – those parts of the papers most interesting to journalists – entirely unread.

'One of the most promising boys Seaforth Grange ever produced.' The High Court judge has now become the Binker. 'Er, bend over, Timpson, will you, while I . . . '

Darnley's chiselled, pitted face creases into its old hilarity. Gorley Swallow looks displeased to have been left out of the conversation so long. He supplies my ignorance by mouthing miserably, 'Bishop Timpson, the Bishop of Didcot. He's a very distant cousin of mine as a matter of fact. A wretchedly sad case.'

'Proceeding in a northerly direction through the defendant's diocese – ' Darnley has now become a police sergeant from *The Pirates of Penzance* ' – and entering the public conveniences on the layby near the Ruislip slipway of the A40 . . . '

'Oh dear,' I say. '*That*.'

'I once asked him to resolve some religious doubts which I was having at the time, but I'm afraid . . . '

'So Timpson had to resign,' says Darnley.

He has appeared to take no notice of Dodie, but in order to escape Gorley Swallow's religious doubts, he has taken us both by the elbow and led us through the crowd.

When Dodie says, 'You would think the police had better things to do with their time', Darnley's face wears its old expression of schoolboy facetiousness, pleased to have got a rise out of one of the younger masters who had not yet learnt how to keep order.

He says, 'What a blessed life you lead, Mr Grainger, not having to worry about bishops in loos. I have to read such unedifying tales, or I'd have nothing to write about in my column. I can't decide', he turns to Dodie, 'whether to take your line, and use it as an occasion for having a go at the police, or whether to make it a decline of the Church piece.'

It seems the moment to introduce Dodie to Darnley; but the attempt to cross the room, find a little space in which we can chat, catch up, is interrupted by an unintended encounter with Deborah Arnott herself.

95

At New Year's Eve parties, in answer to Burns's question (if it is a question rather than a subjunctive), I have always felt that most auld acquaintance are much better forgot. It would be pointless to pretend that Debbie and I still have anything in common; we have both changed into different people from the days when we knew one another.

Her books have not appeared with quite their old regularity since Deborah Arnott – DBE in the last New Year Honours – has been so taken up with committee work. For the last three years she has chaired the Advisory Committee at the Department of Libraries and Heritage, been an active member of the Council at the Royal Society of Literature, an Hon. Deputy President of PEN and, of course, a tireless traveller and lecturer for the British Council. A long time has elapsed since Debbie Maddock and her young 'kids' (one is now Chief Executive of a major television network) used to live in the village. Aunt Deirdre had called her That Wretched Woman; as a child I felt it was deeply unfair, but time, as I have observed before in these pages, causes a revision of almost all one's early opinions.

Those novels she wrote as a young woman, with her lovers thinly disguised, or not disguised at all (I'm the snooty public-school-educated waiter in *Such Fond Return*) have a brio and an innocence lacking in the later work. Reviewers even used words like 'leaden' about her last novel; whether fairly or not, I'm not qualified to judge since it is some years since I managed to slog my way through the latest Arnott.

Deborah and I no longer kiss on those rare occasions when we meet. She has taken to bowing, even to quite old friends like myself, in a semi-ceremonial way, the sort of inclination which might be appropriate when picking up yet another Hon. D. Litt. from some newly created provincial university.

'Where's your nephew?' she asks me.

'Sorry, Debbie, who's that?'

'Kit Mayfield. Your nephew.'

'Victoria Amt's nephew.'

96

Dame Deborah gives me a sharp glance, which is a call to order. There is a wariness in her glance as if my only wish is to undermine her seriousness. Perhaps this is why Darnley sniggers.

'Kit Mayfield's application came up last week and I have been happy to tell him just now that he's been successful.'

'What application was this, my dear?'

'He applied to the grants committee of the Everett Trust at the beginning of the summer. Unfortunately at that date all the previous year's allocation had been assigned; as you can imagine, we have far more applicants than we can possibly satisfy. But we – that is to say, the committee and I – found that this was an extremely interesting proposal, even though there was some doubt about its exact eligibility within the terms of the Trust. As you will probably remember, when Virgil Everett died, one of the happier consequences was the establishment of the Trust, set up, I need hardly say, through the good offices of Raphael.'

Deborah has presumably been addressed so often as 'chair' on her various committees that, with her bulbous crimson velvet coat and her round black bottom and her neat rolls of chins and necks, she seems not so much dressed as upholstered. Her wiry short perm might be composed of that rough horsehair used for upholstering, now bursting from the top of her head as the stuffing might show through a torn sofa.

It is hard to remember that this is the same person with whom I passed boozy evenings in Soho some thirty years ago. I remember that, like the lately deposed Prime Minister, Dame Deborah is the daughter of a northern Alderman. I vaguely remember that Kit, always short of funds, put in for as many grants and bits of cash as he could, in order to buy time to write *The Fairies of Staithe*. At some stage of the year he has probably mentioned applying to the Everett Trust. It is no surprise to find that Dame Deborah sits on – the metaphor seems apt – this Trust, though, given the ways in which Campbell Dilkes managed to blot his copy-book with the Establishment, I am a little surprised that the Headmistress – as she is unkindly called in some quarters – has considered this a suitable subject on which to expend the Trust's money.

'You are probably aware', she says, 'that the Trust is administered by the Council of the Royal Society of Literature on which I chair the Grants Committee.'

I make what is an appropriately deferential grunt.

'Council felt very strongly that Mayfield is a young man to be encouraged. I particularly liked . . . '

The slight pause as we all looked across the room in the direction of Kit's tall snaky figure gave time for snapshots of a younger Debbie to display their flickering magic lantern-show on to the mind's screen. I thought of the night when we had first gone to bed together in Dartmouth Park Avenue, having put Day Muckley to bed in his own squalid lodgings in Leighton Road, NW5; of the thunderstorm which occurred while we made love; and of her disclosure that Raphael Hunter was my wife Anne's lover.

'Oh, you poor, poor boy. It does you good to cry, pet.'

I thought of her own tears when I subsequently failed to keep in touch with her. In this very spot, in the Black Bottle, I had heard her plaintive voice on the telephone.

'Julian, just tell me what's happened. Just tell me what I'm supposed to have done . . . Just tell me and I'll be able to accept it.'

And I had gone round to Dartmouth Park Avenue to comfort her; and Day Muckley had turned up, to find me with my hand inside her blouse.

It was all aeons away; but, as her sentence reaches a natural pause, and we wait to hear what it is she particularly likes about Kit, images of that younger Debbie, with no clothes on, return to the brain. Kit is by any standards beautiful. The mouse-blond hair flops across a brow which looks as if it has never been spotty, never been furrowed. The high cheek-bones, the straight nose, the clear blue eyes, the curling lips, none of these is lost on his company. And Deborah stares. Were these what she liked? The misfortune of her having turned into a staggeringly pompous old bore is no ground for supposing that she is any less highly sexed. I recall her expressing a distaste for poncey men with southern accents, her belief that, for all his boorishness, Day Muckley was a real man. Would Kit, in her own old demanding terms, exactly qualify?

'I liked, that is to say, Council very much liked his . . .'

I think that her sentence ends with the word 'application', but at this point Darnley, for whom the joke had gone on long enough, intervenes.

'Your young negress friend seems very taken up with that young man from the *Standard*.'

Like most of Darnley's utterances, this comes dripping with inverted commas. The High Court judge voice has not merely selected an obsolete noun, but chosen to pronounce its first syllable to rhyme with 'egg'. Dame Deborah bridles, angry, it would seem, to be implicated publicly in racialism, however mild.

'What's her name?'

'Rich. But you must know that.'

'She's extraordinarily beautiful.'

Having earned his living for more than thirty years as a journalist, Darnley seems wholly unfamiliar with what most people, and most newspapers, would regard as the current state of things. He has never been abroad since schooldays, and would be hard put to it to name any politicians outside his own country. He has never possessed a television set. Three-quarters of the people at Dylans would have recognized Dodie Rich instantly. Darnley's wonder at Dodie's appearance is genuine. In forty-five years, I have never heard him make a remark suggesting overt sexual interest in another person – though there were, at Seaforth Grange, some unforgettable anatomical disclosures about Garforth Thoms (now a Junior Treasury Minister) with whom Darnley had shared a tent during Scout camp.

Darnley's expression grows hostile. His jaw sets, as though he has suffered a sudden twinge of pain. Out of the wrinkled face, blue eyes peer suspiciously, on the lookout for snipers. Kit waves to us, strides through the crowd, approaches, places a bony hand on each of my shoulders and kisses me on both cheeks. Some boys at school were shy of being kissed by their mothers in front of the rest of us. I should have given anything for Mummy to come back from the grave and kiss me – at school or at any time. This level of childish embarrassment, however, is what I feel now, in Darnley's presence. I find myself hoping that my oldest friend will not take against a young man of whom I am so fond. Darnley, obsessively undemonstrative, bridles and sniffs, a furious old camel.

'Find out any gossip?' I ask Kit.

Dodie says, 'This party's great! You said I wouldn't know anyone.'

While I try to mumble introductions, Dame Deborah catches on to the fact that Kit is there as a journalist. She does not react suspiciously; on the contrary, it would seem as though she half expected 'media' attention at all times, but merely wished, before speaking in Kit's hearing, to establish which of her sentences were off, and which on, 'the record'.

Kit next does a surprising thing, for I expect him to smile in his teasing way while Dame Deborah proses about her committee work. Instead, he leans forward, and it looks as if he is going to embrace her. Debbie looks far from displeased; in fact, she looks delighted, and in her toothy smile I see again that jolly, randy being with whom, time out of mind, I used to knock around. As he whispers in her ear, she blushes, deeply and girlishly.

'Every day he has to get a "story",' Dodie explains – while this intimate transaction passes between the Dame and the boy – not to the world in general, but quite specifically to Darnley. 'I can't imagine wanting to be a journalist, can you?'

'Not really.'

'Then what's so funny?' she asks.

For a moment, I wonder whether to 'explain' everyone in the circle to one another – to tell Dodie that Darnley is a journalist, for example. All attention, though, is focused on Kit.

'You don't disapprove. If you did, you wouldn't have told me that story about *Planet Venus*.' Kit pauses. 'No, but it would be brilliant . . . ' He pauses again. 'If only you'd let me put it in.'

Both women seem slavishly appreciative of the *double entendre* which Kit so tantalizingly lets fall.

'He'd trace it back to me,' says Dodie excitedly. Like most 'celebrities' – a fact which in the course of the last year I have found increasingly alien – she is obsessed by newspapers as a junkie might be by her supplier; quick enough to condemn the immorality of the trade itself, more than ready to avail herself of the quick thrills which it was able to provide.

Since Dodie is young and sexy, we both concentrate on her, Darnley and I, not realizing that the 'story' which Kit wishes to print in the morning edition of the paper is not television tittle-tattle, but to do with Debbie.

To someone as young as Kit, the story about Debbie would be on the same level of trivial interest as any other 'gossip' item in a newspaper. I am only to discover the content of this story fourteen hours hence, and my night-long preparation for it has only begun. As those who set out on pilgrimage in the days of faith spent the previous night in vigil and prayer, I too need preparation for what Kit – all in an evening's work as a professional gossip – has discovered. When the words have been spoken and the information purveyed, then I shall feel able to sing my *Nunc Dimittis*. My years will be brought to an end as a tale that is told, or, if that is not quite true, the tale which began all those years ago on the morning in Timplingham when we heard of Jimbo's death will at last have reached its strange conclusion. The first I had learnt of James Petworth Lampitt's death had been at church when Uncle Roy celebrated a requiem for this distinguished member of the family which occupied most of his waking thoughts. Both my uncle and aunt had spoken about the death as something 'hush hush', and when, later in the morning, my aunt and I had gone shopping, it had been decided that we should not say anything about the matter to 'the village'. Debbie Maddock (as she was then) had been in the butcher's – a woman of twenty-five who had read about the death in the *Manchester Guardian*, chirping her artless thoughts on the subject over the heads of the other women who were queuing for the last piece of scrag end. How scandalized my aunt had been by Debbie's words – quite incomprehensible to me at the age of twelve – about 'naughty old Petworth'. She had spoken airily of Lampitt's death as if it were an obvious suicide. 'Poor old things. A blackmailer gets hold of them and that's it – or they just get taken over by the sadness of life passing by. They think of the days of their golden youth. It's sadder for them.' Who were they – the ones for whom life was sadder?

I have set out for this evening with my mind focused on my affair with Dodie, my friendship with Kit, and the revels which lie ahead. I am unprepared for the possibility – *you watch, then, you watch?* – that the fifth act of the drama is to be completed. Whatever passed between Kit and Deborah in their whispered confidence, and whatever he wished to 'put in' to his newspaper, could only relate, I imagine, to the here and now. Those past events, those mysteries, those characters, with whom my mind has been so intimately engaged for more than forty years, are not at the forefront of consciousness; I have no sense that a conclusion of sorts will have been reached by dawn.

I turn away my imagination from Deborah and concentrate on Dodie, feeling a wistful sense of regret that our association has come to an end, combined with that overpowering relief which has always accompanied the conclusion of love affairs in my life, a sense of liberation, the illusory feeling that life was once more my own.

Darnley is speaking.

'The best gossip items in a newspaper never have anything to do with sex.' He accompanies this remark with one of his long sniffs. To a male eye there is nothing obviously appealing about Darnley now; but I have noticed over the years that almost all women find him attractive. I watch Dodie, almost instant-aneously, fall for my old friend as he makes this declaration that

102

sex is of no interest. Even Dame Deborah, who has made it clear by facial gesture and body language that she disapproves of all Darnley's anarchic and unserious political viewpoints, allows her lips to quiver over protuberant teeth as she glances from one man to the other, from Darnley to Kit, and back again; the schoolgirl on exeat surveying the sweet trolley in a hotel restaurant and unable to decide between the rum baba and the sherry trifle.

Darnley says, 'Julian here will remember a little paper I ran called *The Spark*.'

He laughs, so Kit and Dodie laugh. I, too. Only Dame Deborah looks grave.

'You'll remember old Pughie, Mr Grainger – Albion Pugh?'

'Naturally.'

'There was this writer –' Darnley expresses himself with full concentration to Dodie; the rest of us merely overhear ' – there was this writer, half a loony, half a bit of a genius, called Albion Pugh. He's completely forgotten now.'

'*Memphian Mystery*,' says Kit.

'My dad's in the Albion Pugh Society,' says Dodie. 'They have a Mass once a year.'

'A Black Mass?'

'Is that supposed to be funny?' snaps back Dodie.

Darnley had obviously not meant any racial pun, and ignores Dodie's touchy response. 'Pughie was a bit of a wizard, wouldn't you say, Mr Grainger?'

Dame Deborah draws herself up. 'He was a terribly bad writer.' She seems not merely affronted, but agitated, by the recollection of his name. 'Towards the end of his life, he became something of a cult, I'm afraid. This did not stop him badgering our literary Fund for financial assistance. Some of the letters he wrote were extraordinarily offensive.'

'Did you give him some help?' I asked.

As a result of a libel case, Albion Pugh (the *nom de plume* of a civil servant named Rice Robey) had been severely stung, not merely by the costs of the legal proceedings, but by losing his job.

103

Presumably, he was no good at managing his money and had outlived his savings. Having always nursed very mixed feelings about Pugh, the man and his works, I now discovered that it pained me to think of him in penury in Kentish Town. I could imagine the strange letters he might have written to such a committee as at the Royal Society of Literature, while huddling in his cold poky house in Twisden Road, concocting a mixture of mysticism and malice as he wheezed on his cigarettes. I see Deborah now as a figure of power, able to punish 'Pughie' for not toeing the line, and I'm afraid I rather hate her as she says, 'We did not consider his applicaton to be a serious one.'

So – Pugh died in penury thanks to her fucking committee.

'That old gent in the corner,' says Darnley.

'The one deep in talk with Clive James?'

'He's called Raphael Hunter.' Darnley sniffs again.

Kit shoots an anxious glance towards Dame Deborah, but I barely notice it. I recollect it the next morning when the night is gone, and with the morn those angel faces smile, which I have loved long since and lost a while.

'Raphael's actually been tremendously helpful to me,' Kit says, 'with my book about Campbell Dilkes . . . '

'Hunter made his name – ' Darnley has decided that we need to be put straight on the story of this once famous, now very slightly faded, literary figure ' – writing this scandalous book about an old bachelor called James Petworth Lampitt.'

'James Petworth Lampitt comes into the book I am writing,' says Kit.

I sense that he is trying to stop Darnley's flow. Since Kit is addicted to all gossip, ancient or modern, this display of reticence is surprising to me. My antennae are dulled.

'He is a sort of cousin – all the Lampitts are,' says Kit, really boringly and deliberately, as if to staunch the flow of words from Darnley's lips. 'And Campbell Dilkes the composer married Lavinia Lampitt who was James Petworth Lampitt's . . . '

'Anyhow – ' Darnley is not to be deflected ' – Hunter over there

– this is ages ago, no one had heard of him – he rose from nothing to tell us that this old writer most of us had never read was a raving poof.'

'I think that in this day and age we should all have grown out of words like poof,' opines Dame Deborah.

'Hear, hear,' says Dodie Rich.

'When you consider', says Dame Deborah, who has probably chaired half-day seminars at the PEN Club on the plight of Gay Writers in different areas of the globe, 'that many of the finest musicians, poets, novelists, painters . . . '

Kit wavers. He knows that he should silence Darnley, if he can, but he can't resist learning what the older man has to say. 'There was some run-in, wasn't there?' Kit is on dangerous ground, and at any minute his foot might hit a mine. 'Did Albion Pugh allege that Campbell Dilkes and Lampitt were . . . ?' He tosses back his floppy hair and ignites yet another Marlboro Light.

Once Darnley finds something funny it continues to make him laugh, seemingly for ever. Hearing from me that he is amusing company, friends have sometimes been baffled to meet him, only to find that he laughs uncontrollably at things which happened twenty, thirty years ago, but never says anything which is strictly speaking witty. Twenty or more years have certainly not dimmed the comedy, as he saw it, of the libel case which closed down his magazine, and he begins to quiver with mirth at the recollection of Raphael Hunter in the witness box, and of Albion Pugh's – certainly, by any standards, very eccentric – defence.

'I had this policy', he splutters, 'of printing anything which I happened to believe was true, and hang the consequences. Pughie stated that Hunter had in fact bumped Lampitt off. Chucked him over a balcony. The really strange thing – '

'I have to say', says Kit, 'that Raphael has been very, very kind to me.'

'It is a most monstrous suggestion – you shouldn't be repeating it even now,' says Dame Deborah. 'Not a shred of evidence was ever produced at the trial and we should not be talking in this flippant vein.'

I say: 'The funny thing is that Jimbo Lampitt's papers were

bought by this American collector. Well, it was Virgil D. Everett – and Hunter wrote a book about him, too, incidentally, but that was much later. It's from his Trust you're getting the money to do your Campbell Dilkes book, Kit.'

Darnley either is a bit deaf or he doesn't listen. At this second or third mention of the composer's name he pricks up.

'Campbell Dilkes?'

'Hunter', I say, 'wrote his best-seller about Lampitt, based on the so-called Lampitt Papers. Hunter was in charge of Everett's collection. It is a mysterious fact that both old gentlemen, Everett and Lampitt, died in exactly the same way, falling from high buildings. First Lampitt, in 1947; then, twenty years later in New York, Everett fell from his penthouse umpteen floors up.'

'I never heard anything so ridiculous,' says Dame Deborah. 'You have read too many detective stories.'

A case could be made out for Dame Deborah's point of view. After a nervous breakdown, I rediscovered my childhood passion for the genre, and I now read little else outside the works of Shakespeare. Most nights close for me at two a.m., with a few more murders solved. (I don't like the ones in which there is no solution.) Well, perhaps the Dame is right, and I should be better employed reading all those great books by Dante or Balzac or Cicero that I've never got round to, but the truth is that I never will; my reading habits are just that – habits. Books are now a narcotic for me, not vehicles for self-improvement – as perhaps they still are for Debbie.

If I had one more drink, and the lights were low, and I rubbed against Dame Deborah's ample form, would I be able to recapture what we had once enjoyed together? It seems cruelly unlikely.

Darnley, always much more musical than literary, is melting towards Kit. For the first time he speaks in his own voice with no inverted commas, but he hates to seem serious, so he mumbles the suggestion that certain phrases in *L'Après-midi d'un faune* were quotations from one of Dilkes's early symphonic poems. Kit – also one of those mysterious people who is not just, as I am, fond of

106

music, but actually musical – enters into this with deep seriousness, and exchanges a few sentences with Darnley impenetrable to the non-musicologist.

'He's actually a much more innovative composer than Elgar or Vaughan Williams,' says Darnley. 'I imagine it's a fascinating story, too.' This was long enough in his own voice, and the headmaster distributing prizes suddenly rounds off with, 'A much neglected figure, we feel. A capital idea for a book. Well done, young man.'

'This is very much what we felt on Council.' Dame Deborah, who retains her old desire to be amiable where she can do so without compromise of principle or personal dignity, seems delighted to find a matter upon which she and Darnley can agree. Finding this a good moment to leave us, she stomps off to beard the London Librarian about a matter of apparent urgency.

'The Dame did not like being told a few home truths about Hunter,' sniffs Darnley.

I reply, 'Perhaps she does not like the idea of the Everett Trust being blood money. After all, she helps to distribute it to deserving cases like Kit here.'

'What's the Everett Trust?' asks Darnley, very much with the air of a man who does not wish to be told.

Repetition blurs the edge of sympathy. Over the years Hunter became a monster inside my head. One of my ways of prodding or subduing this inner demon has been to make him into a joke, shared on occasion with Darnley. In the days when we saw more of one another, Darnley and I devoted hours of cogitation, broken by laughter, to the impenetrable subject of why Hunter was so successful, or attractive, or whatever the right word would be, with women. Anyhow, there were lots of them. The evidence was incontrovertible. Strings of women had queued up to have their lives interrupted by an emotional mess. Most of them, when the tears dried, remained on friendly terms with 'Lover Boy', as Sargie had always called him. ('Mr Clever' had been Debbie's own nickname for Hunter when – in that different era – she had broken to me the news that I was being cuckolded by Hunter with my wife Anne.)

107

My cousin Felicity was unusual in this respect. Kind Quaker lady, impenetrable Wittgensteinian, she has not mentioned his name in my presence in forty years. Fliss knows that whereof we cannot speak, we must be silent. (Victoria's 'fling' with Hunter happened years ago and she continues to speak with respect of his generosity to other authors, his tireless work for 'the arts', his round of travels and councils and committees. Victoria, as the reader will have noted, has her serious side.)

All fallings in love are acts of the imagination. Darnley and I decided, in our talks on the subject, that Hunter's success in the field was a supreme demonstration of this point, his popularity with women stemming from the fact that he was so colourless. He is a *tabula rasa* on which any woman can draw her ideal man. Moreover, Hunter is a kind man. Sometimes, when I have used this word of him, and remembered Fliss sobbing after her abortion, or Anne stomping along the pavement in grief when she had seen Hunter embracing Bella Marno that night at the theatre, I have felt that the epithet is marinaded in bitter irony. The truth is, though, that Hunter has been a very kind man indeed – much kinder than I have ever been. He helped me get my novel published when I was a young man; there were, I am now sure, no ulterior motives behind this spontaneous act of helpfulness. I have no doubt, thirty years later, that he is helping Kit with his researches into Campbell Dilkes in the same disinterested and altruistic spirit. In the days when I thought myself capable of great things, I liked to mock Hunter's transparent desire to get on in the world. Less easy to do so now. No literary historian of the twentieth century is ever going to mark Hunter down as one of the great writers. His prose is as colourless as the persona with whom the women fall in love. You can't deny, though, that Hunter has been a friend to literature, if by literature you mean Literary Funds, Literary Dinners, Committees, Literary Societies, Literary Festivals and International Conferences on the Role of the Biographer, the Future of the Novel, or the plight of the Dissident Writer under the world's less congenial political regimes. Bella Marno, one of the more candid of the ex-mistresses, remarked to me once on the fact that Hunter evidently had only a limited interest in the sexual act, and never looked happier than when slipping back into his trousers at the end of the afternoon, discreetly peeping at his wrist-watch and mentally preparing himself for the next book launch party at six thirty p.m. This did not prevent him from being in all other regards an attentive lover, a great rememberer of birthdays, purchaser of flowers and chocolates, reserver of window-tables in fashionable restaurants – or, in the case of his shyer girlfriends, discreet nooks in unpretentious North London *trattorie*. It was as if he could manage all aspects of love except feelings, just as he was adept in all areas of literature except the ability to write. Given the amount of time which Dame Deborah now devotes to committee work, it is no wonder that she and Hunter should have come across one another, and it is no surprise, at this party in Dylans, to hear her defending him so robustly.

We peer through the crowds for Hunter, but he has evaporated.

I say, 'I can't see him.'

Kit says, 'I had a word with him earlier.'

And Darnley says, 'He's over there. No he isn't. He seems to have gone.'

'He has supplied me with the best *Diary* story I ever wrote,' says Kit.

'Tell,' I say.

'Couldn't.'

This was the flirtatious giggle of the girl who says 'no', meaning 'yes'.

'He must have left,' says Darnley.

'I wonder if I am going to fall in love with Raphael Hunter after all,' says Dodie. 'Julian speaks so much about him, and I've never met him. You know, he even came down to Staithe this summer to see my Titania, and I never even got to meet him afterwards. I came to this party hoping to find a husband and it occurs to me that he might suit me very nicely.'

She cooes this information in Darnley's ear, and he looks delighted.

We continue to stare – the party is thinning out – at the corner of the room, now almost vacant, where Hunter had been.

Dodie murmurs, 'And leaves a gap in Nature.'

Our group, all looking fixedly in one direction for the figure of the departed Hunter, has accidentally focused on Gorley Swallow.

'When I saw you all staring at me, I wondered if my flies were undone,' he says, shuffling up towards us and adding, superfluously, 'I've stayed longer than I intended and now I am slightly drunk.'

He is in the gossip business, so Kit is wise to button up his scoop about Hunter, whatever it may be.

While he could be said to be the maker and sustainer of gossip, the high priest of it, the hierophant who plots how many duchesses could dance on a pinhead in his own arcane theogony of connection and interconnection, Gorley Swallow is still not averse to the cheaper thrills of the trade. It is rather as if one of the Colombian drug barons were still prepared, when he found himself hanging around in London without ready cash in his pocket, to sell a little substance on a street corner or in the lav of a pub. Several times since I have known him, I have spotted 'titbits', directly traceable to Gorley Swallow's willingness to betray his friends, in varous 'diaries' in the newspapers.

But why am I being so unkind about Gorley Swallow? I do genuinely love him! His very vices – his capacity for petty treachery, his avarice, his self-absorption – have all been turned, by some strange magic – *Yours, O Shakespeare? Fairy magic?* – to our happiness, the happiness of us all.

For, in the course of the summer, Victoria fell in love with Gorley Swallow. I cannot make up my mind whether they are the Theseus and Hippolyta of the drama, or the Titania and the Bottom.

There was a night – I suppose it was about a week after the *Dream* finished. I had been up to London, intended to return to Staithe by early evening, been late for my train, and telephoned Victoria who assured me that she would be perfectly content without me. I did not believe her. I was still under the absurd impression that I was a necessary part of her establishment. It did not occur to me that I was merely in her way, that my staggering about with trays and my relentlessly regular preparation of meals, once helpful, had become intrusive and unwanted.

I'd left the car at Sheringham, the nearest station. I remember that night so vividly, the drive back to Staithe through empty roads beneath the enormous blue-black sky. When I parked the car outside the stables, I looked up at that sky. It dominates in Norfolk to a degree which would be unimaginable to a Londoner who, blanketed beneath a haze of pollution and street-lighting, never sees the stars really shine. That night the Milky Way arched and glittered over Staithe with fairground brightness. The whole firmament sparkled ('The moonlight lay on the hills like snow' – Dorothy Wordsworth). The almost full moon shed a bright silver light, sharp enough to cast shadows from trees, topiary, garden statues. I passed the amphitheatre, now so empty, so eerily empty, and thought of my Titania, so lately left in London, the extraordinary intensity of her approach to physical relations. When shared with her, sex was like a spell. Not kidding myself (as she in her blessed unselfishness could sometimes kid me) that I was anything special in that department, I marvelled at how, in bed, people are always themselves; the same energy and brio and desire to show off which made Dodie such a memorable actress are all there in the bedroom. And there, in that bricky Edwardian amphitheatre, now flooded with silver light, I remembered the enthralled silence of the audience, just a fortnight earlier, as

Titania wak'd and straightway lov'd an ass.

O, the wonder of that production, the mystery of it! (It quite outshone *Dark Lady*, which was described by the local newspaper as a triumph for Sir Hubert. It was, I think, one of the most embarrassing evenings I ever spent in a theatre.) In the silence of the moonlight, a fortnight after the final curtain-call of the *Dream*, the mystery seemed stronger than ever. I stood on the brick steps looking down through the shrubbery at the empty stage, which was now lost in the blackest pools of shadow, and heard it all again – the extraordinary touchingness of the young lovers in their quarrels; the hilarity of Bottom; above all – but perhaps I speak with the prejudice of one who played Oberon – the utter perfection of the fairy scenes. If you have only read the play, in the company of giggling and cynical schoolchildren in your childhood, or if you have seen a poorly made production, you might think the fairy scenes are just whimsy. They were never whimsical in Victoria's production. They were, by turns, funny, menacing, touching and mysterious.

No director I have ever worked with has better understood how to direct comedy. She taught us to play it with complete concentration and seriousness. She crafted every syllable, every movement, every appearance of the fairies – and it was extraordinary to think that she could never see the enchantment which she made. That was why the moment when Titania fell in love with Bottom held the audience completely spellbound. They were rapt from the moment when Dodie arose and stared with abject adoration and imploring lust towards the ass-headed Bottom, to ask, 'What angel wakes me from my flowery bed?' As was only right, in the ensuing scene, at the beginning of Act IV – 'Scratch my head, Peaseblossom' – Bottom played it for laughs, and got them. But the initial rapture moved everyone, reminding the actors who took part and the audience who saw them of how painfully ridiculous we all are when we fall under this enchantment.

It all came back to me so strongly as I passed the theatre and crossed the garden in the September moonlight, little knowing that the thrall which held us all imprisoned at Staithe – Victoria's blindness, yes, but Victoria's whole personality, also – had been broken by the same magic which enabled Titania to dote on an ass. My feelings of irrational guilt whenever I was not making myself a slave to her domestic needs; her desire to control and issue directives to 'the children'; the need we all felt to escape her, but our powerlessness to do so – yes, while loving her and admiring her as we did: all this was about to be lifted from our shoulders. And I knew it not.

In my brain as I crossed the moonlit garden there began again the prosaic catalogue – *Something to Do* – of chores which framed my days at Staithe. It was near midnight. I would go to the kitchen and, while consuming a large glass of Irish whiskey with much water, I would 'make up' the Aga from the hod of coke, and assemble Victoria's breakfast tray: the pills, the pills. I would probably smoke a last cigarette, and make sure that the cat was not hungry. Then, glass in hand, I would totter the final stairs to my room. If I sensed that Victoria was still awake, I would go to her room and ask if there was anything she needed; when I could convince myself that she did not need me any more, I could go to bed, and to sleep.

Passing the theatre, I climbed the stone steps into the rose garden and paused again. The moonlight shone so strongly on the lawn that for a moment it crossed my mind that some theatrical lights, left over from the *Dream* production, had been directed towards the fairy ring, the patch of dewy lawn in the middle of the knot garden where, eighty years before, Campbell Dilkes had witnessed the mysterious dance of the Little Folk. And I myself stood there, enraptured by the brightness of the light, which is so unlike sunlight, so strong, but so undazzling, so silver; and I also felt humbled by the thought of those strange presences

> *Whose midnight revels, by a forest side*
> *Or fountain, some belated peasant sees,*
> *Or dreams he sees, while overhead the Moon*
> *Sits arbitress . . .*

Total sceptic though I might be, it was hard to peer at the silvered grasses without hoping for some movement, some footfall or dance, hard not to strain the ear for that high-pitched polyphonic which had been vouchsafed to the ears of Campbell Dilkes's faith. Darkling I listened. Nothing. As with all attempts to penetrate the veil, I was left with the mere sense of mystery but no actual belief that there is anything 'in' or 'behind' such feelings; still less, that I had had an 'experience' which could substantiate such a creed. Instead of being like Milton's peasant, seeing, or dreaming that he saw, the Fairies of Staithe, I had a recurrence of egocentric fantasy that I myself was being watched by some unseen presence. So many people must have nursed such sensations when walking alone in the dark that it would not be worth recording were it not for the irrational thought, which instantly communicated itself to me, that the Presence, or Presences, who were waiting for me were not amiable; they were, it seemed, planning some mischief, playing a game with my life.

It is humiliating to remind readers that I have spent over a year of my life in a mental hospital, and that when the illness was at its height I suffered from advanced persecution mania. The sense that there was a Presence staring at me from the darkened windows of the house made me quicken my pace. I resolved that when I reached the kitchen, I would take a Largactyl. No point in allowing the mind to churn down its dangerous old tracks.

And there, in the moonlight, suddenly, was my vision.

My love, my joy!

The fates, the kind fates, had decreed that before I made my melancholy way to bed, I should be given a glimpse of Leman. White trousers, white shirt, barefoot in sandals, she seemed part of the silver-painted scene. I stopped and stared as she walked past. Her walk broke into a near-run, so my vision of her was brief, no more than twenty seconds, as she crossed from the big house to the shadowy paths leading down to her cottage. The next day, when I confessed that I had seen her, she upbraided me.

'You should have called out, Julian, so! You should! I knew there was someone lurking in the shadows. How could I be sure it was you? I was terrified. I thought if I ran it would encourage him to chase me, so I walked briskly. For the first time in ages, I locked the door of my cottage. I was afraid that Angelo and I would be murdered in our beds.'

When I got into the kitchen, I found a note from Leman on the kitchen table, propped up beside a jam-jar of Michaelmas daisies.

Don't bother to take Victoria her breakfast!! I'll explain in the morning. Hope you did not get up to too much mischeif in London. L.

I spent half the night awake, loving the fact that she could not spell; and, as always, when I read the simplest message in her handwriting, even a shopping list, wondering if there were any rational way of interpreting it as a love-letter addressed to myself. Was it because she was sexually jealous that Leman did not want me to take in Victoria's breakfast tray? I knew that such an idea was preposterous, but the mind can form preposterous notions at four a.m. before drifting into that last unsatisfying pre-dawn sleep.

When I was awake again, the message, like the injunction made to Adam and Eve not to eat the Apple, merely excited curiosity. Was Victoria unexpectedly away for the night? Evidently not. There were always telephoned messages when she stayed overnight in Norwich or London and if this was what Victoria were doing, Leman's note would have made it plain. What possible reason could Victoria have for not wanting her morning tea, her muesli, her pills? As I am myself, Victoria is a creature of routines.

So, the next morning found me pyjama-clad and toothpaste-breathed staring out at the grey dawn over the salt-marshes and then continuing my stage-butler progress towards Victoria's bedroom door.

Sometimes, and today was such a time, I felt skittish enough to announce in Boris Karloff tones as I opened the door, 'You rang!'

It was a surprise to see not one but two heads on the pillows.

Gorley Swallow's eyes were closed in sleep, but his shoulders were bare. Victoria, uncharacteristically, was naked though most of her top was covered. Her unseeing eyes were open, and as usual I felt them focused upon me.

'I asked Leman to leave a note', she said, 'to tell you not to . . .'

Gorley Swallow awoke. Unabashed, he said, 'Tea. How very nice.'

'I'm afraid', I said, 'I brought only one cup.'

Having announced long before that he was leaving the party at Dylans, Gorley Swallow now seems ready to make a night of it. Gorley Swallow's 'nights on the tiles' were a feature of Victoria's loving anecdotes. Behaviour which in me, or in Kit, she would have deplored, seemed positively admirable in her beloved; he was not so stuffy, she seemed to imply, as to eschew the occasional raffish night. Perhaps the reason that they were good for one another was that Gorley Swallow has never allowed Victoria's overbearing manner, nor her blindness, nor her powerful combinations of vulnerability and forcefulness, to create in him those feelings which they awoke in most of her entourage before he 'took her in hand'. He knows now, at this party, that which I know with my mind but not my heart – that Victoria will survive perfectly well in his flat for a few hours without him. He does not care whether he returns home at once or later.

Kit asks him, 'Have you read much Day Muckley?'

I notice that Gorley Swallow is one of those many people who bring out the offensive schoolboy in Darnley, who does not address a word to him, preferring to stand on the sidelines sniggering at everything Gorley Swallow says.

After a few drinks, Gorley Swallow's melancholy face, a child on the first day at a new school who has just wet his drawers, becomes idiotic. The self-absorption becomes so total that it is by no means obvious that he understands any remarks unless they directly concern himself. He blinks at the question Kit has posed.

Gorley Swallow had never met Day Muckley, though as a matter of fact Muckley was just the sort of person he liked to cultivate in moderate doses, such 'Bohemian' or 'artistic' connections, particularly if working class in origin, serving to counterbalance any impression

116

which might be formed in his company that Gorley Swallow was a snob.

'I think,' he murmurs. And we wait to hear what Gorley Swallow thinks. I wait to see how long it takes him to draw the subject of the Yorkshire novelist back to himself. 'I think Deborah Arnott must have been so helpful to Day Muckley, don't you? Reading his stuff, and so on. I have just been talking to her. I don't know if it will do any good. I asked her if she had time to read a few chapters of something I had written myself. Of course, I understand how journalism works, but I am still new to the game of fiction. You must all – ' he gazes around with an assumed, Coco-the-Clown sadness which seemed to implore shouts of contradiction ' – you must all know so much more about it than I do.'

'Much more,' says Darnley rudely. In fact, having blurred the edges between fact and fiction in his journalism for thirty years, Darnley has little time for novels, and it is hard to think of any novelist, except P. G. Wodehouse, to whose work he has ever referred.

'I say,' says Gorley Swallow. 'I'm hungry and I expect you are. Why don't we continue this conversation over dinner? This is just the sort of conversation I like, and it isn't often one gets the chance to pursue it in such congenial company.'

It is interesting to watch Kit, Dodie and Darnley – very different characters – form an instantaneous and silent alliance. Their features all compose themselves in readiness to give a negative response to this suggestion.

'Dodie,' says Gorley Swallow, 'I have not really spoken to you all evening.'

'You have not really spoken to me all summer,' she says, not crossly but factually. 'You have said a number of things in my presence but that is not the same thing as talking to me.'

'I once had a West Indian girlfriend,' he says with a playful smile.

'That was extremely big of you,' says Dodie.

I do hope we aren't going to have one of Dodie's slightly tedious tirades about men who are attracted to black girls being racist at heart.

'I thought it was all going well – oh, thank you.' Gorley Swallow

117

allows a waitress to refill his glass with plonk. He is now indiscriminate about the colour of wine offered, so that by blending the fairly lethal Chilean red with a sharp Australian white, he – or the waitress – has produced a rosé concoction in his glass. Someone barges past as he is talking, and the acidic contents of the glass spurt into the air, some of them showering me, some spattering Dodie's marvellous brocade jacket. Gorley Swallow shows no consciousness at all that any wine has been spilt. He continues to talk.

'Now it isn't called *The Martians*,' he explains to Dodie. 'Your programme.' He says this with a tremendous air of self-congratulation as though she should be grateful for the information. I feel hotly defensive of her, and while I dab her wine-dark sleeve with a handkerchief, I say, 'It's called *Planet Venus*.'

'You see, it's scarcely worth my having television, because I am so often out in the evenings. I was on it once, though.'

'Gorley, my dear,' says Kit – and suddenly he has emerged as a figure of authority, one of those young people, like Prince Hal at the end of the *Henry IV* plays, for example, whose youthfulness actually lends them authority over their elders – 'go home and cook Victoria some pasta.'

There is nothing offensive in this valediction, but Gorley Swallow responds to what it is: a command.

I have this antiquated, almost feudal sense, suddenly, that Staithe will be all right. It has a new young master. The king shall enjoy his own again. Or – another image – one to which Day Muckley had referred on the last day of his life, when I had drunk with him in the Bottle – the sense of homecoming, of Odysseus and Telemachus reclaiming Ithaca from the suitors. Was tonight going to turn out to be a journey in which, at last, old Campbell Dilkes was to be – not exonerated, but exorcized? Could he and his fairy visions be allowed to rest, and his seed to inherit his land? We step out, the four of us, into the night. Gorley Swallow has gone, and I am declaiming:

I am thy father's spirit;
Doom'd for a certain term to walk the night,
And for the day confin'd to fast in fires,

Till the foul crimes done in my days of nature
Are burnt and purg'd away.

In the wet street, headlamps from cars make driving rain splatter golden showers. Above maimed shopfronts neon flashes, GIRLS, GIRLS, GIRLS. Oh, you know the cheap impulses that lead on past beaded curtains to ADULT VIDEOS and teach the heart to yearn for 'material likely to offend'. What syphilitic hag awaits those credulous enough to follow the sign in a doorway which reads: YOUNG MODEL, SECOND FLOOR? *Enjoyed no sooner but despisèd straight.*

Have we decided to go to the Concord, or is Kit leading us there? It is only a very short walk through the filthy monsoon of Dean Street. For the rest of the evening, and the night, Kit will be my guide, my leader. I know about his fondness for the Concord; Leman ribs him about it. He has a taste for the obsolete. Relaxation of the licensing laws for ordinary pubs has made the Concord and 'drinking clubs' like it in central London superfluous. When I worked as a barman at the Black Bottle in the 1950s, the law decreed that drinking stopped in pubs during the afternoons. The more determined of our customers, such as Day Muckley or Peter Carnforth, had naturally gravitated to this seedy pair of little rooms, since most of the other 'clubs' in the neighbourhood were not really meant for drinkers. They were joints where you spent two weeks' wages for an unwanted glass of Babycham while some painted girl, up for the week from Rochdale and half-embarrassed by what she was doing, stroked your trousered leg and told you not to leave the premises until your pockets were empty. For those who preferred the idea of dying of drink, the Concord was certainly the place to be. It would be twisting the truth to say that you could risk cirrhosis in style here, but at least you could do so in the company of various alcoholics who were famous as poets or painters, together – honesty forces me to add – with some of the worst bores in London. If you liked this sort of thing – enough did, apparently, to keep the place afloat – the Concord once had an allure. With most of its 'famous' clients dead, it is difficult to know what allures, if any, it still possesses; but if they exist, Kit, bounding up the stairs in front of us with shocking eagerness, is about to show us.

You see the virtue, Shakespeare, of imagining you as the Director, as Oberon the Fairy King or Prospero the Mage, summoning us up like dreams, fashioning us, pushing us around the stage to play our parts? When you walked the earth, people believed in God; but even you, wholly conformist as you were (right-wing by modern standards), found comfort in abandoning the contemporary Christian outlook for the purpose of drama.

> *As flies to wanton boys are we to th' Gods,*
> *They kill us for their sport . . .*

A fiction, but one which fits experience better than the pieties of your contemporaries, the Puritans and the Jesuits? It has the advantage, too, that when you write in other moods, in other plays, the 'paganism' can be celebratory and cheerful:

> *Laud we the Gods, and let our crookèd smokes*
> *Rise from our altars to their blessèd nostrils . . .*

(lines Albion Pugh liked to quote, not surprisingly).

The fairies are an even better conceit than the gods, the fairies in whom we continue to believe for several days, or even weeks, after any good production of the *Dream*. So, Shakespeare, I see you perhaps more as Puck than as Prospero, ushering us up the stairs of the Concord. Sometimes in Homer, the Gods simply take on the disguise of a mortal; perhaps for the rest of the evening, Shakespeare, you have taken up residence in the body of Kit? Your enigma in Kit's hooded eyes and facetious smile? The Concord is the sort of place, if its Elizabethan equivalent could be imagined, which I can imagine your having frequented in the days of your flesh. Falstaff and friends would have seen the point of it. That staircase, its scuffed red lino; oh, the vomit that's been spattered on it; the remorseful feet, the scarlet, sweated faces that have heaved up and down it. The expense of spirit in a waste of shame.

As if this were his reason for having led us up those stairs, Kit says, 'Pubs get so crowded at this time of night.'

Cyril, my old landlord at the Black Bottle, had made gratuitous insult to the customers (particularly new or female customers) a *specialité de la maison*. In this, he was not alone, however, and the tradition of the Concord, faithfully maintained by the present management, was that any newcomers rash enough to push open the door should receive an English welcome.

Balanced on the bar-stool, the small man clad in an emerald green track suit and matching baseball cap exudes the fumes of a menthol cigarette and barks at Kit with the rich Devonian vowel-sounds of a West Country sergeant. During my years of National Service I heard some pretty ripe insults from the RSMs but the words yelled this evening were strong even by the standards of the parade ground.

'What d'you want to bring those three cunts in here for?'

'Good evening, Sausage. I think we'll have a bottle of champagne.'

'That's more fucking like it.'

It is remarkable that someone of Sausage's particular physiognomy should feel in a position to be censorious about the costume and appearance of his clientele. Not only is he short and fat – a combination which makes the green track suit a surprising choice of attire – but his face, a puckered oval which has not seen daylight for half a century, is a mere background for the nose; the steps at the foot of the column, the lawn surrounding the hill. The nose is the colour and texture of a mouldy strawberry; but even in the sunniest Californian valley, no strawberry of such proportions has ever been nurtured. To say that it is big would imply that it belongs to the same genus as other noses. But it has outsoared the shadow of even the most monstrous proboscis. Cyrano de Bergerac could not have competed with it. At some stage of his life – when, for example, as a young rating in the Merchant Navy, and before his first fateful visit to Soho (he had got his present job aged nineteen and had been in Soho since the end of the war) – the nose was perhaps much like any other noses. Perhaps it was just a snub of a thing, waxy and pale. The revenge which alcohol had taken upon it has been to transport it from contemporary London into the fantasy world of the Brothers Grimm.

I've been to the Concord now and again, but Sausage never remembers my name, still less, one assumes, my face. Each time I see his nose, however, is a new occasion of wonder. The difference between a great work of art and a minor one is that great art seems the greater each time one renews the acquaintance. Familiarity with it is on one level impossible, which is why one can know *Hamlet* or *Lear* by heart and still be surprised by every new performance. By a similar token, when one thinks of the Concord, one forgets the 'mad days' spent in Soho by the likes of Day Muckley or Dylan Thomas, and one remembers only that nose.

The man behind the nose – does Sausage wear the baseball cap, with its exaggeratedly protuberant peak, for aesthetic balance? – has slipped off his stool and waddled behind the bar to fetch a bottle of champagne from the fridge. He does this with aplomb; he lines up five glasses on the bit of dirty towel which drapes the bar, unscrews the cork with a dishcloth and, with the solicitude of a nurse coming round the ward with her trolley of pills, manages at the same time to make sure that the pathetic crocks perched on the bar-stools have a refill of their medicine.

Formulaically, almost kindly, he murmurs, 'Same again?' to the pair who sit there; and, not staying for an answer, he takes each tumbler in turn and applies it to the upended giant of Bell's behind his head.

'I told Terence – of course, he was terribly sensitive. Terribly. Sit it out, my dear. Kenneth Tynan? I mean who the hell is she? I really said that.'

'Completely mad to have invaded Russia, when we were a sitting duck. If he'd decided to launch an invasion offensive against the coast of Kent in 1941, we could not conceivably have stopped him.'

Kit's right. Pubs do get crowded, a tendency not shared by the Concord these days, if this evening is a typical one. Beside the fireplace at the opposite end of the room, four disconsolate individuals sit around a table playing cards. Otherwise there is no one else in. At the mention of Kenneth Tynan, as at the mention of any famous name, Sausage brightens. Perhaps the Concord really had seen such luminaries as he likes to imply. After a handful of visits to the club, stretched over a lifetime, I have developed a sense that these celebrities were more honoured in their absence than their presence. Mention any great name – Sir Winston Churchill, President Kennedy, the Pope – and, with a lecherous piratical leer, Billy Bones remembering Captain Flint and his cronies, Sausage will sigh and say 'Aargh! Do you remember 'im in 'ere?'

The regulars, who sometimes seem in a state where it would tax their powers to remember their own names, always appear to remember the presence among them of the great ones. Their claims to have been goosed by Francis Bacon are brought out with such nonchalant pride as Gorley Swallow might use to boast of an invitation to Chatsworth. There is a difference of approach, however. Sausage is in awe of fame, but he makes no distinction in the way he treats anyone. Had His Holiness or Sir Winston ever been adventurous enough to step into Sausage's kingdom, they would have been greeted as 'fucking cunts', just like everyone else.

'Arrgh! old Ken. I remember him. 'Course I do. Oh, what was the fucking . . . oh, the fucking . . . '

Sausage hits his forehead frantically as if the word he wanted is a penny jammed in a slot which, with sufficient force, could be dislodged.

'Anyway,' Kit says, 'let's have something to drink.'

'It'll come back,' says Sausage, who has hit the grey putty of his forehead so vehemently that a dull bruise, purplish, appears beneath the peak of his baseball cap.

Kit hands one glass of champagne to Dodie and another to Darnley.

'No thanks,' says Darnley, putting his glass down on the bar.

'I don't suppose you do food?' says Dodie.

At twenty-seven, she is of the new generation which believes that it is (even, that it should be) possible to get things to eat when you go out for the evening in England.

Twice her age, I belong to the generation which thinks it reasonable to seek out a cooked breakfast in a corner café if you feel hungry early in the morning. For the rest of the day, unless you have no cooking facilities at home, you rely on things on toast – roes, sardines, eggs, beans. Restaurants played almost no part in English life in my youth. Home was for eating; bars were for drinking.

Sausage is still in Billy Bones mode, the pirate yelling to the quarterdeck.

'Nice bit o' steak and onions. Aaargh!'

Wrinkling his face villainously, Sausage somehow manages to get Darnley's champagne to his lips without breaking the glass.

'With a few chops? Wouldn't that be lovely?'

He could hardly speak with more relish if he were arranging a striptease by a platoon of paratroopers.

Dodie turns an innocent smile on the rest of us and says, 'That'd be fine, wouldn't it? Though I wouldn't want chops as well as steak.'

''Course we don't do food, you fucking idiot.' Sausage sounds truly furious. 'What d'you think this is – Planet Fucking Venus?'

Dodie bridles at his coarse tongue, starts back at the sheer noise as, with much spit, Sausage directs these words at her; but she is pleased to have been recognized. I wonder when Sausage, stuck in this darkened hole, ever has time to watch telly. Then I recollect that the Concord is not open on a Saturday, which is the evening when *Planet Venus* is transmitted. An inevitably sad picture of Sausage comes before me: as a domestic being, he would be vulnerable; solitary in some poky flat, with a plate of steak and onions balanced on his knee as he stared at Dodie, garish in her lurex, speaking from Outer Space through the cathode ray tube.

'I mean.' It is an Ulster voice. One of the old gentlemen at the bar says, 'I mean it. It wasn't as if we'd properly rearmed by '41. Far from it. We couldn't conceivably have known what Hitler was up to.'

Years ago, Darnley introduced me to Professor Cormac.

It is hard to imagine, quite, what his mind's eye sees as he discourses in his strong brogue of the military tactics of the great dictators. A vast audience, perhaps, of undergraduates or a conference of military historians.

Though perhaps a good academic historian (who are we to judge?), Cormac has been driven by some inner daemon (fear of poverty?

boredom? hatred of his colleagues at Oxford?) to set up his brass plate as a media don. It was a role which he played, according to his shambolic lights, quite successfully in the 1970s. Some of the stuffing, professionally speaking, was knocked out of him in the ensuing decade. Men like Cormac thrive on opposition. When he was a young man, his unashamedly right-wing view of things had seemed quirky, adventurous, certainly, by the standards of academic colleagues, eccentric. It must have been irksome to Cormac suddenly to find that the wind was all blowing in his direction, and that even the Prime Minister now shared many of his ideas. (She was rumoured to be a great admirer of his books, and there was talk of a knighthood.) Cormac must have found this disconcerting since so obviously it was his vocation to be an irritant, not an oracle. Attack being his sole mode, he had been forced to concentrate his efforts in recent years on hatred of his old colleague Professor Wimbish. With Wimbish dead, Cormac had accepted a large contract from a London publisher to reassess British military capabilities during the Second World War, a monumental task whose general drift he was willing to share with any drinking crony prepared to listen, but which he had not apparently yet got down to writing.

While Dodie, remarkably slow on the uptake in this instance, tries to assess the likelihood of Sausage preparing her a plate of steak and onions, Professor Cormac, with the use of ashtrays, cigarette packets, matchboxes and a rather sordid wad of paper handkerchiefs discovered in the pocket of his leather jacket, tries to assemble a rough and ready model of the Siege of Stalingrad.

Darnley stares with a strange grin on his face. He has always been impatient of drunks and I wonder why he is bothering to stay in this club, a place meant not just for drinking, but for becoming disgustingly drunk. Perhaps, like the rest of us, Darnley is beguiled by Kit? Certainly, the boy's physical charms are not lost on Sausage, lecherous little goblin; and we know from the summer at Staithe that the other figure sitting at the bar, Hubie Power, finds Kit beautiful.

Sausage is having one more try with that word he has forgotten.

He hits his head with a tremendous thump and the words 'Oh, Calcutta' are jolted from his word-hoard.

'But', says Hubie, taking Kit's long white hand, 'you were too young to have known Terence.'

He pauses, by way of explanation, and stares contemptuously, disappointedly, at Dodie. 'Rattigan,' he adds.

''Course he knows you're talking about Terence Fucking Rattigan, cunty,' shouts Sausage, fortissimo. 'He's not a fucking moron.'

If a stone-deaf person were to witness this scene and could see merely Kit's physical response to this exchange, his charming, slightly goofy smile, they might have concluded that the most delicately conceived compliments were being bandied about.

I stand and think of all the worries which Victoria has expressed about this boy in the years since his mother died, and the memory of conversations held at Staithe, the two of us, late at night, in Victoria's bedroom, brings a whiff of pure air of the salt-marshes. How far away it seems, Staithe, at this moment, the clammy air blowing in from the sea across the grass and the samphire, the cows mere smudges in the dark and sea-mist, the ruined mill, the copse of beeches just blobs of ink on a darkened page. Victoria fears that her nephew takes drugs, will never hold down a proper job, has no idea about money, is treating Leman badly, is possibly bisexual, perhaps wholly homosexual. I think of Leman, and wish I were sitting on the rickety garden chair in her hut, wasting her time while she mended a hoe.

Fluttering his hooded lids, Kit says, 'When I was very young . . .'

'Just listen to him!' Hubie does not relinquish the young man's hand.

' . . . that is, when I was at school, I thought *The Browning Version* was one of the most moving things I'd ever . . .'

'Were you in it?'

'Just a school play, you understand . . .'

I am now drunk, and I want to bore the company with my belief that my best days as an actor were the teenage years, when Treadmill was directing me in slightly off-beam Renaissance dramas. No one listens as I offer some reflections on *The Knight of the Burning Pestle*.

126

They are all trying to guess which role Kit played in Rattigan's mawkish play.

Stroking Kit's bottom, Sir Hubert Power says, 'I bet you were the little boy who gives Crocker-Harris the Browning version of the *Agamemnon*. My God, how can we get this boy to act some more?'

'More? Fucking more?' This is hollered from the quarterdeck by Bosun Sausage. 'What do you think it's doing now if it isn't acting? Posing more like. Fucking posing, aren't you? Ponce.'

Kit makes an overwhelming impression on Sir Hubert when he confides, 'As a matter of fact, I played Crocker-Harris's wife.'

Not to be deflected, Sausage tells Dodie, 'You'd be better off having him on *Planet Venus* instead of that Brad.' An arch wink assures her that he remembers all the characters in her space drama.

'Wouldn't it rather spoil it, having a companion in the space ship whom Roxana likes? The dynamic of the thing depends on the fact that Brad and Roxana are at daggers drawn.'

It is one thing, apparently, for Sausage to show an interest in *Planet Venus*. Quite another for the star of the show to be a bore about it. Sausage starts brushing her shoulder with angry gestures of his palm. She has no scurf, but his harassed expression suggests that no amount of effort on his part will shift the dandruff.

He gratuitously inquires, 'What shampoo do you use?'

Darnley, I see, is on the verge of a schoolboy giggling attack.

'Yeremenko's no idiot. He's a bloody fine general for Christ's sake. So fine, Stalin nearly had him killed in the purges. But now it's November '41. The Germans are surrounding Stalingrad. Vatutin's come down from the north. And we're talking huge numbers here, many divisions . . . '

The Professor is still speaking as the stool on which he had been swaying, while he expounded Soviet military tactics, crashes to the floor.

I have recognized defeat, conversationally. My account of a school production of *Ralph Roister Doister* has petered out, and my mind is filling with unresolved questions.

Most of Professor Cormac's whisky splashes on to my sleeve as he hurtles to the floor. The champagne bottle on the bar, which falls over in the general mêlée, was empty anyway. No one is much the worse for wear as the Professor rights himself.

'Don't forget,' says Cormac, standing up, and perching himself once more on the stool, 'you've got Zukov's bloody Sixty-Second Army coming down to liberate the Stalingrad factory-workers.'

By the time Sausage has fished another bottle of bubbly out of the fridge, and we have all shaken ourselves down, Dodie and Darnley have made an exit, in quest, they declared, of steak and onions.

'Anyway, ponce, what you want to come in here for all dressed up?'

As a matter of fact, Sausage is not alone in being puzzled at Kit's 'smartness'. Normally clothed in whatever came to hand – most usually in a jumper and some baggy cords – this evening he has contrived a frayed but just about clean shirt, a striped tie (a college? a school? bought at a jumble sale or found at the bottom of a drawer?) and black shoes. These shoes, in particular, are rather 'good', made on a last, to measure, but not to measure Kit's feet. The suit does not quite fit either, but that in itself is fashionable nowadays, with the mobile phone brigade all wearing sleeves several inches too long and coats with gorilla-shoulders. This suit isn't from Armani, however; the Mencap shop more likely, or conceivably a hand-down from some elderly relation. Could Campbell Dilkes have been wearing it on the day of his arrest?

Perhaps I was not so intuitive at the time as to guess the ownership of this suit – it has since been confirmed to me by Leman; Kit is to wear it again at the party, a year after this story has come to an end, to celebrate two events: the birth of his first son, and the publication of *The Fairies of Staithe*. It is thickly chalky pinstripe on heavy woollen stuff. The waistcoat, too large for Kit, is buttoned high, leaving only a few inches of the school tie showing. Through a haze of champagne-breath, I survey Kit in this suit and I try to find words for his qualities. (Incidentally, have you ever noticed that, since the bubbles stir up acid stomach juices, champagne makes the breath

128

rank? Every word I utter for the next hour stinks, and it is unendurable to be within range either of Kit's mouth or of Sausage's. Hostesses should remember this before offering champagne to a roomful of people. The fruity mixture of wine and stomach-acid is three-quarters of the way to being the smell of vomit.) But I'm reflecting on Kit's – what is the word I am looking for? A housemaster would call it leadership quality and an Armani-suited executive with a mobile would call it organizational skill. It is much more mysterious than this, though – one is tempted to say that it is akin to magic. True, in some senses, Kit has organized this evening, urged me to come to the party at Dylans for the Day Muckley book, and chaperoned me to the Concord. On another level, however, he could not conceivably have organized the evening as it is destined to turn out. Without Kit, all its different strands would have remained inchoate. His quest for the Fairies of Staithe, his pursuit of his great-grandfather's ghost, are all being relentlessly advanced as he lolls beside the bar smiling.

In the mêlée caused by Cormac's temporary collapse, Kit has extricated his hand from the grasp of Sir Hubert and moved his bottom out of stroking-range. To break the monotony, Kit has told Hubie about his own book, his desire, not to whitewash his great-grandfather, but to resurrect him.

'It's a bloody good subject. Gem of a subject.' Hubie spits these sentiments at Kit through the barrier (as Homer would say) of his teeth, in his case false teeth. 'And you'd concentrate, you say, on the business with the fairies . . . '

Sausage's response to this question, too predictable to be written here, did not deflect Sir Hubert from his sentence.

' . . . and old Campbell Dilkes's vision. That's what we're talking about, isn't it? Visions. It was Tyrone Guthrie's company doing the *Dream* for Dilkes down at Staithe that year. I've bored your Aunt Victoria silly about it.' To keep me in my place, he turns to me and says 'Forgive me, dear boy, but I've known this boy's family a very long time – I go back for ever.'

'I knew you were old, dear, but I didn't think that even you could remember the young Tyrone Guthrie.' This little mincing remark of mine falls flat.

Kit prompts: 'And the appearance of the fairies had quite a bad effect, I gather – I mean on the actors.'

'Oh, completely split the company from top to bottom,' says Power. 'Even when I first went on the West End stage before the war – *just* before the war' – this is his only riposte to my suggestion that he might in fact be as old as the century.

Sausage, never averse to telling a girl her age, decides to rub it in.

'Just before the war? Just? Who's she think she's fucking kidding? Just before the Boer War more like, with Lottie Fucking Collins.'

'People were still talking about it' – in his desire to concentrate all his attention on Kit and to ignore our vulgar interruptions, the Knight Bachelor has allowed a slightly pompous tone to creep into his voice.

Sausage is singing, 'Ta-ra-da-boom-de-ay!'

'People still spoke of it. Oh, yes. You see, it wasn't just this one isolated vision of some fairies dancing about on the lawn. The poor old boy felt he'd seen a vision of England.'

Cormac on his high stool has rubbed the remaining droplets of whisky from his leather sleeve and Sausage has refilled his glass. One assumes he's still deep in the Siege of Stalingrad, so it is something of a surprise to discover that he has a word to throw in on the subject of the Staithe apparitions.

'It's very interesting that fairies were all so right-wing during the period – oh' – he wrinkles his nose as though one of us has been haggling about dates and he wants to strike a reasonable compromise. ' – well, let's be generous and say between 1870 and 1920.'

'Right-wing fairies?' The phrase is deeply suggestive to Sausage's imagination but no one heeds his predictable jokes about Nazi uniforms.

'Now, Yeats is a prime example – mad on fairies and an out-and-out fascist in politics. Kipling's no fascist – he's a British Imperialist, which is something quite different – though try explaining the difference to my moronic lecture-audiences at Oxford. But you find

Kipling turning aside from his tales of Indian civil servants and engineers and soldiers and tea-planters to write *Puck of Pook's Hill.* Which was written when? Turn of the century, let's say.'

'Even in my generation,' say I, 'we all had to learn Alfred Noyes's poem about Robin Hood; some of that seems pretty extreme if you remember the words in today's political climate –

> *Oaken-hearted England is waking as of old,*
> *With eyes of blither hazel and hair of brighter gold . . .*

All good Aryan stuff.'

'And when set to Campbell Dilkes's music,' says Kit.

'I never knew it was,' say I.

Kit tosses back his hair, closes his eyes and breathes out smoke through clenched teeth. This is what I have been trying to suggest about him, this capacity to influence or control in the Prospero or Oberon manner. Before we walked into the bar, Hubert Power, Sausage and Professor Cormac had nothing to say to one another. For the first quarter of an hour after our entrance, their talk had been a clatter of monologues in the country of the deaf. Suddenly we were all interested in Kit's great-grandfather.

'I can remember that song,' says Hubie. 'So Dilkes wrote the music, did he?'

'But that's the march,' says Cormac excitedly. 'I mean – the march! You know what I mean?' His eyes are aflame as Kit sings:

> *'The dead are coming back again, the years are roll'd away,*
> *In Sherwood, in Sherwood, about the break of day . . . !'*

Kit says, 'Perhaps you see why Dodie could not possibly have come with us for the next stage of our journey. Good thing your friend took her out to supper. What was his name? Darnley?'

'Yes, who was that extraordinarily rude man?' asks Hubie Power.

'My oldest friend,' I say.

Admittedly I have grown distinctly tipsy, but none of this

makes immediate sense to me. We had made several leaps – from the appearance of the Fairies of Staithe, to the departure of Dodie. Some explanatory connecting link between these two statements was needed. A sense that something 'creepy' is afoot feeds false signals to my brain and I assume – given present company, a natural assumption – that it is Dodie's gender which makes her an unsuitable companion for the next stage of our pilgrimage. Once again, Kit the magician. He has not forced Dodie and Darnley together. We cannot say – from the perspective from which I write this narrative which is years after the evening – that Kit was responsible for Darnley marrying Dodie. Kit, however, waved a wand.

> Fetch me that flower; the herb I show'd thee once.
> The juice of it on sleeping eyelids laid,
> Will make or man or woman madly dote
> Upon the next live creature that it sees.

Everyone says that Darnley is a changed man since his second marriage. I should certainly agree. I am godfather to Julian, their eldest son. That was just one of the many pieces of magic summoned out of that *Midwinter Night's Dream* of which I write, that comedy in which so many loose ends of the previous forty years were tied up with the neatness of a dramatist.

> And this was not I, but thou, oh unseen watcher!

The Professor says, 'You see, it really was that song. He might have written the music thinking of the Merry Men of Sherwood, but this was the song they were playing when some distinctly nasty individuals, very much not merry men, set out to march down Cable Street in October 1936. Now people talk a lot of rubbish about the Battle of Cable Street when strictly speaking there wasn't a battle at all.'

Hubie shudders and says, 'You wouldn't get me coming along to a thing like that.'

I understand him to refer to the Cable Street disturbance of half a century earlier, and indeed, it is hard to envisage Hubie, even when young, being drawn to the pleasures of fisticuffs.

Cormac is saying, 'I'm absolutely fascinated. Of course, if you are sure, I should love to come along with you both.'

''Course we are, aren't we, Julian? The more the merrier, eh?'

It would certainly seem very unfriendly to disagree, the more since I do not know what I am agreeing to.

I do know enough by this evening about the proposed book to realize that the title, *The Fairies of Staithe*, deliberately and whimsically belies a subject which alternates between tragedy, political seriousness and social farce, as well as much which was endearing about the late composer. It was always felt in the family (by which I mean the Lampitt family) that Campbell Dilkes's musical reputation had been clouded by his unwise political affiliations. It seemed extraordinary to think that this apparently gentle creature had died in prison. Vernon ('Ernie') Lampitt was too freely prepared to denounce as 'an absolute fascist' anyone with whom he happened to disagree, within or outside the Labour Party. He even used the word of Gaitskell who, in his view unaccountably, had been given the Shadow Chancellorship in preference to himself some time in the mid-1950s. When Vernon denounced his cousin by marriage Campbell Dilkes as a fascist, however, he was using the word in its simple sense. After 1936, the Dilkeses were scarcely on speaking terms with the Lampitts – hence the phrase 'poor dear Lavinia'. By describing her in this way, Uncle Roy gave the impression that Lavinia's marriage (touchingly happy, as Kit's book proves) was a terrible burden, and her husband's views (which in fact she not merely shared but in many areas overstepped) a source of pain to her.

No obvious political interest had dominated the musician's earlier life when studying at the Paris Conservatoire. Lavinia in later life said that Campbell's eyes had been 'opened' by the Dreyfus Affair, but, as Kit shows, the young Dilkes, like the majority of Englishmen at the time, had been shocked by the affair and his letters to

Hamilton Harty were distinctly Dreyfusard in flavour. Of later developments there was not the slightest discernible sign in the great central phase of Dilkes's career, the phase which produced *Surrey Rhapsody* – when Dilkes, with Cecil Sharp, enjoyed collecting English folk-songs and working their themes into his orchestral and chamber pieces (witness in particular the First Symphony, and the occasional music for *Twelfth Night*). True, the fairies appeared quite early on – in 1908 – and might be taken as a sign that Dilkes's mind was prepared to absorb what others would reject as garbage. It was not really until the First World War, however, and the death of his son Lionel at Ypres, that the great change came upon him.

While never formally abandoning the Anglo-Catholicism, Dilkes had started to become interested in the theories of the British Israelites, and to form the conviction that the so-called Lost Tribes had emigrated to Britain during the Bronze Age and taken up residence here. This idea, impossible to substantiate since it is by no means clear that there ever were any 'lost tribes', appeared to justify in Campbell's eyes an intemperate attitude to Jewish contemporaries, who were not in his eyes Jews at all. All the promises made by God in the Bible to the children of Israel had in fact been made to the British. The present 'Jews' were a group of sinister Bolshevik conspirators who had, by a series of ingenious plots, contrived, among other things, to start the Great War. They were therefore responsible, with their profiteering, and their arms-trading, and their gambling with international currencies, for the death of Campbell's beloved son Lionel. It goes without saying that these views were – to put it mildly – an embarrassment to Dilkes's Cordelia-like daughter. When she married Rudolf Amt, that charming businessman from Prague in 1938, she effectively banished herself from her father's house at Staithe – hence Victoria's American citizenship.

Momentarily, it seems as if Kit's lost his ability to make Hubie and Cormac dance to his tune. Hubie surprises me – he has been ignoring me all evening – and touches my arm.

134

'Don't count chickens, but I think we've got a film deal for *Dark Lady*.'

It is the last I ever heard of such an idea, which had, very possibly, only that moment occurred to him. I believe him, however. I want to ask him all about it. Already, I imagine myself rich, and able to purchase what I want more than anything else in the world – limitless leisure to write the present narrative. (I do not realize that in six months, Aunt Deirdre will be dead and that her only daughter Felicity will let me live rent-free in the bungalow at Binham.)

My head fills instantly with dreams. Myself as Shakespeare – at last, a famous actor, known to the world. Jason Grainger can be killed off! Hubie is saying something about not counting chickens, and the number of fucking film deals he has seen go up in smoke at the planning stage. He has no sooner whetted my appetite with this idea than he is telling us about the possibility that they are considering casting him in a big feature Sherlock Holmes film. Most of us are too polite to suggest that this notion – of an obese septuagenarian Holmes – has, at least, the advantage of originality.

Even Sausage contents himself with asking, 'Who would you play? Mrs Fucking Hudson, I suppose?'

'What I've said to the director of this film idea is that if *possible* – ' Hubie has reached that stage where he needs to overemphasize, for fear of slurring, his words ' – we should try to recapture that evening we all had at Staithe this summer. I *mean*. That theatre is just a little *darling*.'

He has taken Kit's elbow again, and is massaging it gently as he continues with his theatrical reminiscences.

'I can remember it, of course, since I am so fearfully old.' There is a pause, to allow everyone to contradict this assertion. Twitching with annoyance at our silence, Hubie lights up a Senior Service and continues. 'I can remember that production of *The Tempest* which they put on at Staithe during the last summer of the peace. It wasn't a very distinguished production if the truth is told. Just a little private thing.'

'Always talking about yourself' – Sausage seems proud of this *bon mot*. But he spoils it by adding, 'If your private thing is little, I'd keep quiet about it if I were you. It's what we'd all have guessed.'

'There was an old actor playing Prospero called Antony Highsmith' – the Knight Bachelor was too grand to answer all Sausage's taunts, and proceeded in a particularly orotund manner – 'a fucking dreadful Miranda, about three times too old and with a voice like a corncrake, Fenella something. Quite a lively little Ariel though.' He smiled as at some memory too precious to share. 'Ollie Pitman.'

'Whose real name . . . ' I began. But no one was interested in Ollie Pitman's real name.

'As you can imagine, though, the last act was very moving. Of course, we were all leftish in those days. Well, Ollie wasn't as a matter of fact, naughty little thing.' Hubie sniggers, and we must assume that he is momentarily remembering some example of right-wing bitchery which he is not going to repeat to us. 'Most theatre people were leftish, as they still are, but some people just have to be different.'

'I'm not sure I would be able to accept that,' says Cormac. He looks perfectly capable of delivering an impromptu lecture on 'The Political Sympathies of Actors, 1920–1950', with graphs and slides to prove his points.

The old ham's eyes, however, mistily recall the summer of '39 at Staithe.

'You know, it wasn't so much "Our revels now are ended", which was so moving. It was "Ye elves of hills" which brought tears to our eyes, and, as you probably know, darling Antony Highsmith was no great shakes. He had a terrible vibrato, just couldn't keep it out of his voice.'

Hubie now demonstrates:

'Ye – huh-huh – elves of huh-huh – hills . . .

'He was no good as Prospero; but there we all were, getting cold bums in this Norfolk garden; and we all somehow knew by then that something terrible was going to engulf us all; that some tremendous drama was facing us *all* – as a *nation*, I mean.'

'Kind Jesus, spare us,' asks Sausage.

Sir Hubert blubs slightly as he lights up another cigarette.

'We were there the day that war was declared,' he sniffs.

'The Day God Pulled the Plug out,' I say.

'What? Who called it that?'

'It doesn't matter,' I say. 'It just happens I was on holiday that day not far from Staithe – nearer Mallington – with my parents.'

I have no desire to interrupt Hubie's narrative. It is entirely involuntary, this recollection of that strange day. Mummy and Daddy and me, and Granny and Mrs Webb, waiting on the dunes for the rectory party to come over from Timplingham for picnic lunch. The hunger of Granny and Mrs Webb getting the better of them and their making inroads into the sandwiches before Aunt Deirdre, cross Sea Scout, and Fliss, about twelve in age, came stomping towards us over the sand with their much more austere repast. And where was Uncle Roy, on this day of days? He could not come. Sargie was very much upset. And why was Sargie so unhappy? The world was at war. Staring across the huge empty beach to the sea which was now a mile or more away, I had asked whether God had pulled out the plug. Certainly, for the time being God would seem to have left his creation to its own violent devices. The train of recollection makes my own eyes misty.

But Hubert Power understands my words quite differently. Throughout the summer, with the firm insistence of the *arriviste*, he has been anxious to remind me that he has known Victoria's family 'for ever'. He now peers at me with a momentary glance in which I read anger and fear in almost equal measures.

Has he got me wrong? That is what his expression seems to say. Were my parents on dining terms with old Campbell Dilkes?

'So they were at that *Tempest*, your parents? You were staying at Mallington? At Mallington Hall?'

His tone very much implies that this was information which I should have confessed at the beginning of the summer.

'No, no. They just happened to have taken a cottage about ten miles away from Staithe. I was four years old at the time, and I didn't see *The Tempest*.'

One might presume that the colloquialism 'to look down one's nose' at another person were purely figurative. Hubie, however, now demonstrates that, by pursing the lips, tilting the head slightly backwards and half closing the eyes, it is possible to give the illusion that the object of scorn is surveyed down the lane of one's mottled old nose. He clearly considers that he has well and truly 'seen off' my impertinent claim to have been in Norfolk when he was taking part in the last *Tempest* of the Peace.

'You see, it was when Prospero said:

> *this rough magic*
> *I here abjure; and when I have requir'd*
> *Some heavenly music – which even now I do –*
> *To work mine end upon their senses that*
> *This airy charm is for, I'll break my staff . . .*

I don't know. It was bloody moving. And of course we did all think of the old boy.'

Cormac, feeling the historian had a duty to enter a correction, splutters, 'No, Churchill was completely out of it by '39. It's in '40 that you get . . . '

'Dilkes,' says Hubie superfluously. 'There he was. It was his show. I'm not saying the last production was on the very day war broke out; but you see the rough magic was only about to start.'

We did not listen to Sausage's 'rough-trade' barrage.

After a lifetime of being a not very good actor myself, I've noticed the tendency of actors to wrench your words wildly out of context and demonstrate that though they have repeated them night after night on stage, they have apparently not understood what they meant. Did this happen in your day? Is that part of the joke in Hamlet's injunctions to the players? The idea that 'rough magic' could be applied to the Second World War or that 'rough' in this context meant violent as in 'nasty rough boys' beggared belief.

'Of course,' says the great Knight of the Theatre, 'if we had known. I mean, if we had known the extent . . . we shouldn't have been there! I mean, there he was, this dear old boy in a Norfolk jacket and knickerbockers, collecting his Old English folk-songs: and all the time he was a Nazi!'

'It would seem', says Cormac 'as if you don't understand the position of a man like Campbell Dilkes at all. He was no more a Nazi than you or I might have been.'

'As I say, we were all on the left,' whimpers Sir Hubert.

'That's supposed to be a good thing?' spits Cormac contemptuously.

Kit says, 'No, Hubie, about this matter, the Professor is right. Campbell did not want the war to come; but when it did, he certainly did not want the Germans to win it. The First World War had broken his heart. You can imagine his feelings about the Second. But the idea of him as a traitor is simply grotesque.'

Not one but two scrawny hands now reach out from Hubie's sleeves to grasp Kit's wrists.

'You weren't born, dear. You weren't *even born*. You can't remember. Oh, when I think what Londoners went through in the Blitz. Their sheer bloody pluck. But *listen*. I could tell you so much about that production of *The Tempest* and it really is rather important. You wouldn't . . . ' His voice sinks. Furtive eyes look from left to right. He would have liked to say these words out of earshot, but he knows that Kit is about to leave the Concord, and so he has to speak now. ' . . . you wouldn't like to continue this discussion later this evening, would you, my dear?'

'Lay off, will you, fucking poof!' It is about three minutes since Sausage shouted anything, and the sight of the old man's hands on Kit's sleeve provokes an explosion. 'We leave that sort of thing to the fucking bedroom.' Allowing this information to sink in, Sergeant Sausage pauses. Could it be that he feels he has gone too far? Surely he never thinks that? No! He has been seized with a thought, rather as Socrates, or his predecessors in the Athenian schools, were sometimes possessed by the divine *afflatus*. He certainly looks as if he is going to say something original, so it is a disappointment to watch him fill his lungs and bellow, 'What people do in their own fucking bedrooms is up to them.'

When I was Kit's age, I'd have run a mile had an old man like Hubie suggested a late-evening assignation. But Kit just smiles and says, 'Sure, Hubie. Where will you be? Here? Julian and I, you see, are off to this slightly crazy old get-together.'

'We are?' I say.

'It shouldn't take long. I reckon we'd get the flavour in an hour and then we could all meet up again . . . '

'Where are we going?' I ask.

'We're going to a little fascist reunion,' says Kit with the sweetest of smiles.

Sausage screams.

It looks possibly as if his nose will explode; not a happy thought.

'I wrote to them,' Kit says. 'I was surprised that there are still enough of them around to hold a reunion, but I'd heard of this old boy who vaguely knew Campbell. They wrote back, tremendously chuffed that a member of Campbell's family was at last showing a bit of interest.'

Sausage is laughing uncontrollably.

'They very kindly asked me to the supper, but I thought it was a bit early. They start eating at seven o'clock and one never knows what one might be doing at that hour, with the wretched *Diary* and so on. So, I asked if I could blow in for drinks afterwards.'

Professor Cormac has elected to join our group.

'So they'd be, what?' he is saying. 'Not your young thugs – not the National Front?'

'Rather old thugs if they are friends of Campbell's,' says Kit.

'They're all the same horrible lot of people,' says Hubert, provoking a well-informed disquisition from the Professor.

'You see, all these little neo-Nazi groups like the Front are Little

Englanders,' says Cormac, 'whereas the Mosleyite vision was always pan-European.'

'With Hitler at the top of the fucking pan,' says Sausage.

Kit speaks as if the most pressing matter of concern to himself had been, not the doctrinal, but the sartorial question – the matter raised by Sausage when we had first entered the bar.

'I thought a suit, anyway. A sense of occasion.'

And Kit shows a row of teeth.

It is a long time since I subscribed to any political views; and I am fond of Kit. Nevertheless, it is hard to avoid sensations of extreme distaste; I feel trapped, quietly angry. He promised me a pub crawl, and he has dragooned me into something altogether nastier.

'Did you warn Victoria that you were going to attend this rally?'

'Look.' He smiles so gently. 'It's not a rally. It's a reunion in a pub – OK?'

'Should you have time to fit me in later,' says Hubie, 'I generally look in before closing time at a pub near Marble Arch. It's called the Duke of Leeds.'

'Pacemaker's Arms more fucking like.'

Sausage's words stir flickers of memory. The Pacemaker's Arms. Years ago, staying at Virgil D. Everett's palatial Gothic residence in Connecticut, shortly before my 'breakdown', I ran into Ol Pitman – the man who, we now learned, had played Ariel in that last pre-war production of *The Tempest* at Staithe. He murmured darkly to me of this pub, nicknamed the Pacemaker's Arms. He hinted that Virgil D. Everett, the financier and collector who had bought the Lampitt Papers and entrusted Raphael Hunter with the task of looking after them, had made a point of visiting this hostelry whenever he was in London. John – Mr Everett's slightly sinister butler – had first met his employer in the Saloon Bar there.

The Pacemaker's Arms. Even when I was only in my mid-thirties, and in full possession of my wits, it had struck me, on first hearing the sobriquet, that this was something more than a camp joke. It was not a place to which I had ever felt drawn, but as the years passed, the phrase had lodged itself in my brain, not so much as a pub but as an idea: the fairly obvious one that human passion does not cease when the body starts to decay. 'The Pacemaker's Arms', as an inner conceit, rather than as an actual building never visited, became an emblem – one thought of Hardy's poem about his 'fragile frame at eve' being shaken with 'throbbings of noontide', and realized that, though wisdom, dignity and detachment were to be hoped for, as life tottered to its close, the heart would still continue to play havoc and cause pain – even a heart which required the mechanical assistance of a pacemaker to keep ticking at all.

For some reason – as Sausage shouts, 'All the old faggots go to the Pacemaker's!' – I find myself paying. Not just for our two bottles of champagne, but for lots of other drinks as well. The four card-players by the fireplace wave their gratitude to me, and Sausage pours me a generous Smirnoff on the rocks as I write a cheque. My signature is not quite as usual. It swoops at a diagonal across the dotted line of the little blue rectangle.

'It's not everyone I'd trust to write a cheque,' says Sausage. 'But Jason Grainger – well!'

And he sings the melody from *The Surrey Rhapsody*.

But now the three of us, Kit and Cormac and I, are lurching taxibound eastwards to the murkier environs of King's Cross.

Kit told me at a later date that the White Hart, Stamp Street, a pub which crouched opposite some joyless Victorian tenements south of Argyle Square, had no historical connections with the Mosleyite cause. The venue had been chosen by the faithful merely because the board outside the Saloon advertised – in addition to Hot and Cold Meals, Beers and Spirits – 'Private Functions, Details on Request'.

142

From the look of the building outside, it is safe to assume that the room hired out for parties is not expensive. Kit's smile convinces me that my obvious discomfiture causes him pleasure. Certainly, the potential for embarrassment in what lies ahead is increased by Cormac's apparently inexhaustible interest in it all. During the taxi journey he talks unceasingly about those imprisoned during the Second World War under the 18B regulation. A little heavily, Cormac emphasizes that the suspension of Habeas Corpus was a terrible mistake; an unwarrantable breach of civil liberty, precisely the sort of tyranny to which the Allies, in their war effort, were opposed. He speaks of Jewish refugees from Hitler whose papers had not been in order and who were still officially German citizens, being sent to spend the war in internment camps on the Isle of Man. They were '18Bs'. Professor Cormac opines that very few of the British-born 18Bs were spies, nor did they in his view pose the smallest threat to national security. Kit enthusiastically agrees with him. Lurching about in the taxi is not the moment to remonstrate.

I understand Kit's desire to put the record straight as far as his great-grandfather is concerned, but it is hard to see Campbell Dilkes or his fellow-fascists as victims, pure and simple. Kit shows no sense that rash or even unjust things do sometimes of necessity get done in times of war; that we might deem these people 'harmless' when viewed with hindsight, but that, in the light of the manner in which some of the extreme Right conducted themselves in England during the '30s, it was hardly surprising, once war broke out, that public panic (even if it was unreasonable) should have required assuagement. For that reason, the 18Bs were locked up. But as the two men talk in the taxi, I say nothing. I am slightly drunk, aware that it is one of those occasions, mercifully rare, when, if one spoke, one might lose one's temper, say things one did not mean, or, much worse, things one did.

They came for Campbell Dilkes some time in the spring of 1940.

Ever since living at Staithe – from the mid-1970s onwards – I had been puzzled by a graffito painted on the wall opposite the village war memorial. It is a patch of wall belonging to the estate, conspicuous for the fact that the flint-knapped surface, on which it would have been impossible to daub symbols or words, momentarily gives place to red brick. It is a symbol, rather than a word, which has been painted there – a circle of black paint which encloses a lightning flash not unlike the logo for the modern British Rail. Visually unobservant, politically ignorant, I must have walked or driven past this device on the wall a hundred times before anyone hinted its significance.

Some said that 'Squire', as older villagers still called Campbell Dilkes, had painted the symbol with his own hands. Others believed it had been the work of someone in the village. For thirty years I'd known about Campbell Dilkes as a composer of whom his in-laws disapproved. I'd never known why, and this graffito was the first indication to me. I knew he had been in prison, but Victoria had never told me why, and – assuming, this being England, that it was either a contretemps with the tax authorities or some undignified little offence in a park – I had not liked to ask. When the odd and somehow unpalatable truth began to dawn that Campbell and 'poor dear Lavinia' had been out-and-out blackshirts, I assumed that this fact would be regarded as a local disgrace, something of which the sturdy village folk would have disapproved. Here again, I was wrong. Dilkes's family blushed for his 'views'. The village of Staithe, however, was a blackshirt stronghold; far more locals shared, than deplored, the composer's political convictions. It was no accident that, when almost forty years had passed, that defiant symbol (whether painted by the composer's hand or no) was still to be seen so clearly on the brickwork. (Even now, sixty years on, when I write these words, it is clear and distinct, prompting me to wonder whether there is not, in Staithe, some Old Mortality, who has, in the intervening decades, touched up the lightning flash lest succeeding generations should forget the Good Old Cause.)

Kit persuaded an old man in the village called Sid Shepherd – he was an electrician who lived in the council estate at the top end of the village, as far as possible from the sea – to recollect Squire's last months at Staithe.

There had been an incident at the war memorial. On the first Armistice Day of the war, with the vicar and the leader of the parish council in attendance, the village had turned out to honour the dead of the previous war. An unusually high proportion of the assembly were strangers – men who did not come from Staithe or its surrounding farms. Shepherd believed that the fascist emblem, painted directly opposite the memorial cross where the British Legion were to lay their wreath, had been daubed specially, on the eve of Armistice Day. First a Major ('They do say he came from Swaffham,' Sid told the tape-recorder disapprovingly; his voice hinted that this choice of residence could hardly have been more decadent or frivolous if it had been Las Vegas or Monte Carlo) laid a wreath for the Armed Forces. Then the vicar. Finally, Squire, whose son Lionel's is the first name inscribed on the war memorial.

It was Lavinia, apparently, as her elderly husband stood to attention having laid his wreath, who was the first to raise her right arm in solemn salute. Spontaneously, some of the villagers did the same, followed by two or three old soldiers. Others, however, protested. The scuffle which ensued was hardly in the same league as some of the more spectacular fisticuffs laid on by the Movement in the East End of London before the war, but someone got a black eye, and Constable Larkin's helmet was knocked off.

The next day, Squire received a visit from the village constable and a 'caution', though more properly speaking it was Lavinia, if anyone, who had instigated the minor affray. The authorities thereafter left the Dilkeses alone for several months and it was supposed that nothing would 'come' of the incident.

They came to arrest Dilkes, however, one bright spring morning some four months later. Sid Shepherd had witnessed it.

'Squire was always up with the lark, you might say. And he was, funnily enough, waiting for me, 'cause in those days the wiring in the Hall was, shall we say, prehistoric?' A good laugh. 'There was fuel shortages by then and Squire was wondering whether they shouldn't revert to oil lamps and candles up at the Hall, which they always did 'ave the first, oh, twenty years he and Mrs Dilkes was there. Anyhow. Squire had hit on the idea that electricity were a thing of the past. After the war was over, we'd've used up all our supplies and the future were all going to be gas. So he believed.'

The electrician's voice was completely reverent as he recalled this misjudgement, as though Squire's view had been a perfectly sensible one.

'So I'd been asked up to the Hall to see what chance there'd be of converting all the electrical light-fittings over to gas, see, and I was trying to persuade Squire.' More laughter. 'Well, it couldn't really be done, see.'

One thought at first, as one listened, that Sid Shepherd meant that it was impossible to convert these particular electrical appliances to use by gas. Perhaps this was what he did mean, but one got the sense that it would be as easy to make gas pass through wire as it would to make Campbell Dilkes change his mind once it had been resolved.

'So I'm in the study and funnily enough, he's at the piano, sitting there. Would you know what I mean when I say he had a very florid style? It weren't like the marches, oh no, much more – well, florid is all the way I can describe the noise of that piano. It filled the house, that lovely noise he were making, and Mrs

146

Dilkes is coming down the stairs for her coffee, which you can smell; quite a rarity in those days and I'll always remember that, the smell of coffee coming through from the morning room where they had their breakfast and the door-bell ringing and my going. I suppose there weren't many staff left up in the Hall, though Phyllis was always there, and I remember she were going to make me a breakfast of fresh eggs which was why I'd gone to work so early that day. And I opens the door and in the drive there's two vans and on the lawn there's, like, a great mob of policemen, come over from Norwich, oh, twenty, thirty men I should say; and they come running through the door and into all the rooms of the Hall as though they were looking for a murderer. And Squire comes out, he's stopped his playing, and he stands there, bewildered like. And he says to the senior officer, "My son died for his country." Quite simple. "And I'd die for my country." But they're rummaging here and there, and Mrs Dilkes, she's telling them not to muddle all Squire's papers, 'cause they've got drawers and cupboards open, and they're taking away great armfuls of the stuff – Squire's music – just his music and his diaries, and that. You never saw such a thing. And Phyllis is crying, and Mrs Dilkes, she just stands there stiff as a board. And Squire kisses her and says, "I'll be back soon" – ever so gentle. But I do wonder whether he didn't have a very minor stroke there and then that day. Well, they took him to Norwich and put him in the prison there for a couple of months. And he weren't a well man even then, before they transfer him to the Scrubs. And Mrs Dilkes kept visiting him – she went up to live in London, and they do say she wrote letter after letter to the Home Secretary, nearly drove herself mad writing letters all the while. But he died in the Scrubs, of course, the next winter. Pneumonia.'

Misgivings about the next phase of the evening are not wholly attributable on my part to political prejudice. I've always had a horror of the gas-lit back-street mission hall where nine or ten initiates meet to share the true meaning (denied to the rest of the human race) of the Book of Ezekiel; or the smudged, hand-printed pamphlet thrust into your hand in the middle of a shopping arcade, announcing that eating meat causes wars. The anarchist cranks in *The Man Who Was Thursday* are fun to read about but best, for my taste, kept within the covers of a book. Likewise, seven-page communications, on lined paper, perhaps written in block capitals, sent occasionally to any person in the public eye, however obscure (even an actor on 'The Mulberrys') fail to convince me that all the ills at present besetting British society are attributable to the preponderance of Jews in the House of Lords, or the fact that the Royal Family are all Freemasons. Darnley has always had a fascination with the dingy hinterland in which such views are nurtured. Albion Pugh, with his home-brewed mysticism and his conspiracy theories, used to make me feel as if slugs were crawling up and down my spine.

Cormac is spitting out – literally– the old saw about hating the words you say but defending to the death your right to say them. My feelings, less politically mature, no doubt, begin and end with cringing embarrassment.

But there is another fear, baser and more immediate, which strikes as soon as Kit pushes open the glass door marked SALOON. Within a couple of seconds we have sized up the clientele of the White Hart. For anyone my age or older, the political sympathies to which Campbell Dilkes had felt drawn were synonymous with violence: young Reds having punch-ups with Blackshirts, bricks

148

lobbed through the windows of small bespoke tailors in Whitechapel, ugly words daubed on synagogue walls, makeshift weapons – a splintered plank perforated with six-inch nails and used to scar an opponent's skull. The two or three young men at the pool table in the White Hart, shaven-headed, heavy-necked, acned, would not have much difficulty in bloodying my face with a broken lager-glass should the fancy seize them. In one corner of the saloon, two leather-coated scruffs loll by a bleeping gambling-machine. A mindless thump, thump of pop music blares from the speakers over the bar.

The first mental snapshot, however, is more alarming than the impressions which sink in as we cross the frayed floral carpet to the bar. A stale stench hovers in the air, an atmosphere of old beer, the smoke of cigarettes, the vaguely disinfectant aroma which, with a howling draught, blows from a door marked GENTLEMEN through which an old Irishman is shuffling, and the 'pub grub', the lethal-looking remains of a large, orange meat pie which congeals beneath some bright lights and a perspex cover at the far end of the bar.

Fear has made me look for Nazi thugs at every corner of the joint, but when the barmaid (swabsy, Aunt Deirdre would call her), in her pale grey sweatshirt and her bulging baggy denims, gives a bad-teeth grin and asks, 'Right folks, what can I get you?' I have already decided that we have come to the wrong pub. There must be as many White Harts in London as there are Red Lions, King's Armses, Coaches and Horses. Before Kit has time to make his inquiry, however, embarrassment flushes back. I order a large vodka. Cormac, in no mood to consider the possibility that this drink is meant for anyone other than himself, asks me to make that a whisky and I, anxious to convey that we had only come to that pub for a drink, and that we had no special interest in any neo-nationalist side-shows, hastily allow her to make that two large Bell's, even though I suspect this isn't going to mix very well with what I have already had to drink this evening – the large vodka while I paid Sausage's bill, the two or three glasses of champagne, and the plonk at Dylans. I still feel cringing embarrassment as Kit smiles at her and flutters his eyelashes. If he were about to inquire about the possibility of an erotic floor-show, I could not feel more achingly sheepish.

'Is Mr Smethurst's party here?' he asks sweetly.

Obviously forewarned, Swabsy leans forward. She asks, 'You're not journalists?'

'Lord no,' says the freelance from *Londoner's Diary*.

'Are you Mr Mayfield?' she asks.

Gulping my Bell's, I say, 'Kit, before we go in – better go and . . . '

Spattering against the rank urinal and watching the remains of the day collect around the freshener at the drain – it is one of those curious circular objects the consistency of Kendal mint cakes or mothballs which emit a pungent odour, peculiarly nauseating when mixed with urine – I attempt to assess my level of inebriation. Nothing is actually swaying about yet. My vision remains reasonably clear. There being no mirror on the wall, I try to squint at the end of my nose, which is usually a palish pink, but which tends to go green if I am in any danger of throwing up. The nose I see is scarlet. I shall probably be OK if I take the next hour steadily.

But I very much don't want the next hour to happen. Would it be too churlish to sit it out with the lager-louts in the bar while Kit and Cormac hobnob with the fascists? I can't quite bring myself to propose such an arrangement, so I ask them to wait for me while I make a telephone call.

'So! Julian! What are you doing? You sound drunk.'

'Leman, I . . . I'm not drunk. I just want . . . '

I want . . . to hear that clear bell-like voice ringing from the purity of North Norfolk, down the wires, and into this sordid place. I want Leman's goodness to redeem all my bitterness, and her dear love to redeem all the fascists' hate? No, this is drink swirling round in my head; even by my own mawkish standards, such feelings cannot qualify as thoughts. But, as I stand by the phone, and listen to Leman's voice, half-thoughts half-form themselves in my brain about the question of How to Love, or, rather, How I Wish to Live the Last Portion of Life on this earth. Hitherto, ever since I lost Mummy, love for me has been synonymous with possession; and I no longer want this. My love for Leman is like the love of a Catholic for a saint; I just want to know that she is there, but I do not want to invade her life. A time will come, I know, when I shall not even have her as a constant companion. (I do not know how soon this is to be.) I feel (perhaps I write this with hindsight) that this moment by the telephone, listening to Leman's voice, is the beginning of a New Life, akin to a religious conversion. I want, henceforth, to lead an unselfish life. It is as simple a wish as that. I want to live without attachments, and without dragging others into attachments. I want to be abstemious, sober, non-smoking, simple in my tastes. The long evenings will be devoted to reading, the days to walks and simple domestic pursuits. And I shall write this book, this story of the Lampitt Papers, this petty-bourgeois, English, late-twentieth-century recovery of Lost Time. Twice a week, when Jason Grainger is required, I shall journey to Birmingham by train and do rehearsals and recordings for 'The Mulberrys'. I value – need – the money; and to give up being Jason Grainger would be an act of pride. I wish from now on to be a sort of monk-in-the-world, like Alyosha Karamazov at the beginning of that novel; only this life of renunciation will be a secret from everyone. There will be no show-off 'profession', as if I were entering a monastery; simply a quiet decision to learn, in secrecy, how to be wise, how to be good. And in a way which at the moment I am slightly too fuddled to be able to understand, Leman, and my love of her sweet boy-face, is all part of this.

'Julian! Are you still there?'

'I am.'

'Are you both being very naughty, you and Kit?'

'I'm trying to keep him under control.'

'It doesn't sound as if you are being very successful. The music in the background sounds so loud.'

'It's so loud I can hardly hear you.'

'Kit's told you the news – our news?'

And then the money runs out.

'Come on,' says Kit when I rejoin them. 'We really ought to be going in.'

In the back room set aside for the purpose, a trestle table, paper-covered, shows the remains of – not even a school dinner, but an institutional meal of the cheapest kind. Half an hour ago, painfully hungry, I should have been tempted by the sight of the half grapefruits (most people had 'left' their cocktail cherries) and the uneaten slithers of meat, *rechauffés* in caterers' gravy.

Mr Smethurst, in his mid-sixties, is slightly Bohemian in appearance. Why am I surprised? It isn't that I expected the diners to be wearing uniform; but then, nor had I expected Mr Smethurst to resemble a dishevelled modern languages master at one of the more relaxed boarding-schools. Thinning grey hair sweeps back from a wrinkled brow, a packet of Gauloises is clutched in a brown hand. He wears a check shirt, a navy-blue knotted tie and a suit which Uncle Roy would have considered too pale for the evening. His bonhomie, enlivened by a smiling jumpiness, seems entirely natural and unforced.

'Some of us are having a beer, or there's this awful wine.' He holds up the glass of red which is clearly his preference.

Much more surprising than his appearance is the fact that Mr Smethurst and I have met before.

Venice, ten years ago. A February. He appeared at that dinner of the Usignuoli. An Italian wife? That Venetian visit, undertaken to 'get over' a divorce, was another of those occasions when the strands of existence, so disparate that one would have supposed no comic master could draw them together, were found to be entwined. Childhood and adolescent acquaintances, a future life-companion, and the ubiquitous Raphael Hunter, had all been partners in that particular quadrille.

The stout woman who stood before me in the gallery – sixtyish, impeccable in black – had hardly aged at all in the twenty-five years since I had last seen her. I had been looking at pictures, nothing special, just saints and virgins by the score, relieved by the occasional Hercules. It was all School Of, this gallery. The great masters were absent; no matter; I was not here to see them, merely to kill time. And then, there she was, this stylish, not-quite-old woman.

I merely knew that she was someone from the past, though from which of the compartments in the past she had arbitrarily stepped, memory doggedly refused to reveal. She was too smart to belong to any of my recent years in London. She wasn't a friend of Sonya, thank God! (Sonya was the wife in this divorce; she plays no part in this story.) No broadcaster, no journalist, no actress or politician of my acquaintance was quite so – so – to say so well *turned-out* would have implied dressiness, and this lady was perfectly at ease in her well-cut clothes. The plain black coat, the boots, the white silk scarf and gold ear-rings were all simple but, as worn by her, they had a certain grandeur. My mind was beginning to place her. Was she the parent of some schoolfriend who had once entertained me? No. Her French tones gave it to me.

'Julien!'

'Madame!'

This was the daughter of Madame de Normandin, the old lady in France with whom I spent a memorable holiday in my teens. She and her mother must, over the years, have taken a hundred summer paying-guests, so I was impressed, very, by her being able to recollect my name.

153

Madame de Normandin's method of teaching French conversation to her young English and American visitors was to keep up a flow of consecutive translation of any phrases which might cause difficulty. Her daughter (whose name still eluded me) pursued the same course now, wishing, evidently, neither to insult me by talking English, nor to risk the possibility, in the quarter-century since I stayed at Les Mouettes, that I had forgotten all my French.

'*Tout le monde arrivent enfin à Venise*, everyone comes to Venice in the end,' she announced rapidly. '*Et vous, Julien, vous aimiez toujours la solitude.*'

The fact that she remembered my name presumably meant that she remembered Barbara at the beach hut. At sixteen, I had imagined that I was being so discreet; but 'it' is presumably always obvious to adult observers.

'*C'est tout à fait dans la note que vous choisiez le février pour votre visite.* You always liked to be alone.'

True, my visit to Les Mouettes had been marred by a painful shyness, at least in the company of my coevals, the Birks. To spare Madame – what *was* she called? – the trouble of providing more conversational subtitles I replied in rusty French, and it was in this language that the conversation creaked along. She soon jogged my memory by saying that she was no longer called Madame d'Alifort. Three years earlier, she had become Signora Usignuoli.

'Yes, indeed, I am now a Venetian.'

'And your mother?'

I spoke as gently as I could. When I had been her guest at Les Mouettes, Madame de Normandin had seemed to teenage eyes unimaginably antique; I could only assume that she had long since died. Her clever daughter, catching the needless sympathy in my tones, said, 'No, no. She is still alive. In some ways better than ever. She had her cataracts removed last year. Now she sees better than she has done for years. She is ninety-six; and she is here. In Venice, for a few months. She would, I know, love to see you. She feels cut off from old friends.'

154

'I should love to see her.'

'Normally, she lives still at Les Mouettes, but her maid needed a holiday and Maman decided that she would like to see Venice again. There is not, alas, much to see just now!'

From where we had placed ourselves, at a window of the Ca' d'Oro, it was barely possible to see across the Grand Canal. The thick fog which had crept across the lagoon the previous night had shown no sign of lifting all day.

'What brings you to Venice, Julien?'

'Oh,' I laughed, 'my unsociable temperament. As you rightly conjectured, I thought it would be empty. Not', I added clumsily, 'that it isn't the greatest pleasure to see you, Signora. Truly.'

'Perhaps you would prefer to be left in peace, or could you bear to dine with us? We get lonely here in the winters when Venice empties.'

'I thought you had a carnival?'

She noiselessly threw up her hands in horror.

' . . . but I should love to see your mother again. Love to.'

This sentence was true. If I could have seen Madame de Normandin over a cup of coffee and have avoided the ritual of dinner, I should have been satisfied. I was, however, palpably at a loose end and it was difficult to conjure up an excuse to get out of the dinner. Besides, one has to eat, and in Venice the only thing which palls is the restaurant food. After a mere three or four days I was tired of little bits of fried fish. The chance of a decent meal was inviting. I told her the name of my *pensione* and she promised to leave directions there of her address.

'One never tires of looking at things. I am still a tourist after three years. I see as much of Venice as I can each winter. When the crowds become too intense in the summer months, we go to Les Mouettes.'

We parted amicably. I heard her well-made shoes clunk along the marbly *sala* and down the grand staircase. The encounter had lifted my spirits. Because, or although (I wasn't sure which), so much of the recent past was painful to contemplate, it was good to be reminded of a time of innocence when the worst agony I could suffer was not knowing how to exchange banter with those spotty, open-hearted Americans with whom Madame de Normandin delighted to fill her house in the summer months a quarter of a century before.

My answer to Signora Usignuoli's question – what brought me to Venice? – was simple: failure. Failure to sustain a relationship with a woman. Failure to rid myself of my obsession with my mother and my mother's death when I was a child. Failure of a second marriage. Failure of a career. (But at least I could do something about that! I was only forty, and when I got home I really was going to kill off Jason Grainger and leave 'The Mulberrys'.) Failure of a life.

Not having wished to admit any of this to myself, still less to the Signora, I honestly don't believe it was just morbidity which led me back to the place where I'd spent my honeymoon with Sonya. It was not a desire to pick at old wounds. I was nothing but wounds at that period. I'd had a breakdown; a spell, quite a long spell, in a mental hospital. Then I'd gone through the process of rehabilitation. I'd met, and married, Sonya, and thought that was going to be a way of liberating myself from my old unhappiness, from mental illness, and grief, and the unrequited, miserable love I felt for Margaret Mary Nolan. We're never more greedy, never more destructive, than in 'love'; I had appointed Sonya as the cure-all for these sorrows; no wonder she, who wanted a husband, not a patient, had not been able to endure it for more than a year.

Now of course, as I sit in the bungalow in Binham, having achieved, at sixty-something, a serenity which my younger self would not have dreamed possible, it is hard to recapture the pain of that particular period. I must have been fairly miserable. The lawyers had done their work. The decree nisi had come through. I had wanted to get out of London, and go to a place which was utterly different and yet familiar. I'm not well travelled. It was natural to choose Venice, denuded of its tourists.

'By Christ, I wish you'd join the human race!' Sonya had

shrieked at me once, provoking what I can now see must have been an infuriating silence. She had come up close to me and bellowed it in my ears. 'The human race! You should try joining it some time! See how it feels.'

I'd learnt not to allude to menstruation on such occasions, since it made her scream even more.

I just murmured weakly, 'Not really my thing.'

This had made her scream just as much as if I'd attributed her mood to the cycle of the moon. And who should blame her?

The human race still seemed at this date like an exclusive but coarse-grained club to which I had no aspirations to affiliate myself. As it were, a golf club. Hunter, now. He seemed effortlessly at ease with the club members. Not only was he the welcome guest in so many houses, and the lover for whom otherwise sane women had gone crazy (there were plenty of stories of them leaving happy homes and begging Hunter, pleading with him); but he was also the chronicler who was believed by his readers to know about this human life business, with all the assurance of an expert.

Hunter was also at home in the world of 'men' and adept in his own curious fashion at the exercise of power. Not merely had he lived (the dinners, the mistresses, the tearstained partings at airports, the faraway look, in after-years, which came into the eyes of women when his name was mentioned, as it often was) but he would seem to have cracked the secret of how others lived. Or, so believed those who had devoured the newspaper serializations and extracts from his inordinately long biographies – first of James Petworth Lampitt, and then of Virgil D. Everett – which established Hunter not just as the most impeccable of liberals but also a fearlessly butch investigative writer, at home not just in the rarified atmosphere of Edwardian London (which he had 'exposed' in the Lampitt book) but also in the tough world of mid-twentieth century American politics and finance. The quality of the prose, or even the truthfulness of what it contained, did not, for these purposes, matter. Hunter was established as, among many other things, a 'writer'.

Here again, how unlike me. My literary career had been stillborn. In my twenties I had published a novel, which had felt, at the time of writing, like the most hilarious account of a sensitive boy's upbringing in an English vicarage.

'Your uncle was hurt,' had been Aunt Deirdre's cross little judgement of the book. 'It was so unnecessary to make the little dog like Tinker. Let's hope no one in the village reads it.'

This had been my only endeavour in the field of prose fiction. My aunt was right, really. *The Vicar's Nephew* cheapened me; it failed, as a book, precisely because it was not quite true enough. The crude caricatures which it contained of my uncle and aunt and their dog were only sufficiently like to cause offence to my relations, but conveyed nothing of their innerness, their dignity, their quiet sadnesses. The stuff which you hint at with even the most minor characters in the plays; the stuff inside any of us which allows us (and rightly, even if we are just jokes as far as the rest of the world is concerned) to take ourselves seriously – just sometimes. All I'd done in my novel was to excise this vital part and to parade my harmless uncle and aunt as comic cuts. Like so many bad things I have done, it was completely pointless.

'Let's hope it all blows over and people in the village forget about it.'

My aunt always had a horror of exhibitionism. In this, as in so many other areas, she showed a devastating shrewdness. My novel did indeed blow over. Whether or not people in the village knew about it, I don't know, though one of them – That Wretched Woman as my aunt called her – read it and was kind. Dear Debbie. 'The auntie in your book is wickedly accurate,' she had cackled, that night she and Day Muckley first took me out to supper.

It slightly surprised me that even a fellow-novelist should see works of fiction merely as a quarry for spotting the true-life originals of the characters in the story. A humiliating royalty statement from Rosen and Starmer told me that 512 copies of the book had been sold. It received a handful of tepid reviews, one of them by Darnley. Strangely enough, it got a kind message from Hunter in his 'round-up' of his favourite books of 1958.

Not only had there been a deadly accuracy about my aunt's predictions of literary success. I shared really – always had, always will – her scepticism about the possibility of telling the truth about another human being, or even about a dog, in a work of literature. Unless you're Shakespeare. Where I differed from Aunt Deirdre was in my willingness to try, merely out of fear that my failure should be destined (figuratively at least) to be 'all round the village'. If one succeeded in the case of one human life in telling even a particle of the truth, it seemed to me then, and it still seems to me, that you would have achieved something so remarkable that no amount of embarrassment – 'in the village' – would justify a suppression of that attempt. When I read the great novelists I marvelled that it was in fiction that such achievements most often seem to be carried off.

Hunter would never have written a novel, since he seemed to have so little interest in telling the truth. Like a dogged barrister who did not mind how long he was on his feet in court so long as the judgment went his client's way, he produced item after item of 'evidence'. In the lives of his two subjects, there is not a postcard which Hunter had not perused, absorbed, pondered, or banked in the file index. In consequence, he was regarded on both sides of the Atlantic as one of the foremost biographers of our time. The Everett book, which caused such a storm on its publication in the United States, also won the Pulitzer. Yet, while full of admiration for Hunter's industry as I waded through his accumulations of detail and evidence, I could not feel that he had begun to plumb the mystery of the human beings he purported to describe.

Johnson's *Lives of the Poets*, to my mind the most supremely successful biographical exercises ever attempted, told us more about their subjects in a few brief pages than Hunter was able to do in his ponderous volumes. Possibly he was too cynical or too unimaginative, or too wedded to an empirical way of regarding

159

things, to see the challenge as worth the effort (the artistic as well as the moral challenge – how do you frame the truth, or some part of the truth?). All that mattered to him apparently, was to present the 'material', to collect the 'evidence'. But here one confronted a mystery. The 'material' so punctiliously assembled turned out in so many cases to be false. Everyone who had known Jimbo Lampitt said from the first that *James Petworth Lampitt: The Hidden Years* was an improbable assemblage of information. My own glimpse of Lampitt's diaries, when they were still being kept in the Everett Foundation in New York, those very diaries on which Hunter's revelatory biography was supposedly based, had told me that they were no more than engagement diaries. I have been meditating ever since on the conundrum. Was Hunter a fantasist who did not know he was lying? Or a creative liar? Or a man who had indeed found out some truth which had never been spoken about before? Was the fact that his Lampitt was so unlike the Jimbo Lampitt whom anyone actually remembered simple proof of the fact that Hunter had uncovered the man's hidden self? I had long admired, for example, Jimbo Lampitt's prose poems about the beauties of Venice in *Lagoon Loungings*, though not until Hunter's book did we, Lampitt's readers, guess the extent of his emotional dependence upon a succession of waiters, gondolieri and minor poets while he lounged in the lagoons. Hunter's book had made such a stir because it appeared to reveal a whole homosexual underworld in the post-Wilde era. Lampitt had known everyone, been everywhere. Many of his friends had been well known. The scene, in Hunter's book, of D. H. Lawrence and Lampitt in the gondola particularly caught the imagination of the reading public when it was serialized in the very newspaper, the *Sunday Times*, to which Jimbo in old age had contributed a weekly *causerie*.

From a publisher's standpoint, Lampitt's supposed promiscuity was all to the good. The more trousers fell down in the presence of this apparently insatiable man of letters, the more copies sold. Rupert Brooke had submitted. So, in a moment of youthful indiscretion, had Cosmo Gordon Lang. Hardly a bottom, from Ivor Novello's to Harold Nicolson's, had escaped Jimbo's highly catholic attentions and some of the conquests, if genuine, had called for wholesale reassessment of the characters involved. Gratifying howls of protest had greeted Hunter's wilder assertions, such as his interpretation of what passed in the lift of the Reform Club between Lampitt and Winston Churchill. Coinciding with a period of homosexual liberation in Britain, and a gossipy mania for reading about the sex lives of early-twentieth-century worthies, the book had not merely been a great commercial success. It had somehow given Hunter what he always, in his mysterious way, must have wanted.

To the reader sitting quietly at home with a book, it may seem as if literature is a matter of the open page, the lamplight, the operation of one mind meeting another as eyes pass to and fro over the printed passages. But literature, like almost all forms of human activity, generates its own tedious opportunities for business and the exercise of power. I have never doubted that Hunter's motives for writing the life of Jimbo Lampitt sprang from all sorts of complicated inner needs which I could not begin to resolve until that long night with Kit, and Shakespeare's ghost, in London, ten years after my foggy trip to Venice.

But with the money and the success of his book on Lampitt, there was born in Hunter another desire, so alien to me that for a while I was slow to believe that anyone of intelligence could be tempted by it. Literature Panels, Literary Societies, Literary Conferences, Literary Agents, Literary Festivals, Literary Committees, Literary Prizes. Just as religion of its very nature degenerates into synods and councils, the Papal Court or the General Assembly of the Kirk, so Literature spawns its own grey power games, overlapping, where questions of public finance or influence are concerned, with those for whom politics and the government of the nation are their chief concern. That is why literary power maniacs and busybodies are always on the left, since right-wing people believe that public money does not need

161

to be spent on 'the arts'.

It was into this world that Hunter had walked and in this world that he had shown himself as skilled in the exercise of power as in his ability to make women fall in love with him.

In fogbound Venice, the committees, the women, the whole world which Hunter both inhabited and represented, seemed not just far away but ethereal. The place itself had such power that one felt light-headed with it. Hunter, though, was never far from my thoughts during that period. He had been the cause of my first marriage breaking up. Now Sonya and her ridiculous suggestion that the week with Hunter at the Cheltenham Literary Festival had not 'meant anything'. I was quite aware that this was in danger of becoming an obsession, this pre-occupation with the man; and I was terrified of a return to the loony bin. That was why the encounter with Signora Usignuoli had been so supremely refreshing. The Normandins were in none of Hunter's senses of the word important. Old Madame de Normandin's favourite authors were General de Gaulle, Agatha Christie and Winston Churchill. When in Paris, it is very doubtful that she ever went near St Germain des Prés except to buy a hat or to make her confession.

These things churned in my head during the cold insomniac hours of a *pensione* night. Towards dawn, sleep came and I dreamed of Sonya. Things were all right again in the dream. We were in love. The entrance of a chambermaid with an inadequate breakfast on a tray brought me back to an immediate consciousness of how distant those short months had been.

When I came down into the hall, a message had already been delivered. Signora Usignuoli wrote in detail, and in English. Her mother, she kindly said, was delighted to hear of my presence in Venice and they looked forward to seeing me at eight that evening. An elaborate map accompanied the letter, and a telephone number, and the Venetian postal number. If I came near but got lost, I was to go to a bar called Giasone, where someone would set me on my way.

All this was enough to take me, by winding *calle* and a maze of false turns, to the palazzo where the Usignuoli resided. Madame de Normandin was just as I remembered her. The same hedgehoggy look, as though Mrs Tiggywinkle had been dressed for dinner in a château; the same cut of girlish, sleeved, dark blue silk frock, waisted and full-skirted; the same design of hairnet; the same well-modulated tones saying, if memory served me right, exactly the same things.

'You were so studious that we always thought that you would, perhaps, become a celebrated author,' said Madame de Normandin.

I thought bashfully of the execrable poems which I had written about her maid, Barbara.

'I hoped so, too, Madame, at the time. Our ideas change.'

'But tell me, Julien, if you would be so kind, who is the best – or, if you prefer – who is your favourite English writer of this century?'

This was the very question she would toss out on numberless occasions in her very distinctive manner, part hostess and part pedagogue, to her galumphing teenage paying guests at Les Mouettes each summer. As she asked me the question, I remembered what the answer was meant to be, and also what my own answer had been at sixteen. Madame, it now came back to me, had read *Lagoon Loungings*.

Her son-in-law intervened with his own suggestion.

'Ernest Hemingway, surely?'

'Maman said *English* writer, *caro*,' said Signora Usignuoli.

The husband, though evidently in his way a bigwig (portraits of ancestral doges and cardinals adorned the walls of their splendid but chilly apartment), was a bit of a letdown. For one thing, he was small and fat. For another, although he was expensively dressed, he entirely lacked his wife's sense of style. The jangling of bracelets at his hairy wrist was ground enough for regret even if his suit had not been so blue. The large white silk tie of the 'kipper' design popular ten years before among London dandies, gave to this pudgy old gentleman a faintly gangster air. Yet there was none of the mafioso in his plump, carefully shaven face nor in his innocent large brown eyes.

In spite of the fact that I now remembered how Madame de Normandin's literary conversation went, and therefore knew how completely harmless it was, I did not want it to continue. A good example here of how time makes us into Banquos, bleeding and staring like spectres at former acquaintances who have not changed as much as we. In my teens I had enjoyed her question-and-answer routines from a position of unhesitant intellectual arrogance. I assumed myself her intellectual superior, assumed that I had read more books than she had done. None of these assumptions remained with me at forty. I no longer found anything about goodness funny. The amiability of the women was what struck me now and the slight puzzle of the new hubby. I hated the former self who had dared to feel the slightest superiority to these people who were in every way more civilized than myself; and in return, I felt reproached by that younger self, aware that at forty I had grown into a man whom the sixteen-year-old would have despised. Madame and her daughter, I now heard for the first time, had imagined that I might become a great writer. Now, the name of Madame de Normandin's favourite English novelist excited the clear and painful knowledge that I was forty and that I would never write a book again; or that if I did, it would not be a patch on *Dumb Witness* or *The Hollow*. Before such thoughts could coalesce or form themselves in my brain, however, the door-bell rang, the evening began.

'That', said the Signora, 'might be my sister-in-law and her party.'

She began, while we listened to the noise of voices in the hall, and of guests being divested of winter overcoats, boots, umbrellas, a résumé. Her husband's sister had married an Englishman. Would I remember, at Les Mouettes, their friends the Mount-Smiths, or had I perhaps never coincided with them on one of their frequent visits? Gerard, her husband's brother-in-law, was a cousin of the

Mount-Smiths. (He had been at Ampleforth with Sir Godfrey, Margaret Mary's father.) And with Gerard, was their cousin. And with them, the widow of her husband's younger brother. And this widow was bringing with her a daughter. And a couple of friends.

So much gabbled information about my fellow-dinner-guests was too much to take in, while they divested themselves of their outer garments in the hall. The important thing, which she stressed more than once *sotto voce*, was that the Principessa was not to be addressed by her title. This injunction, easy enough to obey, suggested that the sphere in which I found myself was vertiginously more exalted than anything to which I was accustomed. Princesses, even Italian princesses, might be read about in *Paris Match* or Henry James but they were not to be known in my humdrum circles. How then, presuming I plucked up the courage, should I address this exalted being? Briskly, the Signora uttered that since her brother-in-law's death, his widow had reverted to her earlier name of Mrs Amt.

As the party entered the room there was handshaking and conviviality. The language was chiefly Italian with a smattering of French. Indeed, rather absurdly, the first words exchanged between Gerard Smethurst and myself were in Italian – fluent in his case, scarcely existent in my own. Mr Smethurst and his wife were described as 'artists' and they apparently lived in the Giudecca.

The English words which broke into the murmur of Romance tongues had a strongly American intonation, though one knew at once that the voice originated in the English shires.

'That is some fog. I thought my vaporetto [*vabber-eddo*] would have to quit looking for these mugwumps.'

The Smethursts were indicated with a jerk of Mrs Amt's thumb.

She was a deep-throated, full-bosomed woman with very stout legs: they were so fat that they betokened some glandular or cardiac condition; it was the sort of fat which extended beyond the ankles into the shoes. She wore black trousers and a florid pink bridge coat. Large lobes and goitre-neck were heavy with magnificent rubies and gold. Her daughter, in her forties, could not have been a more contrasting physical specimen. Giacometti was the artist who at once came to mind when I saw Victoria's etiolated and intelligent features for the first time, her short dark hair and her bright all-seeing eyes.

Mrs Amt, in short, was the daughter of Campbell Dilkes. Amt had been the Czech refugee, impoverished at the time of his first, his only, visit to Staithe, but rich twenty years later – seriously rich. His skills as a theoretical engineer, which led to instant employment by a steel manufacturer in Pittsburgh, when he and his wife first arrived in the United Sates, had not gone unrewarded. The Amt Girder had – the little joke was so often repeated in the family – shored up the fortune, which had swollen. Amt Components Inc. had been well established before the end of the war, and by the time of Rudolf Amt's demise, his wife and children were left well provided, but not, as it happened, as limitlessly rich as he had been himself. (By the terms of the will, they were all beneficiaries of a trust, but in the event of his widow remarrying, the bulk of the fortune remained with the company.)

A couple of years after the steel millionaire's death, Mrs Amt had met the younger brother of our host, referred to accurately but not, one felt, without irony, as the Prince. Like the Last Duchess in Browning's poem, Mrs Amt had ranked the gift of a nine-hundred-year-old name with anybody's gift; at any rate, when the charmer died, she reverted to the perhaps no less ancient name of Amt.

'God damn them, what have the Usignuoli ever done to compare with Rudi's achievements?'

Her animated academic daughter (later, I would see this as so characteristic) wanted to tell her mother exactly what the Usignuoli had done. It was a chance for a seminar. The family had not been Venetians – the Venetian connection, and the doges who looked down from their framed portraits, came through the female line. The Usignuoli had been Ghibellines. Or was it, Mrs Amt interrupted animatedly, Guelfs? – one got them mixed. In consequence, they had 'fetched up fairly low down in Dante's *Inferno*'.

'I always think', said Victoria in her gentle American voice, 'that being hated by Dante is something of an accolade. Rather like being excoriated in the English newspapers by that unspeakable Miles Darnley.'

The fact that Victoria mentioned my oldest friend in almost the first sentence she uttered in my hearing, was a signal that she was going to be 'important' to me, that this was one of those occasions when the threads of experience were going to be woven together. There were few points of parallel between Darnley's declamatory attacks on public figures in his weekly newspaper article and the Florentine poet's savage metaphysics. Victoria, it seemed, had spoken intuitively, telepathically drawing Darnley's name out of the air. Before there was much chance to stick up for my old chum, more of her stepfather's family history was outpoured. Another of the Usignuoli had been an anti-pope. A genial conversation ensued once this fact had been mentioned – precisely the sort of anodyne subject of which Madame de Normandin was the mistress. Given the choice, she asked us all, would we prefer to live in Rome, with its magnificent antiquities, or in Avignon? Just the sort of question with which she would keep us talking around the table at Les Mouettes, this apparently trivialized approach to the great schism in the Western Church (only apparent after I'd found out a bit about them and their views) had the effect of keeping the subject of religion at bay. It was one about which Mrs Amt and Gerard Smethurst differed (sometimes, I believe heatedly), Mrs Amt taking a view of Roman Catholicism which would not in any significant particular have differed from Foxe's *Book of Martyrs*, and Mr Smethurst being so dismayed by the liberalization of his Church that he was now an adherent of Archbishop Lefebvre.

167

With the vehemence of an American but with fluty English vowels, Mrs Amt said that if all the Usignuoli had been as charming as their present host, or as her late Prince, God bless him, then Italy would have been a happier place. The Usignuoli had never commissioned a Titian or a Michelangelo – though an altarpiece by Sansovino does depict a Usignuoli Prince and Principessa adoring the Holy Family in the company of SS John the Baptist and Thomas Aquinas. They had, in their history, abused ecclesiastical or civic office no more than other illustrious Italian families. They had grown some half-palatable wine.

'I hope, more than half-palatable,' murmured the Signor to general amusement. 'We are drinking some of it now.'

'In Rome', pursued the Signor's wife a little desperately, still obedient to her mother's conversational agenda, 'there is a torrid heat in summer, but on the other hand, in Avignon they suffer from the mistral.'

Anxious that no one should touch upon a dangerous topic, or that if they did so they should do it diplomatically, both women, Madame de Normandin and her daughter, reverted to Les Mouettes house-style and translated freely as they went, sometimes into English, and sometimes into Italian. Since we were in trilingual company, this was no small accomplishment, and almost took on the nature of a part-song or a madrigal as the contrasting joys of Avignon and Rome were rehearsed and aired.

The sentence which they were evidently hoping to stop before it passed Mrs Amt's teeth, burst, however, into a patch of silence, so that we all heard it. The significance of her remark was not understood by me until a decade later, on my second encounter with Mr Smethurst, at the White Hart, Stamp Street.

'Unfortunately the Prince's family backed every goddamned wrong horse from Machiavelli to Mussolini. So did my father, so perhaps that's what we all have in common.'

'I can't agree with you there,' said Mr Smethurst quietly.

I haven't met Mr Smethurst again since that evening in Venice. And now, here he is, in the extremely different setting of the White Hart, Stamp Street. Kit, Cormac and I have been scattered round the trestle table at which, I suppose, twenty-five persons are seated. They are nearly all male but there is a handful of women and, if I have got the measure of the gathering, it does not seem very different from any other occasion at which the English have assembled together with some arbiter other than class having selected their choice of companions. The parish bun-fight, the regimental reunion – they determine a mixture of ranks; it is not something which happens naturally on the English scene. There is often an atmosphere of strain about such occasions, everyone eager to try their best but no one quite hitting the right tone. That was the atmosphere in the White Hart.

On my right, an old man who greeted me cordially when I sat down, cannot resist resuming a conversation (which my arrival has interrupted) with the man on his other side. I strain my ears, half hoping, now I am here and seated, to be shocked by some real Nazi talk. I do not follow it in every detail, but from overheard snatches – moss control, moles, the necessity of owning a garden roller, and the best months in which to aerate – I gather that a comprehensive colloquy about the care and nurture of lawns is in progress. At first, I try to make it interesting for myself by imagining that it is all phrased in some elaborate code – that moles are the Enemy within, for example – but it is not a fantasy which I feel able to sustain. The serious tone of 'My wife and I put a lot of trust in good old Miracle-Gro' seems too innocently and obviously to mean what it says. This is Aunt Deirdre's idea of good talk.

Meeting Smethurst again – no reason to suppose he remembers me from Adam – is an extraordinary coincidence. Drunkenly, I am happy to have the lawn-talk burbling away in my right ear. If Mr Smethurst married someone related to the Prince . . . I am always bad at genealogical connections, and could not decide whether this made him some sort of relation by marriage to Kit. He was not a kinsman, of course, and nor did the Blood Royal of the Lampitts flow in his veins, so it was only of marginal interest.

'I'm afraid', my Uncle Roy would say very slowly and deliberately – it was the sad tone he adopted when some fault, however minor, had to be admitted in a Lampitt – 'that when old Lord Lampitt, who was a *tiny* little bit of a humbug, went to Italy in the late twenties, he was very much impressed by Musso.' My uncle pronounced the first syllable of Mussolini's name to rhyme with bus or fuss.

I am aware of Mr Smethurst saying something pretty similar, but I could not vouch for when the words pass his lips – is it now in the White Hart, or ten years ago, in response to Mrs Amt's uncompromising 'every goddamned wrong horse from Machiavelli to Mussolini'.

'You only have to think' – Mr Smethurst speaking – 'of the enthusiasm which the English felt for *Il Duce*. Churchill admired him wholeheartedly. But they all did, they came back from Italy glowing with praise for Mussolini. The Archbishop of Canterbury, Cosmo Lang, was absolutely wild about him.'

My ears are half-aware that, at the far end of the table, Professor Cormac is putting them right about a few facts and dates. Grasping the bull by the horns, he has decided to give them a rundown of the Nazi–Soviet pact.

I must be staring into vacancy. Perhaps I have been like this for some minutes, perhaps for a quarter of an hour.

'*Kit's told you the news – our news?*'

Leman's question when I spoke to her in the Gents. Coming out of the Gents. Tonight. Yesterday. Whenever it was. Their news?

170

What did that mean? Had he told me or had he not? I cannot quite remember.

I am not allowing my mind to focus on this, nor on the supper table. Programmed through a wartime childhood – in which my parents were killed by a Nazi bomber – I can't hear the word 'fascist' without a predictable set of responses. There is, for me, no interest in the subject *per se*, as there obviously is for Cormac; and unlike Kit I have no family reason to find it all fascinating.

'I don't think that you remember me, do you, Julian?'

Miss Dare seems programmed to say this to me every ten or fifteen years when our paths cross. During childhood, Felicity and I used to giggle about Miss Dare's crush on Uncle Roy. She attended all the services at Timplingham, sharing Uncle Roy's love of the 'Mass and maypoles' type of religion. A fellow-traveller with Christianity all my life, I should normally have associated this brand of churchmanship – the *English Hymnal*, Gothic rather than Latin vestments, the Sarum Rite, and the revival of Olde Englysshe customs such as folk-song and morris dancing – with leftish politics. Percy Dearmer, who more or less invented this strain of Anglicanism, at the very period when Campbell Dilkes was writing his best music, was a political liberal; Conrad Noel, one of the keenest exponents of Mass and maypole, was a communist. Much of their desire to revive Piers the Ploughman's Fair Field Full of Folk, or the Catholicism of medieval England, as opposed to post-revolutionary Europe, owed its inspiration to Morris's *News from Nowhere*. But now one came to think of it, there was no logical reason why a hankering after Merrie England could not lead those so inclined into just about any political posture.

'Miss Dare, how very nice. I had no idea . . . I mean . . . If you had . . . We seem to meet in such very different places.'

'Is that Mr Dilkes's grandson? The one with whom you came in?'

'His great-grandson.'

171

'Mr Smethurst said that he would be coming. I met him once, you know, Mr Campbell Dilkes.'

In her minor way, Miss Dare shares some of Hunter's gift of ubiquity, cropping up, dotting herself through life like a visitant. An old, rather powdery fairy perhaps (mental arithmetic suggests to me that she must be in her mid-eighties), but a fairy of Staithe all the same? Each of us, enjoying star billing in our own inner drama, has been cast, unknown to ourselves, as a very minor walk-on in the lives of others. Sometimes, though, these walk-ons make links of which the actors themselves may be barely conscious, as though they were carriers of a train of associations and memories. Hunter fills this role most fully and mysteriously in my life. He has been cropping up ever since I was a boy at Seaforth Grange, making a habit of choosing women with whom I happened to be in love or involved. Miss Dare's role in my life is much more tangential, though she must be one of the last surviving links with my rectory childhood. Fluttery, gently whiskery and very white – white hair, white powder, white cardie – Miss Dare has a capacity to be embarrassing which somehow fits with her willingness to attend this supper. She is telling me at some length about our last meeting, with some Roman Catholic friends in Birmingham. She was a brief convert to their creed and she had worshipped at a church which she pronounced, in her mincing tones as the Urra-tree. Homesickness for Anglicanism had evidently been tremendous. When she met me at the Nolans' (Hunter had been there – would she remember? – I tried her and drew a complete blank, she could not remember him at all), she had been assailed by regret at having joined the RCs and having abandoned the religion enshrined in my uncle's airy, light fifteenth-century church, with its seemly old liturgy.

'I have been very happy' – *heppy* – 'ever since. It was too late for Evensong that day, but I went to St Philip's the next morning for the early service; and do you know, when I thought of your uncle and all it had meant to me at Timplingham, I wept. I really did.'

172

She pauses politely and then adds, 'I was very sorry indeed to hear about your uncle, Julian.'

'He was very frail towards the end. You wrote Aunt Deirdre a lovely letter.'

'And how is Mrs Ramsay?'

'She's found a small house near a village called Binham. It's only a few miles from . . . '

'Oh, I know Binham. It has such a lovely abbey, and . . . '

'Just a bungalow, actually' – at this stage, having no idea that the bungalow will become my home, I have no consciousness of what a delightful place it is to live; nor am I imaginative about the relief which Aunt Deirdre, now pushing eighty, must have felt when the responsibility of cleaning and housekeeping her husband's large Georgian rectory was lifted from her.

'She has getting on for an acre of garden,' I say. 'That's why she bought the house.'

That, and the fact that it was all she could afford with the £1,349 which Uncle Roy had left her.

'The rectory garden at Timplingham was always so lovely.'

'The inevitable happened there, I'm afraid.'

I tell Miss Dare the sad story: the sale, by the diocese, of the rectory to a rogue builder, who converted it into 'old people's' flats, the bulldozing of my aunt's kitchen garden, the demolition of those long walls of brick and flint, the ploughing-up of the shrubbery, the erection of four hideous little houses there, with their hardwood doors and metal-framed windows.

While Miss Dare utters predictable expressions of dismay and sympathy, Mr Smethurst has come round to the back of her chair – a wheel-chair, I notice – with Kit at his side.

'Muriel, this is Mr Mayfield. I told you about him.'

'Oh, indeed! Mr Dilkes's great-grandson. Such a pleasure, such an honour!'

The anecdote which she has to share with Kit (though in his words 'quite sweet really') is inconsequential. Some time during the 1930s, Dilkes came to the high school in Norwich where Miss

Dare taught music. She has the score of some of his piano pieces which he autographed for her.

'Ay think it was through Mr Dilkes that ay first had the pleasure of meeting Mr Smethurst.'

'Muriel's been very loyal,' he says.

'It was terrible, what they did to Mr Dilkes,' she says quietly, her thin lips almost disappearing as she purses her mouth. 'We can just be grateful we weren't sent to prison too.'

'I got an even worse punishment,' he laughs. 'My call-up papers!'

'Mr Smethurst is too modest,' she explains devoutly. 'He won the MC at Anzio.'

I want to ask how such an obviously nice man came to be mixed up in such a set, but a smiling reference to Spain supplies the answer.

'I happened to go to a Catholic boarding-school,' he says, taking a drag on his Gauloise and laughing mirthlessly.

'You remember Margaret Mary in Birmingham, Julian?'

'Yes, yes I do.'

'Well, Mr Smethurst was a friend of her father – weren't you, Mr Smethurst?'

'Godfrey was my cousin. So you know the Mount-Smiths?'

The conversation drifts into the safe territory in which we establish how many of this enormous family I have met. Exactly how the eighteen-year-old Gerard Smethurst, fresh from Ampleforth, came to be fighting for Franco's volunteers required no further explanation.

Venice acts on its visitors like no other town. I've sometimes attributed this simply to the movement of the water itself, to the fact that, when you arrive, you need some time to get your sea-legs. Every bus stop, after all, is a raft, bobbing about, often in quite turbulent water. Every main street echoes not to the sound of cars but to the smacking of water against prows. This produces a dizziness. And then there is the whole notorious 'atmosphere' of the place, which inspired some of the purplest passages in *Lagoon Loungings*. All visitors have felt it, and I knew that it would provide a strong antidote to the misery through which, in the previous months, I had been passing.

'I have to ask you this, Mr Ramsay,' the solicitor had said with solemn but ill-disguised enjoyment; 'but, when did your wife and yourself last have er . . . ' He looked at his blotter as if it contained words which he had momentarily forgotten. 'Er, sexual intercourse.'

Truly? He *had* to ask this?

After a month of these interviews, and the letters from Sonya's lawyers, and the bleak discovery that I had nowhere to live and almost no money, I hoped that Venice would 'take me out of myself'. What in fact I found was that my emotions were all jingle-jangle when I arrived and that 'the atmosphere' made me more, not less, overwrought. Or so I tried to convince myself when, waking at half past three after that dinner with the Usignuoli, I found my heart in a flutter.

I did not immediately recognize the old symptoms.

Wandering for a week together, Victoria and I saw old favourites – Carpaccio's *St Jerome in his Study* at the Scuola di San Giorgio degli Schiavoni, and his little doggy; the Tintorettos at the Scuola di San Rocco (for me, the most impressive paintings in the world). Then, Victoria introduced me to things I'd never seen before: the extraordinary marble baroque of Santa Maria dei Miracoli, the delightful gallery (completely deserted) of the Palazzo Querini-Stampalia, and the pictures there of eighteenth-century Venice by that charming, good-bad painter Pietro Longhi.

'You see why Canaletto and not Longhi secured all the big export deals,' commented the daughter of the Amt Girder. Whereas her mother spoke American with a British accent, Victoria spoke English with an American accent.

As we perambulated, never too despondent when we found the greenish or rusted locks of old fanes closed against us, but always turning with some relief to the nearest warm café for chocolate or pasta, she told me about Staithe. Her mother had inherited it, but her mother could not bring herself to go home. It had too many ghosts. She gave it jointly to her two daughters. Victoria told me about her sister who had grown up in England – Dartington Hall – and an early, not completely successful, marriage resulting in Kit. The boy – fifteen or so when his aunt and I first discussed him over Venetian café-tables – was to 'come in' to Staithe.

'Unless there's a miracle and I find myself having a rival son and heir,' said Victoria. 'I am the elder sister, after all.'

It was always difficult, from the first, to guess how much Victoria minded not having children. It's a matter about which I still can't make up my mind.

And we talked, more than we rehearsed our personal histories, or peered into guidebooks, of you. There you were, no doubt, accompanying us over the Rialto Bridge as we debated the character of Shylock, both discovering that we found him one of the most richly sympathetic of your heroes.

'Antonio', I said, anticipating many of the conversations we should have a decade later, 'is Shakespeare – the Shakespeare of the Sonnets. His love for Bassanio exactly reflects . . . '

Her rebuttal of my biographical approach was, in those early conversations, much gentler than it would be during our discussions, a decade later, concerning *Dear Time's Waste*. My life, which had atomized, split up, fallen into a chaos in which none of its constituent elements coalesced, felt very fragile just then. I had gone mad once; I feared that I would go mad again.

The dreadful disappointment of the divorce from Sonya left no purpose, no pattern or shape in which I could cling. The mind, as well as the body, needs furniture on which it can hang its old clothes, a hearth at which it can warm shoeless feet. I was mentally homeless. Victoria, with her Norfolk and Lampitt and Shakespearean interest, brought before my eyes the possibility that all these wasted atoms had in fact been temporarily disturbed in the retort. New shapes and patterns, hitherto unsuspected, were ready to be formed.

I do not know if I loved Victoria or the idea of Staithe, as a place where I might at last find refuge and where the pattern of things could be quietly relearned; where my parents' holidays in North Norfolk, and their subsequent deaths, and Uncle Roy's obsession with the Lampitts, and my own disparate inner history, might all come together in a single story.

On what was to have been my final day in Venice, Victoria planned an outing to the lagoon. Eschewing Mrs Amt's extravagant directive to hire a private boat, we took the ordinary *circolare* to Burano, the tiny island where Galuppi was born. And when we had eaten an excellent *zuppa di mare* (the finest meal I had eaten all week) we went to find a boatman to row us over to an even smaller island called San Francesco del Deserto.

Inquiries at the wharf illicited a number of opinions concerning the possibility or indeed desirability of making the journey to the island that day. Not that I could do more than guess what was being said when I watched Victoria fluently converse with the knobbly old bumpkins on the quayside. Some pointed across the grey, flat expanses of the lagoon as though trying to explain where the island was. Others just grinned yellow semi-toothless grins.

'Ma, Giuseppe, dove Giuseppe?' Victoria was asking.

The bumpkins laughed and made elaborate mimes, lifting their elbows and imitating extreme states of inebriation.

Giuseppe was to be found drinking in the Communist Club, only a short walk away, near the restaurant where we had lunched so well. Both of us felt some diffidence about entering the club which, as far as could be gauged by a glimpse from the door, was no more than a bar where pot-bellied men stood round smoking cigarettes.

'Supposing it's like the Athenaeum,' she said, 'and doesn't like women stepping over the threshold.'

I therefore agreed to enter and ask for the man called Giuseppe, fearing as I did so that they might all have this very usual Christian name, and that it might be like poking one's head round a bar in Swansea and shouting, 'Evans!'

With elaborate gestures, implying imaginary oars and rowlocks, I asked for Giuseppe. The barman indicated an old man with a withered hand and no teeth. The hand had not been lost but, one imagined, deformed since birth, a small circular knot of shiny scarlet flesh from which a thumb somehow jutted out. I repeated the rowing gestures and told him that outside was 'una donna Americana' who was able to speak Italian.

Roars of laughter from his cronies at this, but he consented to follow me. When he spoke to Victoria, she laughed too.

'What's so funny?'

'He says that he can't row us to the island this afternoon.'

'And that's amusing?'

'But his father can.'

Giuseppe senior did not look appreciably older than his son, or more grizzled. His hands were all his own and he stood up a little straighter. Without more ado, he led us to the wharf, helped us down into a small rowing-boat and set out into the flat silver-grey. We sat facing him as he sculled into the mists. About a hundred yards out, the boat started to bob up and down, not from the sea-flow but because we were passing a little motor-launch, propelled by a couple of rotund friars and piled high at the stern with root vegetables, mangel-wurzels, turnip, swede. They waved, these neo-medieval figures, and the old man shouted something at them with a laugh. Victoria asked where the friars were taking the vegetables. She supplied me with a translated précis of Old Giuseppe's replies.

'They usually go to Murano – sometimes as far as Venice – to the market.'

'What about Giuseppe?'

'*Io?*' He laughed and added something.

'*Non e vero!*' exclaimed Victoria. 'He says he hasn't been to Venice since he was a boy. He's been to Murano a couple of times, though.'

This was a life which made Aunt Deirdre's seem cosmopolitan.

'He says he has here enough to eat and drink; a good son, grandchildren and great-grandchildren . . . '

One got the picture.

By now we had pulled up at the little island which, as readers of *Lagoon Loungings* will remember, derives its name from the brief period of residence there of St Francis of Assisi, during the Third Crusade. I read aloud:

'*Remote from the noise of war, the Umbrian troubadour came to refresh his soul with Brother Gull and Sister Hydrangea . . . *'

'It's really a place for the spring,' said the great-niece of this author. 'When the garden is in flower and the geraniums are climbing up the chapel wall. There's nothing to see here, really. I wonder why I brought you.'

She smiled and half closed her eyes.

In winter, grey, dank with dripping mist, this garden felt so far from civilization that it might have been lunar. I took her in my arms and there, on the island of St Francis in the Wilderness, I kissed Victoria Amt.

The first words which I spoke when we recovered, not from the surprise of the kiss, for we had both been preparing for it for five days, but from its wonder and its delight, concerned the author of *Lagoon Loungings*.

'It must be seventy-five years since James Petworth Lampitt came to this spot.'

She had her head rested on my shoulder when I made this observation and now she pushed me away. Having no reason to suppose that Victoria knew Hunter, I suppressed the question which now occurred to my mind: had Hunter, in his relentless search for 'material', his attempt to find gondoliers who might have enjoyed Jimbo's attentions, come as far as this spot?

Time with Victoria was now so short, and the kiss changed everything. I was appalled to hear myself, uncontrollably, telling one of Uncle Roy's narratives about an unsuccessful holiday once undertaken jointly by Jimbo and Sargie in Venice during the 1920s. She giggled politely, and held my hand.

Giuseppe left us alone as we wandered in the damp friary garden and squinted at the unimpressive little church. Hopes that our boatman would not be loquacious on the return journey were soon dashed as we came back across the moon-sea, lapping a path through little islands not much more than scrubs, silver-grey, like the air and the sea, on some of which, despite their smallness and barrenness, life of a kind subsisted – a bush, even a hut, or the huddled shape of a human being recalling Doré's *Dante*.

'*Si, si, sono Americana, ma mio amico e inglese.*'

'And now what's he saying?'

Giuseppe the elder grinned. The gnarled old cigarette no more than half alight glowed through the gloaming and danced on his cracked lips; beyond, an orange dental nightmare and the blackness of mouth and throat; but the whole smile, enlivened by the creasing of leathery cheeks and the brightness of electric blue eyes, suggested that he had summed me up and found me in some way, not merely wanting, but comical.

'What's he saying?' I repeated.

'He says all Englishmen are very handsome. I've said there are Englishmen and Englishmen.'

Loathing the tedium of generalization about whole nations – it is the staple conversational diet of travellers and the strongest argument for staying at home – I switched off. The two of them appeared to have fallen into banality and banter which might have been endurable if set to music by Mozart but which as spoken were tedious. 'I *tedeschi* – they too were handsome; the Norwegians, so so!'

Oh dear, oh dear. This was not how I wished to spend the hour after our first kiss, on our last afternoon together before I went home.

It was when we came within sight of Burano and I was shivering with cold that Giuseppe stood up in his *sandalo* and began a monologue.

'Some twenty years ago,' said the translator, 'he rowed across a young Englishman.'

'*Gentiluomo*,' the communist corrected her. '*Gentiluomo*'.

'OK, so he was a gentleman.'

As Giuseppe's encomium progressed, she laughed. 'Jesus, this is over the top. He says this young man was the very perfection of charm, good manners and good looks; and he was also – oh, this is even better – he was very learned, he was a *professore*; he was writing a book, a great book. And even better, he was a communist. Is that right, Giuseppe?'

'*Si, si, comunisto!*'

Clearly, to be communist in Burano was like being Church of England in Timplingham. He smiled, proud of his respectability.

I assumed this was the end of his story, for by now we were pulling up at the jetty and Giuseppe was occupied in throwing the seaweedy slimy green snake which served him as a rope over a rotten stump which jutted from the water in lieu of a decent landing-stage. The younger Giuseppe was waiting at the jetty, sociably waving his stump and helping with that agile thumb to hold the boat steady while we disembarked.

'*Il gentiluomo*,' pursued Giuseppe the elder.

'OK,' I said testily, 'I think we've had enough of this *gentiluomo* now.'

'You may, he hasn't' – the first sharp remark she ever addressed to me, the first of many.

Had I managed to stop Giuseppe continuing with his tale, would our relationship have developed along different lines? Might

Victoria and I have got married? Might I now be the Master of Staithe?

Old Giuseppe was fishing inside his chest for a greasy pocket-book. As he did so, he continued his relentless tale. I do not think it is hindsight which makes me say that, even at this stage, a worry was passing over Victoria's features as she continued to translate his words.

'Whenever he comes back to Venice this *gentiluomo* returns to see Giuseppe. Now he is very, very famous as an author. He has the name of an archangel and when he was young, oh Rafaello was an archangel!'

Through the gloaming I found myself looking at an old photograph of Hunter which Giuseppe had forced on my attention.

The picture must have dated from the 1940s or very early 1950s, about the time when he came and addressed the Lampitt Society at school and told us of his ambition to edit Lampitt's letters. A wistful young man looking downwards. Hair longer than it has been for years. A polo-neck. Without any self-consciousness, the old boatman raised Hunter's picture to his lips and kissed it. A mother kissing the picture of a son, or the pilgrim who kisses the relic of a saint, could not have been more fervent.

Light was beginning to fade, and by the time we were on the vaporetto bound for home, the lagoon had darkened. The grey mysteriousness of it was lost to a blackness picked out here and there by meaningless twinkling lights. In spite of the intense cold, we stood outside on the vaporetto watching it all, I with an arm on her shoulder.

Of course, we were both wondering whether the excursion would conclude in bed. Had I not been going home the next day, neither of us would have wanted this so soon; but there was something incredibly sexy about the way she pulled down the sleeves of her jersey over her cold hands and held them to her lips. I wanted her, and I suppose if I'm honest I also wanted to prove something to myself – or to that bloody solicitor! After Sonya, it was important to me.

It was about five and completely dark when we returned to the Gritti. Like a coward, I decided to leave the bed question entirely up to her.

'My mother's always asleep in her room until about eight.'

We were standing at the little floating vaporetto-stop by the hotel. I still was not quite sure what she was suggesting; or rather, I was sure, but I wanted her to do all the decision-making. I reached for a hand but got a woollen jumper-sleeve and swung it gently to and fro.

'I wish I wasn't going home tomorrow.'

'I'm frozen out here. So are you. I dare say my bathroom is better than your bathroom at the *pensione*. Can I offer you a bath?'

A hot tub was precisely what was needed after the cold boat trip in the fog. Sitting in the bath facing Victoria was a whole mixture of things. There was this funny sense that we'd known each other for ever, and that this ritual went back to the Garden of Eden. There was also humour, her clever face bursting into a great half-moon of a smile, and those large eyes which in those days could see, could see so very much.

'Uh-uh.'

Victoria, opposite me in the tub, pushed me away. She wanted things done properly, next door in the bedroom. We laughingly dried one another and stood wrapped in one giant white towel, nose to nose. Then, as the towelling dropped away, we walked hand in hand towards the bed.

But although this seemed like a love scene out of dreams, all was not well. Whenever I closed my eyes I saw old Giuseppe grinning and holding up his photograph. And I saw the face of Hunter himself. Hunter kissing Miss Beach, Hunter in Claridge's with Anne, Hunter and the Marno at the theatre, Hunter and Felicity . . . Just as, a decade after this, I have trained myself to imagine you, O Shakespeare, casting your benign gaze

183

on my life, so, as I lay in that hotel bedroom with Victoria, I felt the eyes of Hunter were upon us. We were on the bed now, and it was not long before I recognized that the mechanics of the thing were going badly awry. At first, with kindness and expertise (would this have to do with being American?), Victoria tried to coax life back into a failing enterprise but gradually there passed over her features expressions of bafflement and hurt, and over me a melancholy so crushing that I knew it would be impossible to retrieve the disaster if we lay there all day and all night.

'Is there something I'm doing wrong? Something you'd like?' she asked quietly.

'Dear Victoria.'

'What in hell's that supposed to mean?'

I couldn't tell whether she was very angry or about to burst into tears.

'You know that photograph,' I said, 'the one the old man showed us?'

'Yes?' Her voice was highly suspicious.

'It's someone I know. That's all.'

She sat up in bed and hugged her knees.

'It's someone I know, too,' she said.

Miss Dare did not 'make it' into Kit's book, but I should guess, if asked what that hour or two at the White Hart contributed to *The Fairies of Staithe*, that it was the particular sense, brilliantly captured by Kit, of detached vision. The fairies were the perfect paradigm of this condition, not least because of their harmlessness, their childishness. Fairies are 'silly', in the sense used of Yeats in Auden's poem. There is a place in life for silliness. Those who try to banish it altogether, like those who try to suppress sex, can come unstuck. The reviewers who were aggrieved by Kit's refusal to judge, his refusal almost to be 'serious' about Campbell Dilkes's politics, missed the point of the book.

But I don't think I'm having such thoughts as a floodlit St Pancras Hotel appears Gothic and wild against a night sky, as the green dome of the Planetarium blinks at me, and as I try not to be sick in the taxi which lurches off the Euston Road and weaves through Bloomsbury and down the nondescript regions north of Oxford Street and east of the Edgware Road.

'Is this it, guv?'

'Yup.'

When Kit has paid the taxi, I say, leaning against a lamp-post, 'I'll be all right if I have some fresh air. Mr Smethurst was right. Red wine. Awful.'

We are in a little square. It is bitterly cold. With heavy breathing, I shall probably regain self-control.

'They were nice people.' Kit sniggers. 'Glad we left before the songs really got going.'

'There were songs?'

'Professor Cormac seemed to know the words, which one found mildly shocking.'

'You're having me on. There weren't really songs?'

'They wheeled your old lady to the piano. She played Campbell's March with great gusto.'

A distant clock chimes. The hour? If so, it must be, surely, eleven o'clock by now, and the pubs will all be closing.

'Are you going to be OK?'

Kit has a hand on my shoulder.

'Fine.'

We listen in the cold, biting air. No, it is the half-hour which chimed, not the hour.

Walking towards the pub, Kit says, 'So, you know the

185

Pacemaker's Arms?'

'There was this funny old American actor. Years ago. Ol Pitman.'

'He's a sort of cousin.'

'That's the one. Orlando Lampitt. Changed his name to Ol Pitman when he went to Hollywood. Oh, I met him years ago. When we were staying with Mr Everett. He seemed to hint there were some pretty funny goings-on in Everett's life.'

'That's where Raphael's book about Everett is so brilliant.'

'Is it?'

'Well, yes. On the one hand, there's this redneck politician, and on the other there was this secret, decadent side. Is that what Ol was telling you?'

'More or less. That was the first time I ever heard of the Pacemaker's Arms. Ol told me that old Everett came here to pick up his English servants. He had this butler – really sinister piece of work. Funny thing is, I thought the dinner we've just been to would be full of people like him – fascists, you know. Proper fascists. And as it was . . . '

'Did you hear the conservation between the two retired policemen?'

'They were the two at your end of the table?'

'Well, then. You only met old sweeties like Gerard Smethurst and the lady in the wheel-chair. But tell me . . . Julian? I say, you are OK, aren't you? Would you like me to take you home?'

'No I'm fine.'

'Ol probably explained the point of the Pacemaker's, didn't he?'

'It was a long time ago.'

The chief thing I remember being told was that it was the pub where Virgil D. Everett first met Hunter; it always seemed a slightly improbable bit of malice, so I do not bother to repeat it.

'Come on, then. Let's go in.'

*

186

'I was beginning to wonder whether you'd ever turn up.'

Sir Hubert's words, addressed snappishly and exclusively to Kit, imply he has been waiting for hours, and that the whole arrangement, casual as I recollect, that Kit might join the old man later for a drink, had been as specific as a dinner-date.

'Well, we've had the most extraordinary time, haven't we, Kit?'

Sir Hubert stares bleakly.

'I hadn't realized you were still of the party, dear.' The words are hissed from the corner of his mouth.

It is true that I am out of place, betwixt and between, too young to be one of the old clientele, and far too old to be one of the young.

What are your impressions as you behold this scene, you who made Titania fall in love with Bottom, and who overheard the tipsy old drooling of Shallow and Falstaff? *Lord, lord! How subject we old men are to this vice of lying. This same starved justice hath done nothing but prate to me of the wildness of his youth and the feats he hath done about Turnbull Street . . .*

You got out at fifty-two. By then, you'd been retired some years. When you were in your thirties you wrote about yourself as old. By the time you were in your mid to late forties, you had decided to stop being a writer. By fifty-two, you were dead. This place represents an inversion of all you ever wrote about the beauty and attraction of youth. It isn't – as you'll have gathered – a place where old lechers come to pick up young boys; it is the other way round. It is a place where young men come to find partners ten or twenty years older than you were when you died.

The physical arrangement of the Duke of Leeds is an ideal one for cruising. The pub is roughly speaking a square. The central bar can be approached from four sides. An 'open plan' has done away with any of the booths or stalls still to be found in the old London bars. There is sawdust on the floor, though, reassuring the older clients that this is definitely a pub, not a wine bar. Benches follow the walls around and at the bar there are rows of stools.

187

All these stools are occupied by hopeful elderly gentlemen, as are the benches against the walls. Those young men with a taste for such beauties could find a wide variety of old men leering winsomely through the shadows. A silver-haired Merlin, bearded and kaftan-clad, sits next to the spruce, blazered figure of a man who could easily be the Hon. Sec. of a Yacht Squadron on the South Coast. There are wispy, bespectacled old things, sufficiently aged to have been known in their youth as pansies. Now all trace of the masculine has died in them, and though they have nothing markedly feminine about them, their appearance is indistinguishable from that of old women. Beside them, a Falstaffian creature – loud check suit and handle-bar moustaches – has struck up a conversation with a willowy Japanese of twenty-two. This beautiful young man is stroking the old buffer's moustache with his long lemon-white fingers and staring into his blood-shot eyes with the intent obedience of a geisha.

In and out of the murkiness, the young men hover, glass in hand, surveying the form. Most, by this stage of the evening, have already fixed on their choice and a significant number of 'couples' have been established. The shaven-headed, pencil-thin leather-queen has befriended a man who looks like and perhaps is – the dandruffy black suit, the grey jumper – a Canon Professor of Divinity. The Adonis with floppy, wheat-coloured hair is holding the pin-striped knee of a corpulent, pop-eyed old aristocrat who looks as if he would be more at home in White's.

I feel seriously out of place. Kit's entry has caused a sensation of course and the confusion of signals caused by his smiles gives almost equal pleasure, I should guess, to himself and to Hubie. It seems I'll never get the last train back to Norwich now. Kit's grin inspires me with a sense of weariness. I'm no longer in the mood for whoopee.

The Pacemaker's Arms seems like an image of the human incapacity to see when enough is enough, to know when the party is over. The perverse desire of the young men to find beauty in their ancient companions is matched by the oldies themselves still having the energy, and the lack of vanity, to put themselves on the market. (That old Indian with hennaed hair and too-large false teeth must be ninety, but he has made friends with a shaven-headed eighteen-year-old with clumpy shoes and check shirt.)

My instinct has always been to leave a party early, to quit before the going got good. I'd have been so much better off, this evening, heading for Liverpool Street direct from the fascist beano. Even the greediest of social butterflies, the most eager researcher of lost time, could not complain about the evening I'd spent. I feel as if I've been on a journey which encompasses my entire half-century of life. The act of love in the very road where I was conceived – perhaps in the very bedroom. The walk down streets where Mummy pushed, and then led, me, to Hurlingham Park for those walks of ours together, which I still miss. The garden behind Granny's house where we all huddled in the air-raid shelter.

Dodie and I had planned that this was to be our farewell evening. I'm dissatisfied with the way I allowed her just to drift off with Darnley, without some appropriate goodbye. It is hard to imagine them having much in common – Darnley and Dodie. How extraordinary it was to see them together. How odd to have tasted once more that boozy world of Soho bars which I used to find so exciting in my twenties but which I now find all but unendurable.

(I was right, by the way, to suspect that Dodie would be the last woman to whom I should ever make love. This is also the last night in which I got drunk.)

I think, too, of Debbie Maddock, her artless, toothy Northern smile when she used to live in Timplingham, her sensual kindness to me as a lover. Could she be the same person as Dame Deborah Arnott? The transformation seems terrible. At least in the Pacemaker's the fragile frames are being shaken with earthy throbbings. It would be more dignified if they did not think about sex any more, at their age, but there is also something heroic, defiant about these old dears, which there isn't about the Dame, her desire to boss, her need to exercise control.

It's been a night for scouring the sea-bottom and summoning up spirits from the vasty deep: Miss Dare, my uncle's old parishioner! And now Hubie Power again in this strange pub. And I think not of our recent encounters and his hamming up my Sonnets play. I think of his performance of Uncle Vanya thirty years ago. I was such a very young man, just starting out on a theatrical career – and, oh dear, what happened to that? – and how inspiring I found Hubie's performance. It had absolute distinction and knowledge. Anne who to her dying day hated the theatre had come along with me so reluctantly. She knew, as I realized only afterwards, that Hunter would be there, Hunter with whom she was in love. And she knew, either through gossip or through the telepathy of love, that Hunter had something going with Isabella Marno.

That terrible scene when Hubie Power, clutching at my young elbow – just as he is now seizing Kit at the bar – marched me down the corridor to Bella Marno's dressing-room. And there I saw Hunter. He had his trousers on, but he was standing between her legs.

Years later, when she had come down in the world, more or less fought off the drink problem and joined the cast of 'The Mulberrys', Bella and I had an extended meal and the inevitable subject of Hunter had arisen. She was more candid than any of the others had ever been on the subject – Miss Beach, Felicity, Anne, Sonya, Margaret Mary, Victoria.

'Darling, he'd less interest in sex than any man I ever met. The sheer relief on his startled little face when he knew it was all right for him to scamper back into his clothes! You know, I thought we were going to have this mad, passionate affair, but when it was all over and I looked back, I realized that we had probably not actually done it more than half a dozen times. And this was an affair which went on several months. We were really in love, too. I think we were both very much in love. I've never been so in love in my life.'

'Bella, can you explain his allure?'

'Darling, you remember those cardboard dolls – perhaps boys never play with them? I adored them when I was a child. They were really just blanks, but the joy was putting different outfits on them. You cut out cardboard coats or frocks for them. The clothes had little tabs so you could fit them on to your doll and make it into anything you liked. At one minute you have a guards officer and the next you can make him into a crusader or a crinoline lady. I think that's what women do when they fall in love. They want to transform their little doll men. Usually it's so difficult because the men don't want to be changed. But Raphael – you see, he really is a cardboard doll. He's quite happy to be anything you want. And he is also a genuinely nice man.'

'Yes, he is a nice man. It's what I always forget when I tell myself stories about him inside my head. It's always a surprise to meet him and to rediscover that niceness is his predominant characteristic.'

'Darling, what are you saying? You hate Raphael! You bloody hate him.'

'Yes, but never with any enthusiasm. Perhaps that's the thing we have in common, he and I. He's a lukewarm lover and I'm a lukewarm hater.'

'That makes it better?'

'That makes it different. But this idea of yours that Hunter is simply what any woman wants to make him into: this is brilliant.'

No doubt drunkenly, I tried to explain to the Marno that my life had been punctuated by certain mental icons which represented my experience of loss and the transience of love. The most abiding image is that of my mother, waving goodbye to me on Platform One of Paddington Station when I was a boy. Even as she waved and wept, and I was steamed and chugged away to Seaforth Grange, I half knew I should never see her

191

again. This shattering loss has shaped my life. It seems as if the fates had prepared me for it: years before my parents were killed, I used to scream at the prospect of going to sleep unless one or other of them was sitting at my side. Boarding-school – from my first term onwards – haunted me with the fear that Mummy would not be at home when I returned for the holidays. These fears must have made my parents' lives intolerable; sometimes, during the holidays, I would weep, or try to follow her if my mother left me alone for half an hour while she went shopping. Something was warning me of an impending disaster. Friends and doctors have told me that I have 'read back' these fears into my early childhood, in the light of the subsequent bereavement. They have told me that had my parents not been killed, my fears that I should lose them would have been forgotten, or replaced by adolescent wounds of a different kind. Perhaps. Who can vouch for the authenticity of recollected emotions? Since Mummy's death, however, I have tended to believe irrational fears.

Another image which memory or imagination has fashioned into archetype is the open bedroom window of Miss Beach at Seaforth Grange. The fact of being twelve does not prevent one from being seriously in love. No need to cut such love down to size by gluing condescending adjectives on to the front of it: 'calf' or 'puppy'. Its anguish and torment can be just as great at twelve as at twenty-two or fifty-two. Every time it has happened to me since Miss Beach, whether it has been a fortnight's crush or *une grande passion*, whether it has been a case of fancying someone and striking incredibly lucky (rather what happened with Dodie) or yearning for them and turning them into goddesses (M.M., Leman), each 'love' has something in it of my passion for Miss Beach. Hers is the *echt*, the Platonic form of love of which all the others have been ideas. Looking up at her lighted window I had seen the back of her head and realized that she was being embraced. When the head which had been pressed against her own came into view, I saw the face of

Raphael Hunter for the first time. Miss Beach was then perhaps in her twenties – more than ten years older than me; and what she did in her spare time was no affair of mine. Nevertheless, I felt, immediately, not simply hurt or jealous, but betrayed by this vision. In all the ensuing drama – when Darnley and I spotted Hunter in a tea-room in Worcester with one of the under-matrons, a girl to whom he was supposedly engaged, his abandonment of Miss Beach, the punishment inflicted by the Binker on Darnley and myself for spreading scandal – I continued to feel betrayed.

Hunter, it transpired, was an old boy of Seaforth Grange. No boy in my time, except perhaps the unfortunate Timpson, ever spoke of the Binker, our sadistic headmaster, in anything but terms of loathing. The sexual perversions and cruelty practised by this prissily intoned Scotchman left an indelible impression of distaste on almost all his former pupils (though Garforth Thoms, now in the Cabinet, amazed me by sending all his sons to Seaforth Grange!). When I came to know Hunter in grown-up life, and to follow his career, his success in the literary world, and when I came to observe the reverence with which his books were received, when I came to recognize his importance as a committee man, and reflected on his eminence as a reviewer or broadcaster, it seemed all the more remarkable that he retained so conspicuous a loyalty to the Binker. Wonder was occasioned, partly by the thought that the Binker was not a wholly savoury character with whom to remain on terms, and partly by the more important fact that, in order to confirm his position as an Ambassador, Boring for Literature on a thousand panels and delegations, it was necessary for Hunter to establish himself as a man of the left, who would, one might have supposed, have wished to play down his privileged educational background. The Binker was certainly not left-wing in any of the views he expounded to the boys of Seaforth Grange. Hunter's periodic news of the old man, repeated to me on the occasions we met until the Binker's inevitable demise, suggested admiration for our old headmaster's ability to solve the crossword in the *Daily Telegraph*. His choice of breakfast newspaper did not suggest on the Binker's part any radical shift in old age; I was still foolish enough to believe that kinship of opinion was an essential ingredient in the success of relationships which span generations. Hunter's father (something in the confectionery line) had lived in Malvern, quite near the school; and one always assumed that this partly explained why Hunter had been well treated at Seaforth Grange. No one who spoke as affectionately as he did, in grown-up life, of 'Robbie Larmer' – the Binker's actual name – could have been subjected to the wandering hands, nor to the instruments of correction – canes, sticks, slippers, all whimsically nicknamed 'Wee Tammie the Tawse'. Most of those educated at this hellish little establishment – 'Seaforthers' in the Binker's own terminology – did what we could to keep this nasty old man out of our thoughts. That Hunter sought him out – I last saw the pair of them arm in arm at the funeral of Mrs Paxton, the Binker's sister – was one of life's impenetrable puzzles.

There are things one has always known, without knowing, revelations which come as no surprise even though they contradict all the evidence, accumulated over decades, of the senses. The discovery of truth can be retrospective. How my adolescent brain, unstocked as yet with hindsight, derided this idea when Uncle Roy expounded it from his pulpit! Some of the rambling thoughts I have set down here came to me entire and sudden that night in the Pacemaker's. Others, no doubt, have focused themselves in the years since that evening and the time of my writing down these words.

I have paid another visit to the Gents. It's quite a hazardous undertaking at the Pacemaker's since some of the elderly customers, despairing of good fortune in the Saloon Bar, have retreated to the lavatories to fix with shameless stares anyone unzipping or zipping at the urinals. The fact that this was not my sort of thing inspires less disgust than surprise that we can all go on nursing such ridiculous feelings deep into old age. It is a sobering sight, to watch these old men displaying themselves with all the priapic wonder of twelve-year-olds.

'Told me what?'

I am outside the Gents now, and speaking into the telephone.

'You sound even drunker now.'

'Kit has taken me to a gay bar.'

'I knew it, so! You are both going to abandon me and run away together.'

'But – Leman. When we spoke last time. A few minutes ago . . . '

'Two hours ago.'

'You asked me if Kit had told me. Told me what? That's what I did not ask. Should have done.'

'Julian, are you sure you are OK?'

'You are not about to go away, are you? You aren't going to leave Staithe?'

'Of course not, Julian.'

I wonder if I can put into words what I am feeling. It is something like this – that Leman is the last attachment; I'm not going to make myself ridiculous with love any more; I'm not going to go in for slavish adoration of women like Leman and M.M., nor am I going to indulge in unsatisfactory affairs with the other women who come my way. I have demonstrated that I am incapable of marriage, incapable of maintaining a serious relationship with a woman, and that I should be much better off on my own. But my 'crush' on Leman can in a mysterious way help me. I can focus on her, not in an outwardly mawkish way, but secretly, as 'the one I love'. And my great love for her will remain undeclared to anyone, and it will in some mysterious way – not quite clear to me as I stand there by the phone outside the

Gents – purify me, and make me capable of loving all people and all things.

'Are you still there?' she asks.

'Darnley – you remember Darnley?'

'Of course. Is he with you in the cottage?'

'He's gone off with Dodie.'

'Do you mean gone off or just gone off?'

'I don't mean gone rotten.'

'Darling Julian, go back to Kit. And don't ring me again, even though I know you mean it sweetly, so! Goodbye.'

By the time I return to the bar, the dizziness has steadied and I am in that state where vision has become more sharply defined than when one has not been drinking at all. Sobering up in this sense is to become soberer than sober. It is a shock to find Hubie Power standing at the bar without Kit.

'You shouldn't bring a lovely boy like that in here if you want to keep him all to yourself,' says the Great Actor petulantly when I inquire after Kit's whereabouts. One has complained to the swimming-baths attendant that some piece of jewellery or far-too-expensive watch, left in the changing-rooms, has been stolen. I feel myself to blame for putting temptation in the way of other patrons.

'Anyway, it's time Mother went home for her Ovaltine and biscuits,' says Hubie. He seems sharply nettled; in fact, furious. I cannot tell, in this tired old formula, whether it is he or I, who should be destined for the biscuit feast.

'As I told you, dear, I shall let you know at *once* about *Dark Lady*. Films take ages, and then, quite suddenly, bingo! All the money is in place, and it's time to do casting and locations. You just can never tell. Thank God I thought of that perfect title, though!'

The last sentence is enunciated in the tone of a parody mincing queen. The line being spun, evidently, is that my own outpourings were fey, camp, lightweight, until the butch Sir Hubert came to my rescue. I do not much mind his believing this if he wants to, but I do know that it will be impossible to remain good-humoured if he thinks I am going to listen to another of his ignorant disquisitions about the Sonnets. I am desperate to find Kit, and to get out of the bar before closing time.

Slithering off his stool, Sir Hubert says, smoulderingly, with nicotine fumes pouring in thin beams from nostrils and lips, 'He's behaving absolutely in character tonight isn't he – Mr W. H.? Fucking little queen. He'll break your heart, you know. They always do.'

I am so anxious to avoid being marooned at the Pacemaker's that I do not completely listen to what Hubie is saying; could not care less that he believes Kit and me to be lovers. My eyes, however, involuntarily follow the line of his furious stare. His gaze has fixed on the bench against one of the walls, and on the pair who sit there. One is Kit who is, as usual, giggling. Now that the eye comes into focus one can discern that the other party is classic Pacemaker's Arms material, a slightly made figure, perhaps seventy years old, in blue jeans, a check shirt and a leather bomber jacket.

'Good night, dear,' says Sir Hubert Power. ' I really shouldn't try and break them up if I were you. It will only cause unpleasantness and they are obviously set up together for the night.'

Improbable as this sounded, Kit and the old queen did look, from a distance, very much at ease with one another.

I say, 'Good night, Hubie, dear.'

Immediately, I disobey his advice, since I am determined that Kit, who got me into this pub, should get me out of it.

Kit smiles up at me.

'We thought we'd lost you. Poor old Hubes came on a bit heavy; very luckily, I spotted Raphael, who rescued me.'

'Hello, Julian.'

That soft, feminine, bland face creases into a smile, as it has so often done when we have met. I read in it relief that its secrets no longer need to be concealed, but perhaps some other

197

psychological process is at work?

Ever since seeing him in the arms of Miss Beach, forty years ago, I have been haunted by the thought that Hunter is destined to dog my footsteps: to be loved by those women I love; to achieve the very accolades and prizes which I have most coveted. It has never occurred to me to wonder until now if Hunter in turn feels haunted by me; whether he thinks it rum that I should keep cropping up in his life, as he has in mine. The discovery of Hunter in the Pacemaker's Arms reveals something about him which should have been obvious to me years before. Seeing the matter so entirely from one viewpoint, my own, it does not occur to me that Hunter, meeting me in such a place and at such an hour, will be undergoing a similar 'enlightenment' concerning myself. The true explanation, that I have tagged along with Kit to meet Hubie Power and talk about Campbell Dilkes, would sound lame, and even downright improbable, should I get the chance to voice it.

If Hunter does not immediately assume that I too am 'dong le mouvemong', 'on the committee' (to use phrases which Ol Pitman had coined to me when this matter was under discussion), he will certainly not speak to me as he does for the rest of the night; nor will he unlock at last a mystery which has held me in its grip ever since that morning in the spring of 1947 when I heard of James Petworth Lampitt's death.

I ask Kit, 'Did Hubie have anything interesting to say about Campbell Dilkes?'

Hunter presses the table in front of him with flattened palms. His woman's hands have hardly aged since I first saw them, save for the fact that they are mottled now with a few brown spots. He speaks as though I had addressed my remarks to himself.

'I put most of my Dilkes material into *The Hidden Years*.'

'It's so useful that you have done all the groundwork,' says Kit without apparent irony, 'I feel that if I don't know something about the Edwardian cultural scene, I simply have to look it up in the first volume of your Lampitt book. It is encyclopaedic.'

'Well, that was the idea.' That familiar gesture with the palms. That pressing of the table flat. One feels that those matronly hands are exercising power, keeping all those Edwardian gentlemen in their place. The palms could be those of an insane undertaker shoving down the coffin-lids on the resurrecting bodies of old poets, composers and bellettrists who are struggling up for air to tell their own story.

'Time!'

Mine host, a glistening red recording angel, rotund, with a curious bald tonsure in the midst of a fringed, pudding-basin haircut, resembles Friar Tuck. He rings the ship's bell which is suspended over the jar of pickled eggs.

'TIME, GEN-TEL-MEN! TIME!'

This was a scene for Mr Pilbright's brush: *The Day of Judgement in Quebec Street* or *The Trumpet Shall Sound at Marble Arch.*

'TIME! TIME!'

Without conscious decision on my part, I find myself walking eastward along George Street. A final whisky, coaxed from Friar Tuck just before he threw us out, has induced one of alcohol's old tricks: blotting out the brain's capacity to measure or punctuate time. I do not know whether Hubert Power left the pub twenty minutes or four hours ago.

Here we all are, lurching along a street of terraced houses. I am perfectly, acutely conscious, by no means slurred in my speech nor blurred in visual perception. The dizzy phase is long past. Motorists, when they reach this state, believe themselves to be more observant than when sober; they are very likely right, though what they cannot judge is the speed of their reactions.

Hunter and Kit have been talking as I watched the paving stones scud past beneath our feet.

'Julian knows all this backwards, of course, which is why you're so lucky – that is – lucky to have him. Julian knows far more about the Lampitts than I ever did.'

He too thinks Kit and I are lovers. Let him. As I watch Hunter ingratiate himself with Kit, I am taken back to the time when he first flattered me by enlisting my help in organizing the Lampitt Papers. It was the time when he 'made' – as I saw things at the time – my wife fall in love with him.

'The Lampitts were always much, much more left-wing than my great-grandfather.'

I speak in reply, but it is as Uncle Roy's trained parrot and not as myself.

'Oddly enough,' I say, 'it was Vernon's father – old Lord Lampitt – who first took Campbell Dilkes to hear Mosley speak. Mosley was in the Labour Party in those days, a party to which – it goes without saying – all the Lampitts belonged. Except – ' I harrumphed with amusement at the very idea ' – Bobby and his tribe.'

These aren't memories. They are monologues of Uncle Roy's, surreally snatched from the brain and puffed in steamy breath into cold London air. As I speak, however, actual memories return, of Uncle Roy saying these words, or of Sargie holding forth about the Mosleyite phenomenon. With thoughts, come memories of young Hunter and his strange arrival on the scene as the 'expert' on Sargie's brother, James Petworth Lampitt.

So now we have come to the kerb of Gloucester Place, that whizzing northbound street where traffic is still roaring towards Regent's Park, past blackened Georgian façades which glow ethereally in orange lamplight.

I can hear myself asking, 'How did you ever come to meet Jimbo?'

Such a basic question.

Sargie's wife Cecily had asked it often enough, but I have never, so to say, asked this question of my imagination. Hunter the young man – perhaps at the time when he was so enchanting to the older

Giuseppe in Burano – had come to give a talk to our Lampitt Society at school. By then, he was established, in his own eyes at least, as the Lampitt expert. He had made Jimbo into a 'subject'. Obviously, he was a young man in a hurry: that much, from the unsympathetic perspective of the Lampitts, was clear. As a subject for an aspirant biographer in the 1950s, James Petworth Lampitt was an ideal figure, one who had 'known everyone' but who had not himself been 'done'. Cecily told stories of Hunter rifling through Jimbo's desk on the very afternoon of the old man's demise. Her testimony at the Albion Pugh libel trial would even suggest she lent credence to the outlandish notion that Hunter had done the old man in.

'Careful,' says Hunter. His leather-clad arm has come round my shoulder as we pause on the kerbstone. We are standing by some traffic lights. No need for his solicitude. I wasn't about to step in front of the traffic when he seized me so wildly. I remember, suddenly, all those rumours which were aired at the time of the libel trial. I think too of Virgil D. Everett, and the really rather extraordinary fact that, having bought Lampitt's papers, he should have suffered the same unusual death as Jimbo – namely falling, or being pushed, from a high building.

'I am all right,' I say, although I mean to say, 'Please unhand me.'

I hear Kit say, 'I think he's a bit pissed.'

'Do you think we should try to get him into a taxi?' Hunter is saying.

What would be the good of that? I can't get Leman to answer the telephone. I've missed the train. I don't want to go to an hotel.

And I didn't imagine it. Hunter had been trying to push me in front of the traffic. There really had been pressure on my shoulders and in the middle of my back.

The lights are red now and we cross over. The next big thoroughfare looming up is Baker Street. It is quite obvious what Hunter intends. He wants to spend the rest of the night with Kit and it is a matter of indifference to him whether he pushes me into or under a taxi, so long as he can get rid of me somehow. Yes, I am pissed. So are we all. It does not hurt on these occasions to overact a bit. So, I hit Hunter's arm and turn myself into a bit of a bore and ask, 'Tell me. How? How did you meet? Did Jimbo used to go to the Pacemaker's Arms or wasn't it quite that sort of place in those days? Virgil D. Everett used to go there, another of your friends. And do you remember John, his butler? He was there.'

'Tonight?' asks Hunter anxiously. 'We're not far now.'

So we are going somewhere.

'You see . . . ' Kit really wants to talk about his book, his version of events. Having no idea that Kit can write, or that he has such an extraordinary gift of narrative, I think, How arrogant he is, how impossibly young!

'You see, I've got this idea that the Lampitts are, if you like, the Liberal establishment . . . '

What was to distinguish Kit's book from Hunter's? I now believe that Hunter had no idea that he was imposing himself on what he called his material. He allowed two rambling volumes of 'evidence' to amass under his name while never once bringing Jimbo to life. Jimbo's supposed promiscuity (in which I don't believe), the thing which sold the book and which most surprised those who had actually known the man, was something which I have long suspected to have sprung from Hunter's brain, rather than from the evidence. Only lately have I realized how terribly difficult it is for artists to concentrate on anything except their own selves, and that Shakespearean detachment in a writer is the rarest of qualities and not even a very interesting quality unless you're Shakespeare.

My own attempts to write a history of the Lampitts floundered for a number of reasons: my own mental instability, my inability to decide whether I wanted to be a writer or an actor, my commitment to 'The Mulberrys', my laziness. But the simple reason which encompassed them all was egoism. I could not look for long enough to see other people, without wishing to make them part of my own interior drama.

Kit, with his book, discarded self; seemed in these capacities to be as flavourless as water. The resultant book is not flavourless, far from it. He could see into other people's lives, he had the capacity –

Well, it is your capacity. I wonder sometimes if we are right to see you merely as the narrator of the Sonnets. Sure enough, you knew what it was like to make yourself a motley to the view, to be embarrassing, demanding, foolish; but you also knew what it was like to be the young man, didn't you, unmoved, cold and to temptation slow? And did you not also know what it was like to be the woman?

– and the preparedness, Kit's, to shape his story with the detachment of a craftsman making a fiction. Many of those who rightly praised *The Fairies of Staithe* said that it had the qualities of a good novel.

' . . . I feel that Lavinia Dilkes and all her Lampitt siblings and cousins, if they'd been alive today, would have been very much the sort of people we saw this evening at Dylans – friends of Deborah's really; the sort who'd care about the Arts Council.'

'Would you really say . . . ' there is something cooing and flirtatious about Hunter's question, 'that Deborah is the Liberal establishment?'

'Without doubt.'

Kit makes a twirly hand-gesture, the Elizabethan courtier about to throw his cloak over a puddle. It gives Hunter evident pleasure that Deborah Arnott might say, '*L'état*', or at the least, 'The Arts Council Literature panel – *c'est moi.*'

Failing to read any of the signals which have been given out, I say, 'She used to be fun, that woman. She lived in Timplingham with her first husband when I was a boy. Aunt Deirdre couldn't stand her.'

Kit, for some reason, has begun to dance on the pavement just behind Hunter, making elaborate semaphore gestures as he does so.

'I think of the Lampitts as the grown-ups,' Kit gabbles, 'and my poor great-grandpapa as the child. A brilliant composer, but in the face of all those bright sensible people who thought all the right things about the setting-up of the League of Nations, and giving their support to the Labour Movement, he just couldn't aspire to such plateaux of sensibleness. There was a sort of opera going on inside his head . . . '

'Absolutely hated her,' I persist. 'Aunt Deirdre. Hated Deborah. That, I suppose, must be the Freudian explanation for the fact that almost as soon as I'd grown up and the occasion presented itself, I jumped into bed with her.'

After one last unsuccessful attempt at semaphore, Kit leads Hunter away, so that my words will be out of earshot.

I continue to speak to the back of their heads.

'She used to be such fun. When I got to the party tonight and I saw this pompous old bore with double chins talking about all her fucking committees, I thought – my God! Did I really once go to bed with that?'

'Aren't you running a danger there', says Hunter, studiously avoiding my line of talk and turning his head to Kit, 'of people mistaking you? I mean, you don't want to start out on your literary career seeming to support fascism.'

Dear Kit, of course, isn't looking for a literary career. He is trying to find out something about his great-grandfather; he is trying to tell the truth about a complex series of human experiences.

'I'm not trying to apologize for Campbell at all. But Julian would bear me out if he would only stop talking gibberish – ' when he turns round and takes my arm, this does shut me up ' – I am not defending anything which anybody thought during the 1930s. I wouldn't defend Lord Lampitt's visit to Moscow in '31, the year of the worst of the Ukraine famines, when he so wholeheartedly endorsed Stalin's Five Year Plan. How did he define Uncle Joe?'

'A Peter the Great with Wat Tyler's Common Touch,' supplies

Uncle Roy's parrot.

'No one thinks Lord Lampitt approved of mass murder,' says Kit.

'Of course not,' says Hunter. 'All the same, it would be disastrous if you were tarred with the fascist brush. Reviewers . . . '

Hunter is one of those people who believe that those who, during the 1930s, were hoodwinked by Stalin were all slightly lovable, in no way at fault for disbelieving the stories of the genocides, the concentration camps and the show-trials. Those who were guided by a comparable idealism into believing a different variety of nonsense were, by contrast, to be left for ever in the dock beside the butchers of Nuremberg.

Hunter's earnest avuncular tone with Kit at this moment leads my mind down familiar channels of thought. His anxiety lest Kit should write anything which might make him appear sympathetic to Campbell Dilkes's politics encapsulates what makes Hunter such a very bad writer. He has always been more concerned with cultivating attitudes than with – as Kit is to do so brilliantly in his short book – observing another human life sympathetically. ('It was by loving her that he knew her not by knowing her that he loved', as Henry James remarked in a comparable case.) *The Fairies of Staithe* has some of the poignancy of a Browning dramatic monologue. Kit's Campbell Dilkes is an absurd character, undoubtedly, but he is seen as an individual, one whose perception, whether seeing fairies dance on his lawn, or imagining his Wagnerian political ideas, was profoundly askew. Dilkes, in Kit's book, is an artist who does in an extreme form what we all do – he fails to see things straight, he makes a mess of things. Fascinatingly, he falls foul of England just because he thinks he's found the salvation of England's soul. The disparity between vision and reality, poignant, pathetic, repellent as this might have been, was never something on which Kit needed to pass judgement; he was writing too well for that. But then, Kit was not setting out on a 'career in literature'.

That Hunter, while never writing a single original sentence or producing a work of even the smallest literary merit, had been dead set on such a career from early manhood was obvious from the first.

But a revelation is about to occur. The very myopia which made Campbell Dilkes such a fascinating character in Kit's pages, has been afflicting me, all my life, when I contemplated the figure of Hunter.

I have seen his career – both as a triumphant womanizer and as a professional literary bureaucrat – as an object lesson in the futility of success. Confused, however, by jealousy, rage, resentment against him for so many years, and confused even more by the fact that, when actually met, the monster painted by my imagination was quite a pleasant fellow, I have never been able to envisage what Albion Pugh would have called his 'life illusion' – how Hunter saw himself. Weaving eastwards down one of the streets off Baker Street, I am still seeing him as this other Hunter, this seducer of women, this time-server, this Booker Judge, this presenter of 'Perspectives' on telly, this man who has seized on Literature as others might have gone into politics or investment banking as a way of furthering a career. And I have only seen Hunter as a figure making an impact upon others. What had it all been like, all those years, to *be* Hunter? That's the deep, the Shakespearean thing which you would have seen at once as the important question. And you'd have conveyed it, too, absolutely at once, in the first scene in which Hunter appeared.

We have come into Manchester Square. Now we are walking southwards, against the huge brick palazzo-wall of the Wallace Collection, and Hunter continues to talk of Campbell Dilkes and James Petworth Lampitt. We cross Hinde Street and stand on the corner. Further south, in all its tawdry neon-lit roar, where rowdies reel from pubs to discothèques and where buses and taxis throb to and fro, Oxford Street continues its nocturnal life. But where we are, two hundred yards north, the square is deserted.

Twiggy black against the orange glare, the trees reach above us into the impenetrable night as we turn to survey the alien beautiful façade of the Wallace, a palace which has arrived by mistake from some other European capital and was never meant to stand at the top of an English Georgian square. To our right, the Georgian terrace of Hinde Street is interrupted by two larger houses converted to a block of flats called Hinde House to whose stucco side was affixed one of those blue plaques declaring that a famous person had once inhabited those walls. The roundel says: JAMES PETWORTH LAMPITT (1874–1947) LIVED AND DIED HERE.

'Your generation', Hunter is arm in arm with Kit as he speaks, 'simply can't imagine what it was like in those days. A place like the Duke, or the Turkish baths, they were like underground resistance cells in a country over-run by the enemy. It really was like that.'

'The fuzz hovering everywhere. Beastly.' Kit giggles sympathetically.

'There was this sort of unwritten code. Of course, if a place became too wild . . . '

It was the same measured tone in which I'd heard him discuss his literary-bureaucratic concerns. From the timbre, he might have been mulling over the fact that someone else on the committee had suggested that an old novelist, obviously worth no more than an OBE, should be given a knighthood, or that Public Lending Right be increased or curtailed (whichever at that moment happened to be the fashionable view). I slowly recognize, however, that though the voice is the old voice, it is speaking of something much more important to Hunter than the composition of the Arts Council. The right 'chemistry' of the moment explains, if such things need explanation, why, after forty years, my ears are at last to be permitted to hear what happened on the day of Jimbo Lampitt's death. Hunter must feel at ease in our company. We had all met in the Pacemaker's. (I wondered how many people shared Hunter's habit of referring to this pub as the Duke, or whether this was comparable with his belief that Jimbo's family and friends called him 'Petworth'.) The shared meeting-ground surely betokens a shared sympathy and a shared secret. Clearly, Kit's company is highly congenial to him and draws forth personal disclosures which I had never been able to prise. I am drunk, perhaps not as drunk as Hunter supposes, but perhaps too drunk to realize that we have all been drinking for hours and that words are determined to burst forth, however unwise this might be. No doubt the importance of this evening in Hunter's own life makes him particularly voluble. This, and the fact that Kit knows and indeed wrote the item of gossip about Hunter which will appear in the first edition of the *Standard* tomorrow morning. Those who are cagey with acquaintances, and even with their friends, are often the most indiscreet when it comes to talking to the press. It is a time for taking stock, for punctuating; time for revisions if not for visions.

'Had they not turned the blind eye some of the time, there would not have been enough hours in any magistrate's day to deal with it,' he says, seeing the question of homosexual persecution very much from the point of view of the meetings and paperwork it might generate. 'So, obviously, there were specially assigned places, to which police turned a blind eye on condition that things never went too far. The Duke was always a highly respectable pub in its way. You remember old Robbie, of course, Julian . . .'

Kit says, 'I'm not sure that Julian is quite with us.'

'It seems strange that my first visit to a gay pub was with my old headmaster; but I always did like . . . Well, Julian and I were programmed. You could say that. But it must be a deeper thing. After all, not every Seaforther turned out like us. There was some deeper thing about our temperament, wasn't there, Julian? I've long suspected it about you, but never dared, until tonight, to say anything.'

'He's OK,' says Kit. 'He was nearly sick earlier, but he's OK.'

If, on earlier occasions in life, I've been mildly surprised to think of anyone being on social terms with the Binker, I am now reduced to stupefied silence by Hunter's misapprehension. What words strong enough can be found to contradict the idea that the Binker had initiated me into the sexual life? But the moment has passed, and my silence is taken for assent.

Thereafter it seems unkind to interrupt Hunter or disabuse him of his grotesque idea; and that's one reason, I suspect, why Kit and I will not feel the smallest desire in Hunter's lifetime to make his strange confessions public. We are deterred by a sort of decency, not just by a fearful memory of how swift Hunter had been to sue when a whiff of the true story of Jimbo's death had been aired in Darnley's magazine over twenty years ago. I've had my chance to yell out that I'd rather have died with my head stuck in a bucket of sick than spend an evening – still less have a 'date' – with the Binker.

Having let the moment pass, it would seem as though we were tricking Hunter by allowing him to speak further. His tongue liberated by alcohol, he now feels an abandonment; he has entered that safe territory, which he has described so knowingly in *The Hidden Years*, that was provided in the old days by those few pubs and Turkish baths where men of certain tastes felt they could be open, take risks, which 'above ground' would have led to their prosecution.

'In those days – probably this is something to do with my relationship with Robbie – my tastes were very much for the older man. After I'd left Seaforth Grange, I found . . . I found I missed him. Of course, one grows up, we all change. I did not have any partners, of either sex, during my teens. I was not hankering after what I'd enjoyed with Robbie either. It was all changing, evolving . . . I suppose I was first taken to the Duke during the war. And it was there that I found . . . found out about myself, as it were.'

It is not perhaps so very cold a night for December, more a clammy one. In ordinary circumstances I should have longed to be indoors at home. But Hunter's words fix me to the pavement where I stand at Kit's side and look up at Hinde House, Jimbo's last dwelling.

'You're too young, of course, to remember Maurice's boys?'

'E. M. Forster?'

'No, no. There was an old journalist on the *News Chronicle*, one of the most civilized journalists of the old breed, he always had his special table at El Vino, and his silver beaker of champagne – though that got rather hard to come by during the war – and he had a circle of young men whom he liked to bring on. Maurice Seymour-Booth. Well, I started as one of Maurice's boys. That's what they called us, Maurice's Boys. I liked older men, simple as that. Of course I did not like them only for physical reasons, they were able to introduce me to people, and to have much more interesting conversations than boys of my own age. I simply, well . . . Maurice knew I wanted to be a writer, and he was the one who first took me to the Duke. He was the man, incidentally, who introduced me to Petworth.'

'In that pub? In the Pacemaker's Arms?'

'No – ' he laughs ' – not in the Duke. Petworth was hardly a man for pubs. In the Athenaeum. I suppose I was in my very early twenties and he was, what? Seventy or thereabouts. I was enchanted, absolutely enchanted. The anecdotes poured out of him, Oscar Wilde, Henry James, the Bensons, Max Beerbohm, he'd known them all. Here was a man, sitting beside me during the Second World War, who had really known Henry James rather well. Imagine the excitement of that. I longed to put down on paper some of what Petworth told me. I suppose you could say, if you were using the language of a speculative businessman, that Petworth was a shell ripe for takeover and development. All this stuff was wasted as anecdote. It needed to be written down, chronicled. I wanted, in the rather vulgar American phrase, to "do" Petworth. I wanted to rule a line under that particular phase of literary history and draw out what I believed to be its hidden thread – its gay undertones. Unfortunately, Maurice led me quite up the garden path in one particular direction.'

'How so?'

'How is one to explain such things? I had a very simple view of human character. There were certain aspects of life in Maurice's circle; one assumed that this was what all his older friends wanted too. As it happened, at this time, the war was ending, London was getting back to normal. I was beginning to wonder about getting a job. Maurice informed me that Petworth was looking for a secretary. "Jimbo" I remember he called him – it must have been some private nickname. By now, you understand, I was becoming obsessed with Petworth. To tell you the truth, he had come to symbolize in my mind what was wrong with British literary culture; it was effete, it was played out. I mean – while he was producing those later essays what was going on in the world? You had Brecht revolutionizing the theatre – Brecht is out of fashion now, but I happen to think he is a very fine playwright – you had Sartre and Camus coming along; you had Beckett.'

You had 'the buggers', in short; but I am determined not to interrupt Hunter's narrative, nor to explain the rather specialized use to which Sargie Lampitt sometimes put this term.

'Petworth as a critic simply wasn't aware of these people. He seemed intent either on looking backwards – do you know, one of the last *Sunday Times* articles he wrote was about Fanny Burney of all people! – or on chit-chat, gossip, anecdote. These were all things which had initially attracted me to him, but I came to feel that they weren't enough. And you see, much as I disapproved from a politico-cultural point of view, I couldn't help myself being fascinated by the memories. I became convinced that what was sapping the life out of that generation of English writers was the need to suppress and bury their sexual nature. The story of Petworth was going to be, for me, archetypical. The story of his life was to be The Decline of the Man of Letters. Well, I started as his amanuensis. I became aware that the flat – that flat . . . '

211

Hunter points towards the façade of Hinde House and the round blue plaque with Jimbo's name upon it.

' . . . was full of papers, invaluable research material, if I could only persuade Petworth to let me get my hands on it. I was young, I thought I was pleasing him.'

'How were you pleasing him? What do you mean?'

'I've never spoken of this before. Why am I saying all this to you, Kit?'

'Because anything you say to me will be quite safe. I shall never tell anyone. And because poor old Julian is now out of his head. And because you and Julian have been Lampitt-watching all your lives. Because I've got Lampitt blood in my veins, and like you, I'm writing a book in which I'm trying to tell the truth about the past.'

'It's because, Kit, you understand.'

By now Hunter's voice is so slurred that I am afraid that the essential, the last memory will be denied to us.

'You do understand, don't you, Kit?'

'Just a little.'

'Do you think you love me, Kit? Just a little.'

Like the kindest of school prefects, Kit says, 'Go on with your story, Raphael.'

'Well. One afternoon. It's as simple as that. One' – oh, the agonizing pause! – 'afternoon. I'd come round to do the letters. I suppose it was the fourth or fifth time I'd ever met Petworth – Mr Lampitt as I called him – and we were definitely starting to develop a rapport. He was on the sofa – in his flat – it was the sofa which had belonged to Beardsley, damn it. How was I to know or guess? Half the people Petworth talked about – more than half, three-quarters – Wilde, Gide, Morgan Forster, Willie Maugham, Mr Proust, Lytton, T. E. Lawrence, Arthur Benson, Hugh Walpole – had one thing in common. Was I to blame for leaping to the wrong conclusion?'

'You mean, you made a pass at James Petworth Lampitt?'

'Yes.'

'What was his reaction?'

'To call it an over-reaction could not convey the half of it. He was standing up, very red. All I'd done was to sit beside him on the sofa and place my hand on his cock. He was furious. He was talking about sending for the police. He asked me to leave the flat. I remember the kettle was boiling on the little gas cooker in his kitchen. It came to the boil at about the same moment he did, and he left it alone, whistling and shrieking. He walked out of the sitting-room, I remember. He had opened the french window, which led out on to the fire escape. He said he liked standing there; he'd get a view of the Wallace and the tree-tops. Italianate, he called it. Well, I came into the kitchen, and I suppose – what can I say? You could say that my mind had ceased to behave rationally. All sense had been suspended, including common sense. I knew I had blundered. Terribly. But – one hand-gesture! One palm on an old man's flies. It's absurd to think of it, but that one gesture could have deprived me of everything – my subject and my career! And I tell you, when people in 1947 talked about going to the police, they meant it. My way of life would be investigated. They might even have brought Robbie into it. So I panicked. I did not mean to murder Petworth. Of course, I didn't. But I ran at him as he stood there on the fire escape.'

One of the unforgettable details of the libel trial over twenty years ago was the moment when Rice Robey told the court that Mr Lampitt had been five foot five inches in height and that the railings on the fire escape had reached to his chest. When we heard Cecily Lampitt corroborate Robey's evidence, it was impossible to credit the coroner's verdict of accidental death; nor could one believe, from all that had been said and written since of Jimbo's character, that this septuagenarian man of letters, as abstemious and as innocently self-satisfied as he had been unathletic, was either drunk or suicidal. One can't forget that Jimbo was found upside-down in a dustbin in the area outside Hinde House. It is the sort of fact which lodges itself in the mind.

We have stood long enough outside Hinde House. With Hunter's confession, a whole cycle of my own inner experience has come to an end. The day when the news of this death reached Timplingham had begun in me a fascination not merely with the death (which I saw almost at once as a mystery to be solved in the manner of Sayers or Christie), but also with the Lampitts and their world. Since the death of my parents, I had seen the world through the eyes of Uncle Roy, and absorbed his Lampitt bias. All had changed since then; the vision and re-vision had constantly been readjusted. Something like a feeling of focus flickered on my eye as we stood there, drunk and cold, Kit, Hunter and I, on the edge of Manchester Square.

From the Day Muckley Memorial Party in what was once the Black Bottle and is now Dylans, from the Concord Room, from the Fascist Reunion in Stamp Street, and the odder reunions effected in the Duke of Leeds, we have traced a tortuous route. I still haven't decided what to make of the old man who now takes both our elbows in a gesture far from characteristic.

I realize – we are crossing an empty Oxford Street and it could be any time of night – that Hunter is weeping; and that he is drunk, amazingly drunk, drunker than myself.

Kit and I laugh when Hunter says we must go and have one more drink before coming back to his place. He insists that it is his Stag Night – not a remark I take seriously – and that when we have looked in at one more bar, he is taking us back to his flat. There would have been a time when I should have been extremely interested to see the inside of Hunter's flat. Kit told me, after Hunter's death, that it was a curiously impersonal service flat just behind Broadcasting House. Hunter was found dead there in unmysterious circumstances two years or so after this story ends. He simply died of a heart attack.

Now, still alive, and reeling across Oxford Street, he makes me and Kit laugh by announcing that if the pubs are shut he knows of a drinking club which will be open until the small hours. It's called the Concord.

The cold and the thoughts provoked by Hunter's strange narrative have sobered me up. My mind races back through forty years of misapprehensions, false starts, nice tries. At the same time, I have begun to panic about the immediate and practical question of where and whether I shall ever get to bed.

Feeling Hunter's stubbly cheek against mine – and he has always looked so smooth that I've sometimes wondered whether he needed to shave! – smelling his foul breath, and with the weight of the drunkard falling against me, I have no sense of camaraderie with my fellow-sot. It is obvious that he has reached the end of his confessions. Having confessed to killing Jimbo, he hardly needs to explain to me how another old gentleman who was ultimately a nuisance to Hunter – Virgil D. Everett – happened to fall off the top of a tall building in Manhattan.

It is Kit who holds the final secret up his sleeve. It is not spoken for several hours.

Weakly, I consent to a return to the Concord Room. Sausage, quite reasonably, perhaps, wonders what three silly fucking cunts should want, on a wet night in December, to be coming to his club at half past one in the fucking morning. Inebriation, which seemed to fade in Manchester Square, rages back when I 'top it up' with one or two glasses of whisky.

Some time later, I am curled up in bed in Shepherd's Bush. Underneath are the everlasting arms. They are the arms of Shakespeare, my inspiration, and my God. Or am I with Mummy again at last? There is no need any more for anything to be spelt out. Young as they are, Kit and Leman will parent me. Under the shadow of their wings shall be my refuge until this tyranny be over-past. Leman is at Staithe, and I am still half asleep, but her bright face shines in my dreams. Kit is beside me, he holds me as if I were his child. Before waking, I know that a new life is beginning, one in which I do not need sex, nor money, nor success. I've come home.

Presumably, before climbing into bed, we both kicked off our shoes. Or did Kit do this for me, before cuddling me into his bed? We are both fully clothed and very smelly when, with hard hammer blows to the skull and a mouthful of dung, the hangover wakes me.

The shower, while Kit boils some coffee; the thought that if I don't drink coffee I shall die, and if I do, I shall vomit; the stench of my clothes, and the sense as I sit there, towel-clad, that I have nothing else to change into: all swill around in my consciousness, while I return to the waking world.

While I sit in my steamy daze, Kit has had the energy to go to a corner shop for milk and newspapers.

'I wasn't sure', Kit says, 'whether they'd use the story or not.'

He is young – he is thirty years younger than I am. Of course, I forgive his egotistical obsession with whether or not the newspaper has printed his little piece of tittle-tattle; but this can be of no interest to me, as consciousness returns to focus. Shaken to the point where I no longer quite existed, some constituent particles of awareness have begun to settle. I am taking in – not only the flat, and the mug of steaming coffee, but also memories of forty and more years, as it were a tale that is told.

'In the light of how we spent the evening, it seems quite odd,' said Kit with a light laugh. 'But perhaps when I grow up, I shall discover that all life is odd.'

The headline, and the photograph of the happy pair – Deborah's grin, it was a photo taken at some Booker dinner, creating a great ruff of chins; Hunter, a different photograph, taken at some international PEN meeting – had a curious aptness. One could no longer be surprised.

Deborah and Hunter were married a few months later, in the same week, as it happened, that Leman married Kit.

I was, I must confess,
Great Albion's queen in former golden days . . .

There is no doubt that Dodie made a magnificent Queen Margaret. She aged splendidly. There is something disconcerting for me, however, about seeing on the small screen those once known in the flesh. The Homeric wraiths, gibbering in the underworld, have more solidity than telly, which manages to reduce all who appear on it to two dimensions. No wonder Hunter was such a success on it. In latter days, I believe he took his television work even more seriously than his time on committees.

I looked to the only other armchair in the bungalow. Felicity's serious old face was concentrated completely on the screen as she watched *Henry VI*. Hardly the greatest of the plays, though I remember a splendid version of Part Three, directed by Treadmill, in which I took the role of Gloucester – the future Richard III.

I left my cousin absorbed in front of your play, and went to the kitchen to put the finishing touches to our meal. There are several sophistications which I have added to the rectory diet, and of which my aunt would probably have disapproved. For example, I curried the cottage pie, and served it with green tomato chutney, bought at the Women's Institute stall at Fakenham market; and I put a liberal grinding of nutmeg on the rice pudding. I can hear my aunt now saying that this would make it 'too rich – you don't want people being bilious'. Indeed, not.

What's a life? Mine's gone. I now have something better, which is happiness. I potter, barely aware of myself for most of the time. I don't read the Bible much – private, silent wanderings round the

Norfolk churches and the shrine at Walsingham serve for my religious devotions. The works of Shakespeare are read and reread; otherwise, novels from the library van, which comes round quite regularly. Detective stories, mainly. Memories swim in and out of my head, but they seldom oppress.

On the kitchen table, I laid out a place-setting at each end; and one of my aunt's large white napkins beside each place. Unlike her, I like to offer wine to any guest, though I am all but a teetotaller myself; so there is an open bottle of some Chilean stuff from a supermarket which Fliss says is perfectly OK.

In case the reader wonders, I should say that things have happened in my life which had nothing to do with the Lampitts, nothing to do with Staithe, nothing to do with any of the events or persons described in the foregoing pages. Whatever those things were, however, I am happy to say that they have faded out of focus. Lives of plants and of the lesser mammals simply go. It is only a fiction that our lives are any different. I have no hope of seeing Mummy again, though perpetual regret that so much of my life has been spent without her.

Felicity's eyes were tearful when she came into the kitchen from the sitting-room.

'It was brilliant,' she said eagerly. 'I'd never seen that play before.'

'You have. You saw me in it at school fifty-odd years ago.'

'Well, I forget.'

Our conversation at the kitchen table was desultory. It was about arrangements; the ordering of some more oil for the central heating; the satisfactory nature of the new roof-lagging, which kept our little house warm. When I opened the stove to produce the second course, Fliss said, on cue, 'Good old rice pud.'